The Witch and the Dead

A WISHCRAFT MYSTERY

HEATHER BLAKE

BERKLEY PRIME CRIME
New York

BERKLEY PRIME CRIME
Published by Berkley
An imprint of Penguin Random House LLC
375 Hudson Street, New York, New York 10014

ISBN: 9781101990131

First Edition: October 2016

Printed in the United States of America
1   3   5   7   9   10   8   6   4   2

For Mom and Dad
and
Mama and Papa.
Thank you for the strong roots.

ACKNOWLEDGMENTS

As always, I'm so grateful for all the help given by Jess Wade and everyone at Penguin Random House who help bring Darcy's stories to life. A big thank-you to Jessica Faust and the BookEnds team as well for your endless support of Darcy and me.

I'd also like to give a special thank-you to Kristin S., Gayla H., Kim M-B., Corrine D., and Christine B. for their help with French phrasing. *Merci!*

Chapter One

It was one of those crisp New England autumn days that begged for hot chocolate piled high with whipped cream, a good book, and a cozy spot in front of the fireplace.

Beg as the day might, however, this witch didn't have time to indulge at the moment. I glanced at all the plastic bins and cardboard boxes that needed to be relocated from this space to my new home and pushed up my sleeves. My dream of curling up in front of a fire tonight was never going to happen if I kept dragging my feet.

As much as I tried, however, I couldn't seem to get going. I flitted from one side of my aunt Ve's garage to the other, accomplishing little as early-October sunlight filtered through grimy windows, spotlighting every dust particle in sight.

As well as my hesitance.

I wasn't known for procrastinating, but today as I

transferred all the belongings I'd been storing in this space to my new house two doors down the street, I was taking my sweet time.

My puttering had nothing to do with actually moving the twenty or so boxes and assorted bits of my previous life and everything to do with leaving behind Aunt Ve and the house I'd lived in since arriving in this village a little more than a year ago.

Today was moving day. Tonight, I'd sleep in my new bed, under a new roof.

I'd eventually have to deal with the emotions lurking under the surface, but for right now I fortunately had help with the move: My younger sister, Harper, and my aunt Ve had both volunteered to assist with the process.

"It should all go!" Velma "Ve" Devany said, tossing her hands in the air. "All of it."

She wasn't referencing my belongings, though I suspected the ghostly outlines left behind by my moving boxes had triggered the desire to banish everything else from the garage as well.

"A yard sale! Tomorrow, just in time for the weekend crowd." Spinning around, Ve faced me, her golden blue eyes alight with sparks of purpose. Her coppery hair was pulled back in its usual twist, but she'd accented the style with a red bandanna. It was tied in a knot at the top of her head like Rosie the Riveter's. Round cheeks glowed with good health as Ve pushed up the sleeves of her white long-sleeved thermal henley and then bent to cuff the hems of her denim overalls. She was in her early sixties and had more energy than I'd ever possessed.

"I think she means it," Harper stage-whispered to me, a trace of horror hovering in her voice.

"Oh, I mean it," Ve stated firmly. "Think of all the space I'd have in here if it were empty. I could turn the garage into a craft studio!"

"You don't craft," Harper pointed out as she wrestled a tall box into the driveway. The box was almost as big as she was. At just five feet, twenty-four-year-old Harper personified Shakespeare's line, "though she be but little, she is fierce." Her brown eyes glinted in the sunlight as she looked back at us. "Well, not in a *studio* kind of way."

Technically we were all Crafters, witches with a unique set of abilities. My family happened to be Wishcrafters, who could grant wishes, but there were dozens and dozens of other witchy varieties that lived and worked among oblivious mortals here in the Enchanted Village. This charming neighborhood of Salem, Massachusetts, was a tourist hot spot . . . and the place I now considered home.

"Fine," Ve said, relenting with her quick response to the truth of the matter. "How about a yoga studio?"

Shooting her arms out to the sides for balance, she placed the sole of her right foot on her left inner knee, attempting, I presumed, the tree pose. Her arms windmilled wildly as she swayed to and fro. I resisted the strong urge to shout "Timber!" as I grabbed hold of her to keep her from tipping over.

Flicking me a wry look, she said, "Maybe not yoga."

"Maybe not," I agreed.

"Well, I'll think of something." With a sweeping wave of her hand, she added, "But first, this all needs to go."

By "all," she meant the decades of flotsam that had been stashed and stored in the massive garage. Floor-to-ceiling stacks of boxes, bags, trunks. Christmas and Halloween decor. A tattered love seat and other assorted furniture, dust-covered bookshelves, and side tables. Simply sorting through everything could take weeks. "Maybe it's best to wait until spring for a yard sale," I suggested.

By then this particular flight of fancy of hers might pass.

I hoped.

"No, no." She strode over to a clothing rack stuffed with zipped dusty black garment bags. "An impromptu yard sale is just what I need to take—"

Abruptly, she bit off her words, and I swallowed over a sudden lump in my throat.

To take her mind off the fact that I was moving out.

I sent Harper a pleading look. She gave me a sympathetic nod and said, "You know what could occupy your time, Aunt Ve? Helping me. Marcus' parents arrive back in the village tomorrow morning, and we're supposed to have dinner with them tomorrow night." She pressed her hands together, pleading. "Help me figure out how to get out of it. *Please.*"

With a grateful smile I said, "Tomorrow night? You mean you're not going to the auditions for the play?"

One of my best friends, Evan Sullivan, was directing his first musical at the village playhouse, *The Sound of Music.* Evan was understandably nervous. Though he had a fondness for the theater, as half Bakecrafter his true gift was creating delectable miniature delights at the Gingerbread Shack, his boutique bakery. To bolster his confidence, he'd recruited some friends to help with the production. As I couldn't sing or dance, I had been assigned to lead the scenery team. We'd already had our introductory meeting, and tomorrow afternoon we would commence with building the sets at the large scene shop inside the playhouse. Afterward, I'd agreed to help Evan with auditions.

He'd bribed me with devil's food mini cupcakes.

He knew exactly how use my weaknesses to his advantage.

"I don't sing," Harper said with a shudder. "Or dance. Though if it gets me out of that dinner, maybe I should reconsider. It would be less humiliating. What time are the auditions?"

"Four to seven," I said, watching her carefully. After Harper had moved to this village and become the owner of the Spellbound bookshop more than a year ago, her confidence had grown by leaps and bounds. It was rare to see her nerves on full display.

Looking crestfallen, she said, "That won't help. The dinner's at eight. Maybe I can come down with scurvy or something by then."

I laughed. "Scurvy?"

"I'll take anything at this point. The Debrowskis don't like me as is, and you know how I get when I'm nervous. I'm bound to spill or break something."

I tried to reassure her. "They like you."

"No, they don't," Harper returned, perfectly calm and absolutely serious.

I picked up a plastic bin. Its label said only BEDROOM. Sheets and blankets, I figured. "Of course they do."

Ve unzipped a garment bag. "No, Harper's right. They don't. They don't like any of us." She'd said that as though it was common knowledge. "I'm sure they're having a full-sized cow that Marcus fell for Harper in the first place."

Harper looked at me with a smug smile. "Told you so."

She loved being right.

Still disbelieving, I stared at our aunt. "Why don't they like us?"

I knew the Debrowskis by sight, but I had never officially met Penelope and Oliver. They'd retired from their law firm a few years ago, handing it over to Marcus to run once he graduated from law school. The pair traveled a lot, spending hardly any time at all here in the village. A few weeks here and there. I hadn't yet had occasion to run into them.

"That Penelope has always been a jealous prune," Ve said, wrinkling her face to resemble the dried fruit. "She fancies herself a free spirit and was always most annoyed that I could grant wishes while she had to practice law. Not that I blame her. I'd be jealous, too. Law is so dreadful. She's a Crosser, you know. Half Colorcrafter, half Lawcrafter. Despite Color being her predominate Craft, her father threatened to cut her off if she didn't join the family law firm. She almost flunked out of law school but somehow managed to graduate."

Witches who had parents with differing Crafts inherited both abilities; however, one ability was definitely stronger than the other. We called these witches Cross-Crafters, or Crossers, for short.

"Well, the free-spirit thing explains her love of bohemian clothes," Harper said dryly.

"Don't let her bother you," Ve advised. "Just focus on that man of yours and all will be well."

Color rushed into Harper's cheeks. "He's not *mine*. . . ."

Ve met my gaze and we both burst out laughing.

Harper, who until she met Marcus had compared marriage to a prison sentence, shot us an annoyed look. She then picked up another box and carried it out to the driveway, stomping the whole way. She hated being wrong about anything. Especially about strong beliefs such as marriage and lifelong commitments.

Ve unzipped another garment bag and laughed as she pulled out the frilliest wedding gown I'd ever seen. "Well, lookie what we have here." She held it up to herself, nearly poking her eye with a wayward ruffle. "It's the dress I wore to my wedding to Godfrey."

Cloakcrafter Godfrey Baleaux owned the Bewitching Boutique here in the village and had been the third of Ve's four husbands, the one she once referred to as a rat-toad bottom dweller. She didn't call him that anymore. Not often, anyway. I considered him family. An uncle of sorts, though he liked to claim he was my fairy godfather. He'd rescued me from more than one fashion disaster.

"Did Godfrey design that, Aunt Ve?" Harper turned to me. "Because if so, maybe you shouldn't let him be in charge of *your* wedding dress, Darcy."

I couldn't imagine that dress was one of Godfrey's creations. He preferred classic, timeless fashion. That gown was . . . neither. "Aren't you getting ahead of yourself? I'm not even engaged."

"Yet," Ve and Harper said in unison, both with big smiles.

I couldn't help smiling, too. Police Chief Nick Sawyer and I had been dating for more than a year, and a few months ago we'd had the Talk. I knew a proposal was just a matter of time, and thanks to a slip of the tongue by his teenage daughter, Mimi, I knew he already had the ring. The anticipation of what he had planned—and when—was killing me. Part of me wondered if he was waiting to pop the big question at the housewarming party next weekend, but then I immediately ruled that out.

Nick was rather private. He wouldn't put such a special moment on full display in front of our family and friends. And I wouldn't want that, either. It should be just the two of us. . . .

"Honestly, I don't know what he's waiting for," Harper said. "Do you want me to talk to him?"

"Definitely not," I said. "He'll ask when he asks."

Harper *harrumph*ed.

I grabbed a box and set it next to the others in the driveway, near a spot where my dog, Missy, lay stretched out in a puddle of sunshine. The mini schnoodle—half mini poodle, half mini schnauzer—watched us with sleepy eyes.

She'd been extra tired lately, and I was starting to worry. I added making an appointment with the local vet to my to-do list. It probably wasn't necessary, but I didn't want to take any risks with her health.

Glancing at my watch, I noted that Nick was due here soon to help move these boxes. My new place had been recently renovated top to bottom, which included adding a new stacked-stone fireplace in the family room addition. I had high hopes that Nick would end up with me in front of that fireplace tonight. . . .

"No, no, this was all me, my design," Ve said, eyeing the dress with pity. "The fact that Godfrey still married me despite this atrocity rather proves how smitten he had been with me. Perhaps I shouldn't have divorced him." She *tsk*ed.

"I thought you two hated each other by the end of the first year," Harper said.

"That's true," she said thoughtfully. "But I don't hate him now."

Aunt Ve had monogamy issues.

And loneliness issues.

With my moving out of her house, I had the feeling she was casting a wide net to replace my daily presence in her life.

"Don't forget about Andreus," I reminded my aunt. "Isn't he coming back to the village this weekend? He'll have your days occupied in no time."

"And nights, too," Ve mused with a wiggle of her eyebrows.

Harper clapped a hand over her mouth and said through spread fingers, "I think I'm going to be sick."

"You and me both," I added.

"Oh, you two," Ve said with a laugh. "He's a good man." She paused. "Mostly good." Another pause. "He's a man."

Charmcrafter Andreus Woodshall was the director of the Roving Stones, a traveling rock-and-mineral show that visited the village several times a year. Despite the fact that he was the scariest man I'd ever met, he and Ve had hit it off the last time he'd been here. Whether he was good or bad was one of those questions that had yet to be fully answered. From what I knew of him, it was a mixed bag. He was a complicated man.

Ve frowned. "But he'll be leaving again soon enough. He has only a week off before traveling to a show in Florida."

"Live in the moment, Aunt Ve." Harper sounded more cheerleaderish than I'd ever imagined she could.

Lifting her chin, Ve smiled. "You're right, Harper. That's exactly what I should do." She moved aside a dusty bookcase and wiggled behind it. "And the first order of business is to get this garage cleaned out for that big yard sale tomorr— *Oh.* Oh dear. Oh my."

"What is it?" I asked, watching her face lose all color.

"What? Did you find the veil that went with that hideous wedding dress?" Harper asked, chuckling. "I can only imagine what *that* looked like."

One of Ve's hands flew up to cover her mouth as she stared at something deep in the recesses of the garage. "No. No veil." Over her shoulder, she said in an unnatural high-pitched voice, "Darcy dear, would you please give Nick a call?"

I glanced at my watch. "He should be here in fifteen minutes. . . ."

"We need him now," she said, still using that odd falsetto.

"Why?" Harper strode over and leaned on the bookcase to catch a glimpse of whatever had caused Ve alarm.

Harper's eyes went wide. "Is that a . . ."

"Yes, dear," Ve said. "It appears so."

"It's not fake?" my sister asked. "I mean, there are Halloween decorations all over this garage."

"I don't think so," Ve said. "You see, I recognize that hat. I'd know it anywhere."

Hat? Halloween? I marched over to see what was going on for myself. I shimmied against the shelf next to Harper. "I don't see . . ."

Ve pointed.

I gasped. In a once-hidden nook created by a tower of boxes lay a skeleton fully dressed in men's clothing. By the thick layer of undisturbed dust covering the skeletal remains, I guessed he'd been there quite a long time.

Harper glanced at me, her eyes full of excitement. She was an exceedingly morbid witch. Then she said to Ve, "Who is it? You said you recognized the hat?"

"That," Ve said, wiggling back out from behind the shelf, "is Miles Babbage. My second husband. And hand to heart, if he wasn't already dead, I'd kill him myself."

Chapter Two

Half an hour later, there was a small gathering of people inside Ve's family room, a large contingent of law enforcement in her garage, and a big crowd of rubberneckers on the village green across the street from her house.

Emergency vehicles tended to draw a crowd. Especially the van used by the medical examiner's office.

Voices from outside filtered in through an open window. We were waiting for Nick to come inside to tell us what to expect next, but we all assumed Ve would be under investigation. Her ex-husband had been found dead in her garage. If it was discovered that he hadn't died naturally, it was logical that she'd become a suspect in his death.

Harper had already called Marcus, the best lawyer in the village, on Ve's behalf. He was on his way over.

"Miles Babbage disappeared the night after we

eloped," Ve said as she sat on the edge of the stone hearth. She held a beautiful floral-decorated cloisonné chest on her lap. As she spoke, she began sorting the box's contents, seemingly looking for something in particular. "I figured he ran off and that was that. Good riddance. Bon voyage. It took me forever to get a divorce granted since he was MIA, but it was the best time and money I ever spent."

"I never did care for Miles," my mother, Deryn Merriweather, said from where she sat in an oversized, cushy armchair. "He was weaselly."

She wore a pristine white cashmere V-neck sweater and white slacks. Silver strands sparkled in long auburn hair that hung loose about her shoulders. Twin rosy spots of color had settled on her high cheekbones, and her Cupid's bow lips pursed in dismay. Fine lines crinkled the corners of her golden brown eyes as they flashed with vitality.

Which was rather an amazing feat considering she was . . . dead.

And had been for twenty-four years.

Every time I saw her, spoke to her, *hugged* her, I had to remind myself that this was real.

She was *real.*

My mother might technically be dead, but her spirit was very much alive and well here in the Enchanted Village. A place where magic made the impossible possible.

As I'd learned only a few short months ago, when my mother died in a car accident all those years ago, she'd become a familiar, a witch who took on the form of an animal after death in order to live an immortal life. That day, my mom had taken the form of a mourning dove. And not long after that, she'd become the Elder, the governess of the Craft, which allowed her to use *any* form, including her human one. No other familiars had the ability to do the same.

Two things had prevented Mom from telling Harper and me that she was still around. The first had been my father and her pledge to him that his girls would never know of their magical heritage until after he passed away. The second was her role as the Elder. No one—including family—was to be informed of her identity without having lived in the Enchanted Village for at least one year.

This past June, I'd figured the secret out on my own, though I freely admitted I should have probably put the puzzle together much sooner. The pieces had all been there. We'd had an emotional family reunion and were still adapting to the change.

Aunt Ve glanced up and raised a thin coppery eyebrow in her younger sister's direction. "Fat lot of good that does me now. You could have warned me back then, Derrie."

My mother pressed her hands to her chest. Long, graceful fingers laced together. "I did. You called me in Ohio to tell me that you and Miles Babbage planned to elope as soon as possible. I reminded you that *you* were the first one to compare him to a weasel. Remember?"

My mother had chosen to have her human form age-progress at the same rate it would have if she hadn't left the earthly world. As far as I knew she'd keep on aging like the rest of us for as long as she held the role of Elder.

And just how long that would be wasn't known. I'd asked. In fact, I'd been peppering her with nonstop questions pretty much since I'd learned her identity, but I'd quickly discovered that some things never changed: There were still a lot of Craft secrets I wasn't yet privy to.

And might never be.

I was trying to accept that fact, but it was proving difficult.

Ve frowned and turned her attention back to the contents of the box. "I don't remember any phone call, but of course I remember how I felt about him and the way he weaseled his way into the hearts of the women in this village, then left them high and dry. It was shameful."

Harper and I sat on the couch next to each other, bookended by furry friends. On my left lolled my cat, Annie, a black ragamuffin I'd taken in a couple of months ago after her owner had died tragically. On Harper's right sat Tilda, Aunt Ve's fluffy gray-and-white Himalayan.

Tilda was usually a cranky puss, but today she was allowing Harper to pet her with nary a hiss. Missy was curled up on the floor in front of my mother's chair, looking as if she was asleep, but her ears were perked as though she was listening to every word being spoken about Miles Babbage.

Looking utterly bewildered, Harper said, "You really didn't like him, Aunt Ve?"

Ve continued to sort through the box. "Honestly, I didn't know him, other than by his reputation as a ladies' man. I wanted nothing to do with that. If anyone was to do any heart breaking around here, it was *me*."

"And has been," my mother said with a smile.

Ve waved her off with a laugh. "One or two, here and there."

Or three, four, five . . . Ve had left broken hearts scattered all over this village.

Bracing her elbows on her knees, Harper leaned forward. She opened her mouth, then closed it again. Her forehead furrowed. Finally, she said, "I don't understand. Then why in the world did you marry him?"

Ve adjusted her red bandana and sighed. "I wish I knew."

At the word "wish," I bristled, ready to cast a spell. However, we could not grant our own wishes or those of other Wishcrafters. Not even the Elder had that ability, because she'd once been a Wishcrafter, too.

"It's all a bit fuzzy around the edges." Ve winced as though struggling to pull memories from a distant corner of her mind. "I recall that Miles came by As You Wish onc Friday afternoon, completely out of the blue. It had been a year since anyone had last seen him."

My sister asked, "Wasn't that cause for alarm? That he'd disappeared for a year?"

"Not really," Ve answered. "He was often out of the village for long stretches of time."

"Miles was a transient clay artist," my mother explained. "He traveled with the Roving Stones, so he was in and out of the village a few times a year. He had no ties here otherwise." She uncrossed her legs, shifted her weight, and then tucked her bare feet beneath her. She didn't wear shoes. Ever. Her feet never touched the ground—she floated everywhere.

Not wearing shoes was something she passed off as a quirk of the Eldership, but I had the feeling it held deeper meaning.

Another secret I had yet to uncover.

Ve added, "You never knew when Miles was going to show up. Or leave again. After a year passed, we'd all come to believe he wasn't ever coming back, that he'd finally hooked up with some woman who hadn't let him go. Served him right."

"What did he want with you, Ve?" Harper asked.

"He wanted to hire me."

"To do what?" I asked. What could he have possibly needed Ve to do?

"I can't remember," she said with a shrug. "I'm sure

I took notes, as I do with all new clients, but I've never found a file with his name. It's a mystery."

Harper scooted to the edge of the sofa. "What do you mean you can't remember?"

"Just that, Harper dear. I have no memories from that Friday afternoon after hearing him say he wanted to hire me until the next evening, when I woke up next to a marriage certificate."

My stomach dropped just imagining the situation. I couldn't fathom having lived it. "Had you two been drinking?" I asked.

"Not that I can recall," she said with a smile, "though I don't doubt there was alcohol involved at some point during that time period. Wedding nights often involve champagne. I had no hangover when I woke up, however."

"Do you think he *drugged* you?" Harper's shoulders slid back, and her chin came up. Vengeance shone in her narrowed gaze.

It was probably a very good thing Miles was already dead.

"That's always been my theory," my mother offered. "There's no other explanation to lose more than twenty-four hours of your life."

"Could it have been the Craft at work?" I asked. "Perhaps he cast a spell on you?"

Using spells was something I still wasn't wholly comfortable with, but I was slowly coming around. At some point before she had died, Nick's ex-wife, Melina, who'd been a Wishcrafter, had penned a diary that listed dozens and dozens of spells, among other Craft secrets, and it had eventually found its way to her daughter, Mimi.

Creating the diary had been a direct violation of the Craft laws, and I often suspected Melina had done so deliberately, her intent to teach her daughter her Craft from beyond the grave. When the diary's existence was discovered, the Elder had graciously allowed Mimi to keep the journal but had appointed me to safeguard it. I'd been scouring those pages lately, learning things I never dreamed possible. All thanks to a woman I'd never known.

Speaking of Mimi, the thirteen-year-old was going to be quite displeased when she was released from school today. She loved being in the thick of village happenings, especially ones that affected those she loved. I, however, was glad she wasn't here right now. She didn't need to hear these sordid details. Yes, Mimi was mature, but she was still so very young. I loved her, and I didn't ever want her to know firsthand the ugly truths of the world. Honestly, if I could stick her in a bubble, I would.

I wondered if there was a spell for *that*. . . .

Ve still sifted through memories housed in that beautiful box. "Miles was a mortal, so he couldn't have used a spell."

"I suppose that also rules out the possibility that he memory-cleansed you," I said. A memory cleanse could have explained perfectly Ve's missing day. But not if Miles had been a mortal. He wouldn't have had access to the magical memory eraser.

Ve said, "I don't know what happened. And I couldn't even question Miles about it. When I woke up, I found a note that said he'd had to run an errand and would be back later. I never saw him again. Until today, that is."

Today. When his skeleton was found in Ve's garage.

"Aha. Here it is." Ve pulled a photograph from the box, then carefully set the box back on the bookshelf. She carried the picture over to Harper and me. "This was Miles, apparently on the day we married, in front of the New Hampshire courthouse where we eloped."

I had planned a few spur-of-the-moment elopements

through my business, As You Wish, which was a personal concierge service, so I knew why Ve and Miles had crossed state lines. Massachusetts had a three-day waiting period from the time the marriage license was issued until the wedding could take place. New Hampshire did not, making it much more elopement-friendly.

Harper eagerly snatched the picture from Ve's hands, and I leaned in to study the photo as well.

The man in the image certainly hadn't dressed for a wedding. He leaned against a brick courthouse column, wearing ripped blue jeans, a white V-neck T-shirt, a black leather choker with a round white pendant, and worn biker boots. A tattered straw fedora with an emerald green band sat high on his head, while the ends of long curly brown hair brushed against his shoulders. He was broad chinned, with a long, crooked nose that had obviously once been badly broken. Intense eyes peered out from beneath the brim of the hat, and his half smile revealed a chipped bottom front tooth.

He wasn't what I'd consider to be attractive necessarily, but he wasn't hideous, either. There was something compelling about his looks. Something that insinuated he hadn't had an easy life. It was as though his outward appearance told me a story about what was going on inside of him. A story that didn't have a happy beginning . . . .

Next to Miles glowed a bright white starburst—Aunt Ve, I presumed. Until recently, Wishcrafters appeared only as white auras on film. Fortunately, we now possessed a wonderful spell that allowed our images to be captured. Though I imagined Ve was probably plenty grateful that she couldn't be seen in this particular picture.

Harper shook her head. "This man is . . ."

We all waited.

"He's . . ."

It was unlike my sister to be unable to come up with a word. Any word. Her vocabulary was impressive and extensive.

"He's . . . haunting." She handed the picture back to Ve. "That look in his eye . . ."

"Haunting" fit for both his appearance *and* the shadows in his eyes. If the old saying about eyes being the windows to the soul was true, then we were looking into a very somber place.

"I agree." The buckles on Ve's overalls clanked as she plopped onto the love seat with a hearty sigh. "His broken spirit appealed to a lot of women. Women flocked to him whenever he was here, lusting after him as though he was some kind of sexual Pied Piper."

I absolutely hadn't needed that image in my head.

But as she spoke, I was a little surprised Ve hadn't liked him right off the bat, considering she had a tendency to be drawn to men who needed fixing.

And Miles Babbage looked like he was a fractured mess.

I asked, "When was all this?"

"Thirty years ago." She frowned. "Oddly, it was thirty years ago this very week. It feels like it was a lifetime ago, really."

Aunt Ve would have been in her early thirties. I'd have been a year old, and Harper hadn't yet been born.

Ve glanced out the window in the direction of the garage. "Do you think he's been out there this whole time?"

We sat in silence for a moment, pondering that scenario.

"The bones certainly looked as if they'd been there for a while," I finally said, "but wouldn't you have stumbled across them by now?"

Ve lifted her shoulders in a who-knows kind of way. "I can't remember the last time I was in that corner of the garage. Most of the stuff that's back there belonged to your grandparents. I've never had need to move it."

"Surely you would have smelled him decomposing," Harper said matter-of-factly.

I suddenly felt queasy.

"Perhaps not," Aunt Ve replied. "The garage is detached and solidly built. I hardly ever go in there. I spent the end of that month in Ohio with Derrie, so I didn't need my Halloween decor. I wouldn't have gone in there until Christmas, for my decorations. If I smelled something odd, I might have thought a mouse or squirrel had somehow been trapped inside. . . . It was so long ago that I can't recall."

I shifted to face my sister. "It was also heading into wintertime. If temperatures were low enough, wouldn't that have affected decomposition?"

Harper slowly nodded. "It would have slowed it down."

"It was unseasonably cold that month," Ve said. "That whole winter, actually."

"When was the last time you cleaned or emptied the whole garage?" Harper asked as she continued to pet Tilda, who was still (astonishingly) allowing it.

"Heavens." Ve tapped her chin with a finger as she thought about it. "The last time it was thoroughly emptied and sorted was when your mother moved to Ohio. That was a few years before I met Miles."

We let that sink in.

It was a sobering declaration. I said, "Then, yes, I'm guessing he could have been there the whole time."

Ve shuddered.

My mother said, "The question in my mind isn't necessarily how long he has been in the garage. It is *why* he is in there."

"Obviously, someone dumped him there so Ve would get blamed for his death," Harper said. "Probably someone who doesn't like Ve very much, since it's a cruel thing to do."

I thought so, too.

My mother glanced my way. "You'll look into it?"

It wasn't so much a request as an order, and not from my mother but from the Elder. I'd been working under her direction as a Craft investigator for almost a year now, looking into criminal cases within the village that involved our magic in one way or another. Though Miles wasn't a Crafter, Aunt Ve was.

I nodded. It would be my first case knowing the Elder was my mom, and I kind of liked knowing that I was working for my mother. I was a big believer in family businesses.

"Good," she said with a smile. "The sooner we can figure this out, the—"

In a blink, she dissolved into a cloud of sparkles that narrowed into a thin contrail that shot out the open window and disappeared.

A second later, there was a tap at the back door before it swung open, its hinges creaking. Missy jumped to her feet and ran off, barking at the visitor.

"Harper?" Marcus called from the mudroom.

"In here," she said, tearing her gaze from the window. She stood up and went to greet him.

I glanced at Aunt Ve. Concern deepened the fine lines of her face as she bit her fingernails.

"Don't worry, Aunt Ve," I said, trying to reassure her. "We'll figure out what happened."

She steadily held my gaze. "Darcy dear, that's what I'm afraid of."

Chapter Three

Twenty minutes later, I took Missy outside to the side yard, leaving Ve, Marcus, and Harper inside, mapping out a legal course of action for my aunt should she need it.

When I had questioned Ve as to why she worried that Miles' case *would* eventually be solved, she'd given me only a vague answer of having bad feelings about the matter.

I wasn't sure I believed her.

Which had left *me* unsettled, wondering if Miles' skeleton was some sort of bony Pandora's box that would have been better left undiscovered.

Over the fence that divided Aunt Ve's property from the yard next door, a beautiful scarlet macaw named Archibald, Archie for short, poked his head through an opening in the iron filigree of a large, ornate cage. The tall gazebo-like structure took up nearly an entire corner of the yard, and it had been there so long it appeared as though the yard had adopted it as its own. English ivy that continually needed pruning twined around iron curlicues at the base of the cage, and moss grew on its northern side. Protected by a waist-high fence, the enclosure sat close enough to the sidewalk that tourists often lingered, enraptured by the colorful bird's perpetual need to put on a show.

Archie cleared his throat and said in deep, somber tones, "'And now there's evil rising from where we tried to bury it.'"

Despite the fact that I wore a sweater, goose bumps rose along my arms as I walked over to the cage. The quote, I was quite sure, had been deliberately chosen to reflect the grim discovery of the day. *"The Dark Knight Rises,"* I declared.

"Curses!" Archie exclaimed, his feathers ruffling in dismay.

Lately, he'd been on the losing end of our long-standing movie-quote trivia game, and he wasn't taking it too well. His ego bruised easily.

I kept my body angled, facing the back of the yard, so the gawkers who remained on the village green couldn't witness me having a conversation with the vibrant scarlet macaw.

What they didn't know—unless they were also Crafters—was that Archie was no ordinary bird. He was a familiar. Once upon a time, he'd been a London theater actor, but that had been more than a hundred years ago. He'd eventually ended up here in the Enchanted Village, but his love of performing had never left him. These days, he favored singing the soundtrack for *The Sound of Music* to passersby. He was a big Julie Andrews fan, and it was a small consolation to be able to sing the tunes to tourists, because there was no role for him in Evan's production.

At this point, I wished Evan would write him in. A witch could take only so many renditions of "Do Re Mi" before she lost her mind.

Fortunately for all, mortals have never suspected that the charmingly long-winded bird was anything other than a parrot who watched a lot of TV.

"Did you know him? Miles Babbage?" I asked Archie as I watched Missy roam the yard, chasing after newly fallen leaves.

It had been a long summer, a true New England gift, and the trees had only just started to turn colors with the drop in temperature. The climbing red roses that gripped the arbor above the side gate had finally begun to brown. Soon enough the grass would be littered with discarded petals. Before long, everything would be covered in snow.

"Yes. What an uncommonly vile creature he was." Archie had a deep baritone voice and a rich British accent that lent an air of authority to anything he said.

"He wasn't that bad looking," I said. "Or was there something else you're basing your opinion on?"

He huffed in outrage. "Do I seem the type to judge a person's character on appearances alone? 'Tis the height of shallowness."

I raised an accusatory eyebrow.

"Oh, fine. It's rather true. I'm nothing but a puddle of superficiality," he conceded with reluctance. "However, I judge Miles not upon his countenance, but because he was a callous lothario who mocked my performances relentlessly."

In all honesty, the mocking alone had probably sealed the less than stellar evaluation.

Missy caught a leaf, pounced on it. Then she spotted another falling and chased after that one instead. She seemed to be acting like her old self. Maybe I could hold off on that vet appointment after all.

I leaned against the fence. "I don't suppose you have any theories about how Miles ended up in Ve's garage?"

His gorgeous plumage, with its deep reds, saturated blues, and bright yellows glowed in the sunshine. "Alas, none. No one seemed to openly despise the man. Well, except for me. I am an excellent judge of character, I might add."

I couldn't help smiling. "Did *you* stick him in Ve's garage?"

He laughed, a deep, throaty chuckle. "If only. Did I mention the mocking?"

Out of the corner of my eye, I caught sight of a shadow in the window of the house behind Archie, where he lived with Terry Goodwin. "How did Terry feel about Miles?"

Craft familiars belonged to no one, but many had caretakers. For Archie that person was Terry, a Numbercrafter who worked from home as a CPA. Rarely leaving his house, he was an elusive Elvis look-alike and also notoriously nosy. He was almost always peeping out a window.

Terry also held the distinction of having been Aunt Ve's first husband. And very nearly her fifth. Their attempt to rekindle their relationship this past spring had failed, due mainly to Ve's monogamy issues. They ran deep. Ocean deep.

Fortunately they both rebounded quickly. Terry with his second ex-wife, Cherise Goodwin, whom I counted as a dear friend, and Aunt Ve with Andreus Woodshall, whom I counted as someone I couldn't trust.

Archie fluffed his wings and sidestepped along a branch inside the cage, an enclosure that was purely for display. He could come and go as he pleased. As he edged as close as he could to me, he whispered, "Although Terry was married to Cherise at the time, once word leaked that Ve had eloped and had no memory of the union, it is my belief that *if* Miles had returned to her I highly suspect he would have disappeared again quickly. Knowing Terry as I do, trust me when I tell you Miles would not have been found a second time." He sidestepped away again.

Terry was the protective sort. I knew that firsthand, as he'd come to my rescue a time or two in the past. I had the feeling it was the root of his nosiness. He was the village guardian. "But it *didn't* happen that way?"

"He didn't know of the marriage until well after the fact. Ve kept a tight lid on the matter. It might never have been known except she had to eventually place a notice of divorce in the local paper. It was the only way to proceed with the dissolution since Miles couldn't be found."

"I don't suppose you have the names of any of the women Miles had been seeing?" I asked. "Ve said he was something of a ladies' man."

"It's true, he was regular Casanova. There's no accounting for taste," he squawked. "However, now that you ask, I do recall one relationship in particular. . . ."

"What is that twinkle in your eyes?"

He fluffed his wings and loftily said, "How badly do you want to know?"

Knowing this game well, I sighed. "What's your price?"

"A role in Evan's play."

"Impossible."

He pressed a wing to his chest and weakly said, "My memories . . . they're fading . . ."

I gave him a wry grin and sang, "'We extort, we pilfer, we filch and sack . . .'"

With a groan, he hid his head under his wings. His deep voice rumbled out. "I know it. I know I know it. . . ." He hummed the melody; then he popped his head out. *"Pirates of the Caribbean: The Curse of the Black Pearl!"* Wiping a wing across his brow, he added, "My love of Johnny Depp is deeply ingrained."

"I know. As are your piratelike traits."

"I rarely filch," he protested. "Extortion, however, comes in handy from time to time. As in right now. When one wants a role in the village play . . ."

"Good grief. Fine. I'll see what I can do with Evan, but I cannot guarantee a stage role. Deal?"

He let out a whoop. "'Tis a deal."

"Now, spill."

He chuckled low and deep. "All right, all right. Miles had quite the scandalous affair with none other than . . ." He paused dramatically.

"Archie."

With a tinge of glee, he said in a rush, "It was Dorothy Hansel Dewitt!"

My eyes widened. Dorothy? The wickedest witch in the village? "No way!"

"They were perfectly suited, in my humble opinion. Of course, she was Dorothy Hansel back then, and had left her husband to be with Miles. It was all wickedly salacious. She and Joel Hansel eventually reunited, but their marriage was touch-and-go for a while."

Dorothy Hansel Dewitt was a witch I could do without. We hadn't gotten along since the day I moved to the village. Much of our animosity for each other had to do with my dealings with her daughter, Glinda, which were complicated to say the least. But part of it, I suspected, was simply because Dorothy enjoyed causing trouble.

Missy let out a happy yip, and I turned to find her racing toward the man walking through the backyard from the direction of the garage on the other side of the house.

He bent and gave Missy a hello, then glanced up at me and smiled.

Archie sighed theatrically.

Or that might have been me.

I smiled back at village police chief Nick Sawyer.

He was dressed in his uniform of a black polo shirt and khaki pants, and he also wore a lightweight jacket embroidered with an Enchanted Village Police Department logo on its sleeve. His dark hair was a little longer than usual, curling up at the ends around his ears, and his deep brown eyes never looked away from mine as he strode over to where I stood.

He cupped my cheek with his warm hand and gave me a quick kiss.

"*Sto-o-o-p,*" Archie begged. "I can't take the cute factor. It's making me nauseated. I might hoik." He started making gagging noises.

I laughed. "You should be used to it by now."

"You'd think," Archie replied sarcastically.

Nick said, "Don't worry. I can't stay. I need to track down the village dentist to see if she has any dental records for Miles Babbage. And with that, hopefully a last known address as well."

"If it is him, dental records shouldn't be too hard to match. Ve showed Harper and me a picture of Miles on their wedding day and he has a chipped front tooth. Does your skeleton have any broken teeth?"

Nick's eyebrows dipped. "The skeleton does have a broken tooth. There was also a wallet in his back pocket with an ID in Miles Babbage's name."

"It has to be him," Archie said.

Nick shoved his hands in his jacket pockets. "I think so, too, but I still need to get official verification." Nick glanced over his shoulder at Ve's house. "I'm going to need a copy of that picture."

"I'll get it before you leave." I wrinkled my nose.

"Any idea of how Miles died? Is it too much to wish that it was of natural causes?"

Nick said, "You might actually get that wish granted, Darcy. There are no glaring injuries to the skeleton. No bullet wounds. No stab marks. Until we get more information from the medical examiner, the cause of death is a complete mystery."

Chapter Four

The cause of death.

The phrase was still foremost in my thoughts a few hours later as I carried a moving box toward my new house.

In front of Terry's place, I carefully scooted around a cluster of tourists gathered on the sidewalk in front of Archie's cage, glad I'd decided to leave Missy and Annie at Ve's for now. It was hard enough to navigate with just the box.

Archie was singing "Climb Ev'ry Mountain" in appropriately dramatic fashion and winked at me as I passed by.

Which reminded me that I needed to talk to Evan sooner rather than later about finding Archie some sort of role in the play. Knowing Archie, he undoubtedly wanted a lead. Knowing Evan, he wouldn't give it to him, even if it had been a play about a chatty scarlet macaw. The two had a bit of a love/hate relationship.

I had an idea for something that Archie would be great at, but getting Evan to agree to it might be tricky. I wasn't above begging, however.

A police car rolled by, and I wondered how long it would take to learn how Miles was killed or why his body was in Ve's garage. She and Marcus had gone to the police station to answer questions, and Harper had tagged along for moral support. I had high hopes Ve would be cleared soon enough. As far as I was concerned, my first step in making that happen for my aunt was talking with Dorothy Hansel Dewitt.

Unfortunately, discussions with Dorothy rarely ended well, so I wasn't looking forward to the conversation in the least.

I glanced ahead and noticed a pickup truck parked in my driveway. The vehicle had been a familiar sight over the past few months since it belonged to Henry "Hank" Leduc, the contractor who'd been in charge of renovating my house. He stood at the truck's tailgate, one hand on his toolbox, the other on his hip. He wasn't alone.

I slowed my steps, watching the pair carefully. Hank, the nephew of Terry Goodwin, looked a lot like his uncle. Which was to say he looked a lot like Elvis. If Terry was a dead ringer for the singer, Hank could pass as a decent impersonator. In his mid-thirties, he had the same dark wavy hair, prominent jaw, high cheekbones, and full cheeks as the famous musical icon. Under the brim of a ball cap, heavy-lidded blue eyes intently studied the woman next to him. A woman who happened to possess eyes even bluer than his own.

Starla Sullivan, one of my best friends and Evan's twin sister, had her hands shoved into the pockets of her coat as she talked to Hank a mile a minute while rocking on her booted heels. Her long blond hair was tied back in a simple ponytail that swung as she continued to chatter and flash broad smiles. A camera hung from her neck, and a purple multipocketed waist apron was tied around her hips. As owner of Hocus-Pocus Photography, she often roamed the village as part of her job, snapping pictures of tourists that they could then purchase at her shop at the other end of the square. She also freelanced for the *Toil and Trouble*, the local newspaper.

By the looks of her, she was either flirting shamelessly or asking a favor.

I leaned toward the latter, but I wasn't certain. Even though Starla had been dating Vincent Paxton, owner of Lotions and Potions, a bath and body shop, for nearly a year now—and they cared for each other deeply—they had some issues. The first and foremost being that he was a mortal and she was a witch. Her main craft was as a Wishcrafter, but she was half Bakecrafter, too. The exact opposite of her brother.

And Vince wasn't just a mortal; he was a Seeker, a mortal who was obsessed with witchcraft. When I first met him he had been convinced—despite the Craft's best efforts to keep itself a secret—that witchcraft truly existed and wanted nothing more than to become a witch himself. After becoming a suspect in the murder of another Seeker, he'd cut back on talking about witches.

And since dating Starla, he'd toned down his obsession even more, but he hadn't stopped Seeking completely. Every once in a while he tried to engage one of us in a conversation about witches. We always shut down the talk quickly. Telling a mortal of our powers, even accidentally, was a huge violation of Craft law, and the penance was often the loss of powers.

Despite Vince's desire to become a witch, he was out of luck. Crafting was hereditary. There was no way to become a full witch without having been born with magical abilities. Vince *could* be adopted into our culture, albeit with no powers, if he married Starla. But only if she was willing to give up her own magic in exchange for telling him.

Many Crafters opted to share the Craft secret when marrying a mortal because the price of lying to someone you truly loved was too high. My mother had told my father; Nick's former wife, Melina, had told him. But so far Starla wasn't willing to make that sacrifice, but she was growing more and more weary of keeping the secret.

Neither Hank nor Starla noticed me as I approached.

"Hi there," I said tentatively, giving both a quizzical glance as I placed the box on the ground. "Everything okay here?"

"Everything's great, Darcy," Hank said. "I just stopped by to finish up the punch list."

Hank was a witch, with Manicrafting being his primary ability. As a Mani, he could work magic with his hands, and he put his talent to good use with his construction company.

"And I," Starla added, "was on my way over to Ve's when I saw Hank. I made a quick detour so I could attempt to sweet-talk him into joining your scenery crew. He'd be a natural at building the sets for the play." She smiled at him, a thousand watts of enchanting charm. "But he hasn't given me an answer yet. What do you say, Hank?"

So it *had* been a favor she'd been asking. He hadn't stood a chance, poor guy. I was pretty sure there wasn't a man alive who could say no to Starla's smile.

Hank didn't prove me wrong.

He tipped his head back and laughed. "Okay, okay. I'll do it. Tomorrow afternoon?"

"Two o'clock at the playhouse," she said, her face alight with happiness. "You've already missed the initial meeting of who's who and what's what, but that's the boring part anyway."

"Hey!" I protested.

She said, "You know I'm right." Then to Hank, she added, "Don't forget to bring your tools."

"Actually, we have tools," I explained to him. "We have all the supplies you'll need."

Starla smiled that enchanting smile again. "But I bet Hank's tools are better. He's probably more comfortable with them."

I slid her a look. She didn't notice because she was still grinning at Hank.

Maybe she'd been asking a favor *and* flirting.

If so, it was going to make the gathering tomorrow a bit awkward, as Vince was going to be there as well.

"I'll be there." Hank smiled back at her, a long, lingering look, then turned to me. "What's going on at Ve's?"

Starla said, "Someone told me an ancient burial ground was found in Ve's backyard, the bones of old witches that had been burned at the stake." She shuddered dramatically. Archie would have been proud.

This village and its gossip were impressive at times. "It was the garage. Bones yes, witches no." I explained to them about finding the skeleton.

"Who is it?" Starla asked.

"We don't know for certain, but we think it's Ve's second husband, Miles Babbage. He disappeared shortly after they eloped thirty years ago."

"Poor Ve," Hank said.

I nodded, because I didn't want to get into the dynamics of the relationship.

"What happened to the guy?" Hank asked. "I mean, why was he in her garage?"

"Million-dollar question," I said.

"Did you say Babbage?" Starla asked.

"Yeah, why? Do you know a Babbage?" Starla would have been a baby when Miles disappeared, and the surname was unfamiliar to me. There wasn't another Babbage in the village that I knew of.

She said, "No, I don't think I do. I just feel like I know that name somehow. I can't place it, though."

"Well, if it comes back to you, let me know. I've been asked by the Elder to investigate the matter."

Frowning, she nodded.

All the Crafters in the village knew I worked for the Elder, but not many knew the Elder was my mother. Starla did, but Hank did not. The order of secrecy was in place to protect the Elder's powers from being used or abused, but now that I knew who she was, I suspected the directive was created to protect her family as well.

Starla said, "If anyone can figure it out, you can, Darcy. Your track record speaks for itself."

"Thanks. I'm hoping it's an easy case, for Ve's sake."

"Give her my condolences, will you?" Hank said.

I had the feeling Ve would be receiving lots of condolences she didn't want. "I will."

He closed the tailgate on his truck, then turned to me and handed me a key ring. "Your keys. I'm done here, so I won't need them anymore. Just call if anything comes up."

"I can't thank you enough," I said, meaning it. Four months ago my house had been a dilapidated mess. Hank and his crew had practically rebuilt it from the ground up, using a little bit of magic along the way. Okay, a lot of magic. The house had been a disaster.

"You're welcome. I've got to head out, but like I said, call if you need me. See you tomorrow."

Starla and I waved as he backed out of the driveway.
As soon as he was out of earshot, Starla turned to
me. "Okay, Darcy Merriweather, what's really going on
with the bones in Ve's garage? Because I know you well,
and you didn't tell us everything. I want all the details."

Chapter Five

Starla did know me well.

She said, "I heard something in your voice earlier. What's the real story?"

I picked up the box at my feet; then I motioned for her to follow me into the house. As we slowly walked, I quickly told her about Miles' sketchy history, the mysterious elopement, and Ve's dislike of the man.

"That doesn't bode well for Ve, does it?" she said softly.

Painted a dark purple with gold lettering that visually popped, the beautifully carved AS YOU WISH sign hung from a bracket on one of the front-porch columns. The sign had been moved from Ve's to here, where I'd added one alteration. A smaller version of the original now dangled from a chain attached to the bottom of the sign. Its golden letters read BY APPOINTMENT ONLY.

When I took over the company, I decided the days of drop-in clients needed to end.

"On the surface it doesn't look good for Ve, but hopefully there will be some kind of evidence that will clear her name right off the bat. That way the police can focus on other possible suspects."

The front door opened into a wide entryway flooded with sunlight. To my left, Craftsman-style pocket doors closed off my office space, keeping As You Wish separate from the rest of the house. To my right was a wide set of turned wooden stairs. They were protected by an aqua-and-cream floral carpet runner in a subtle daisy pattern that would hopefully not only keep the treads safe from the dogs but the dogs safe from the slippery steps. In the angled nook below the staircase, Nick had designed and crafted custom bookshelves. Currently the shelves were empty, and I couldn't wait to fill them. When Nick moved in, we planned to add a couple of upholstered chairs and a side table from his current house to the space.

I'd been moving in slowly over the past couple of weeks and was still getting used to this new space. Tonight was to have been the first night I slept here, but now with what had happened with Ve, I wondered if I should postpone that. . . .

As if reading my mind, Starla said, "Are you still planning to move in here today?"

"I don't know. I'm leaning toward staying with Ve, at least for the weekend."

"She probably shouldn't be alone."

I nodded. "I'm also hoping that during that time she'll elaborate on why she's afraid the case will be solved."

"It is rather odd that she wouldn't want to know what happened." Starla looked around the entryway and said, "I know I've said it a hundred times, but this place is incredible."

I placed the box down on the area rug near the door. This space had once been the main living room, which had been relocated to the back of the house, in the new addition. "Hank works a special kind of magic."

Hank and his crew had outdone themselves, creating something I didn't even know I'd wanted. He'd taken my ideas to add "an addition" and Nick's suggestion of "more windows" and Mimi's plea for a "reading nook" and he designed a dream home.

My and Nick's and Mimi's dream home.

Even though everything was brand-new in here, the design had kept much of the original Craftsman-cottage feel of the old house. Unlike the original, however, most of the ornate woodwork was now painted a soft white, with only a few natural-wood touches, like the floor, Nick's shelves, and the butcher-block top on the kitchen island.

Tall flat-panel wainscoting decorated the hall and stairway, the white panels contrasting beautifully with the creamy sand-colored paint. There was a storage closet and a small powder room at the end of the hallway on the right, just before the hallway ended, opening dramatically into the vaulted main living space.

"He really does work magic," Starla said as she followed me down the hallway, our footsteps echoing on the sun-soaked oak floor. "He's amazing."

I turned and looked at her head on. I lifted an eyebrow.

Redness bloomed in her cheeks. "What?"

"What, what?" I asked, teasing.

She darted past me into the kitchen. "Why are you staring at me that way?"

"You like him."

I knew her well, too.

"Like? Who? Hank?"

"Of course Hank."

She adjusted her camera strap. "I don't know what you mean."

Oh boy. I dropped my voice and singsonged, "You really li-i-i-ike him."

Her cheeks now flamed red. She opened her mouth, closed it. Finally, she said, "He's just a friend. Vince . . ."

I grabbed the teakettle and filled it with water, and then set the kettle on the stovetop. "How is Vince these days?"

As I waited for her answer, I crossed the room and grabbed two mugs from the built-in hutch behind where she sat at the island, which was one of my favorite pieces in the house. Nick had designed it and Hank had built it. While the rest of the cabinetry in the kitchen was ivory white and the countertops a sparkling gray-and-white quartz, the island stood out with its deep Nantucket blue base and its dark butcher-block top.

Starla sighed. "He's . . ."

Grabbing two tea bags from one of the four colorful owl-shaped canisters on the counter, I waited for her to finish. Mimi had chosen the ceramic owls, and I loved them almost as much as I did the island.

When Starla didn't answer, I faced her and prompted, "He's . . . ?"

She turned her hands palms up as she shrugged. "Things have been a little strained lately."

I knew. "Has it worsened?"

"I've been thinking about going to see the Elder about him."

Even though she knew my mother was the Elder, she still referred to her as such. Old habits died hard. "Why?" The kettle began to hiss. "What happened?"

"I think he's Seeking again. A lot. I'm starting to question whether he ever cut back at all."

We all thought he'd changed his ways when he fell for Starla. And maybe for the most part, he had.

Except for the Seeking.

I had personally gone to bat for Vince, convincing him to stay in the village after he and Starla hit a rough patch last winter.

I didn't want to believe I'd made a mistake believing in him, but I was starting to think I had.

It made me feel sick to my stomach.

She went on. "He keeps wanting to take pictures of me. I have to recite the Lunumbra spell every single day now. I've always memory-cleansed him in the past when my photos didn't turn out, because of all his questions. Now I wonder if he's been taking pictures of me when I didn't realize it. Why else would he be so fascinated with taking my picture?"

The spell was the one that allowed Wishcrafters to be visible on film and video. As she explained, I went about gathering spoons and napkins, and because I didn't have a sugar shaker yet, I put the whole sugar-filled owl canister on the island. "It's a good question."

"And lately I've been finding witchcraft books in his house," she went on. "Not just one or two but ten, fifteen. I've seen Web pages bookmarked on his computer for witchcraft sites. And not only that, but sorcery sites as well."

The kettle whistled and I quickly pulled it from the heat and shut off the flame. The witchcraft fascination was one thing, because Vince wasn't likely to find anything related to our particular Craft. There was very little out in the world related to our kind of magic. I think Harper had found the only book in existence about it, hidden in the basement of the bookshop, and she had that one under lock and key.

Sorcery, however, was another matter altogether. Much of it was dark magic that anyone could practice with no rules. And it was powerful. Extremely.

This was a disturbing twist.

"Do you think he's been using any of it?" I poured water into the cups and steam plumed. "The sorcery?"

"I don't think so. I mean, I'd feel it, wouldn't I? A disturbance in my force, or something like that? I think it's just a matter of time, though. But right now, that's not the most upsetting thing about this. . . . As you know, his birthday was a few days ago."

I smiled. "That's upsetting?"

"It's what he *wanted* for his birthday, Darcy."

I sat on a stool. Ordinarily I'd have wiggled my eyebrows and teased her, but her demeanor told me this wasn't a laughing matter. "Oh?"

"He bought two of those DNA kits that trace ancestry and wanted me to do one with him. I couldn't. I'm not sure anything wacky will show up because I'm a witch, but I can't take that risk. Crafting is hereditary. There has to be something within us that's not quite normal. Vince and I had a huge fight about it because I refused to take the test. He's not just a Seeker, oh no. He finally admitted to me that he's convinced he's a witch—or, in his words, a 'warlock.'"

Crafters didn't use that description for males within our society. "Witch" was used universally. "Did you try to talk him out of it?"

"Not really. I was too scared that in the heat of the moment, I would say something that as a *mortal* I shouldn't know. I was hoping that ignoring him would work, but then he went off and hired Glinda to help him trace his ancestry."

Glinda Hansel was a former village police officer turned PI. We'd once been adversaries but were slowly piecing together a strange sort of friendship. As a witch herself, surely she wouldn't string Vince along. . . .

"I'll talk to her," I said. "See if she can convince Vince to let this all go."

"I was hoping you'd say that, because you know I don't want to do it. Talk to her, that is . . ." Starla bit her lip. "She finally apologized, by the way. In person. With flowers. And what looked like actual remorse."

"She did? When?"

"A few weeks ago. She said she was trying to make things right in her life and had a lot of regret for what she'd done to me. She said she'd been wrong, plain and simple, and that she was very sorry."

Glinda didn't like to admit when she was wrong, let alone apologize.

"Did you accept the apology?" I asked.

Glinda had made her bed, so to speak, with Starla last January. It had been an emotionally painful experience that had taught us all some valuable lessons.

"I did. Darcy, you know I forgave her a long time ago, but it was nice to get the apology. What she did to me . . ." She took a deep breath. "Although I didn't agree with her methods, of course, when I put myself in her shoes and looked at that situation through her eyes, I could understand—a little—why she'd done the things she did."

It was part of Starla's inner magic—her ability to look outside herself, her feelings, and understand someone else's point of view. It was one of the things I loved most about her.

"But," she went on, "I'm not sure I'll ever be able to be friends with her. I'm not entirely sure how you're able to do it."

We'd had this conversation before. I'd been afraid Starla would see my relationship with Glinda as being disloyal, but Starla had set my heart at ease. I laughed. "It's getting easier."

"She does seem different lately. You think it's Liam? Or Mimi?"

Glinda had fallen in love with Liam Chadwick, Starla's former brother-in-law. They lived together with their dog, Clarence, who was a lovable golden retriever. As for Mimi . . . when they'd first become friends, I fully believed Glinda had insinuated herself into Mimi's life solely to get closer to Nick, as she'd had a crush on him at the time. And maybe that had been true. But somewhere along the line, Glinda had come to love Mimi deeply, and Mimi loved her like a favorite aunt.

"Love is powerful motivation to change. But I like to think she finally recognized she wasn't the person she wanted to be and decided to live a different life."

"I hope that's true. Because to truly change who you are, it has to come from within."

I nodded.

"Anyway," Starla said, "if she can convince Vince to drop this witch-hunt of his, I'd like her a little more."

Smiling, I said, "Sounds like it's been rough between the two of you lately."

"We've been fighting constantly, and not just about the witch stuff. It's wearing on me."

Starla added a little bit of sugar to her tea and dunked her tea bag mercilessly. "His Seeking isn't necessarily a secret, but I highly suspect he believes I'm a witch and is looking for confirmation."

Suddenly chilled, I held my mug between my hands for warmth. I didn't know what to say.

"And not only that," she added. "I'm now questioning whether he's always suspected it. Is it why he pursued me so relentlessly? Was I so desperate to be loved again that I was blind to his true motives?"

"No," I said firmly. "Don't even think that. There's

no question that Vince is a complicated person, but if there's one thing I know for certain about him, it's how much he cares for you—whether you're a witch or not."

She sighed. "I don't think I can be in a relationship where I'm going to have to be constantly on guard. Is he going to try to get my DNA some other way? Is he going to pluck a hair or test my toothbrush?"

If he was on a quest, I wouldn't put it past him. Seekers tended to have one-track minds.

With a spoon she scooped up the tea bag, then wrapped the string around both, effectively wringing out the bag. She placed the spoon on a napkin and looked at me, her sky blue eyes filled with confusion. "I don't know what to do."

"If you take his Seeking out of it, how do you feel about him? Do you still love him?"

She slid her mug from side to side between her hands. "I'll probably always feel something for him, but . . ."

"What?"

"I'm just not *in love* with him anymore. In fact, I've been thinking about it, and I don't even like him very much these days. I don't think I can be with him anymore *and* keep the secret that I'm a witch. And if I have to choose between the two, I choose being a witch." She held my gaze. "And I think that tells me all I need to know about the relationship, because if I truly loved him, heart-and-soul loved him, like I did with Kyle, then there wouldn't be a moment's hesitation to tell him the truth about the Craft."

Kyle Chadwick, who'd died last winter, had been Starla's ex-husband. Theirs was a tragic relationship that had nearly destroyed Starla . . . twice. The fact that she had been willing to open her heart to Vince in the first place told me how much she cared for him, but caring and loving were two very different things.

She took a sip of her tea and stared out the windows that looked into the backyard. "As much as I know what I need to do, I don't want to hurt Vince by doing it. I need to figure out how to break up with him in the least painful way possible. It's not going to be easy."

I had the feeling she'd been wrestling with how to do that for a while. I'd seen the signs over the past few months, the distance.

"It never is. I'm sorry," I said.

She sighed. "It was really good for a while."

It had been. She'd been happy, and Vince had been good to her. I wondered what had changed. Wondered if we'd ever know. I had to remind myself that sometimes relationships simply didn't work out.

"I don't regret being with Vince," she said, "but I'm kind of relieved to move forward without having to watch my every word. It's been a bigger burden than I ever imagined. The sooner I break it off, the better." She took a deep breath. "Tonight. I'll do it tonight."

Once Starla set her mind to something, it was done. I just hoped Vince would handle the breakup well. He had his faults, but I didn't want to see him hurt, either.

Starla glanced around. "Now, do you need any more help with moving in here? My afternoon schedule is flexible."

"Not really. Most of my stuff was in Ve's garage. It has to stay there until the crime techs are done. I just have a couple of little boxes left to move from my room at Ve's, which I should leave there if I'm staying the night."

"I've been thinking about her memory or, more accurately, her lack of memories. Do you know if she's tried the memory spell to recover those missing days with Miles?"

That spell had worked wonders on me when I was trying to recall memories of my mother, but I'd *wanted* to remember. I wasn't sure Ve did. "I'll ask her. It's worth a try."

Starla set her mug in the farmer's sink. "I should probably get back to work. But first, I think I'm going to send a note to the Elder. She should know about the sorcery stuff—don't you think?"

A cold chill went down my spine. "Definitely. Sorcery is not something we want here in the village. That kind of evil is scary. Speaking of, that reminds me I need to go see Dorothy Hansel Dewitt about Miles Babbage."

Starla laughed as she headed for the front door. "Scary is right. Good luck with that."

She gave me a hug, and I squeezed her tight.

"Thanks for listening," she said.

"Anytime."

I leaned against the doorjamb and watched her head down the sidewalk toward Terry's house and Archie's cage. As the Elder's messenger, Archie would see to it that my mother received Starla's note.

As I headed back inside, I could only hope that Vince wasn't in over his head with this sorcery nonsense.

But I had a bad feeling about it.

A very bad feeling indeed.

Chapter Six

Half an hour later, I checked to see if Ve had come home yet (nope) and also called Nick for an update on the case (he didn't answer). I had washed and put away my and Starla's mugs, unpacked the box I'd carried over from Ve's, and now had no other choice than to go talk to Dorothy Hansel Dewitt.

It was probably best to get it over with.

The sun hid behind low clouds as I headed out, and with the shade had come a steep drop in temperature. I looped a dandelion-printed cotton scarf around my neck and buttoned my short pea coat to ward off the chill.

Only one emergency vehicle remained parked in front of Ve's house. It looked to be a crime scene van. A few people still gathered on the green, trying to see what they could see. I couldn't blame them. It was human nature to be curious about such things.

I turned left at my front gate, heading away from the bad memories of the morning. A stiff breeze sent leaves tumbling along the sidewalk as I walked along, heading into the heart of the village's business district.

Tourists huddled against the sudden cold as they hurried along from one shop to the next. I took a second to watch four kittens romp around the window display of the Furry Toadstool and waved to the pet shop's new owner, Vivienne Lucas, who stood behind the counter.

There was a certain scent that permeated the village this time of year. It was crisp and earthy and reminded me of endings and beginnings and the magic all around me. I bent and picked up a perfectly formed acorn that had fallen from a tall oak tree near the playhouse. Some would see the nut as yard waste and rake it up and throw it away. I saw it as a treasure. Acorns were prized by the Craft, mostly as protection charms. On a whim, I gathered a few more and tucked them into my pocket.

"I hope you aren't hoarding those as protection from me," a faraway voice said, the humorous undertones clear despite the distance.

I turned and saw Glinda Hansel and Clarence headed my way. Instead of galloping ahead of her, tugging her along as he usually did, Clarence trotted beside her like a perfect gentleman.

"Do I need to?" I asked with a raised eyebrow as they reached my side.

Glinda had angelic looks with her ash blond hair, clear blue eyes, and fair skin. She was just a hair taller than I was, and I assumed her height had come from her father, since her mother was just a bit taller than Harper.

Glinda carried herself like the cop she once was, with her shoulders drawn back, her head held high. She exuded confidence, but when I looked deep into her eyes, the confidence vanished, replaced with a hint of insecurity. In the past nine months, she'd changed a lot. The old Glinda had been arrogant and self-righteous. That self-doubt I saw in her eyes was the biggest sign there was that her recent personality changes were real and not for show.

I hoped and wished that the changes were permanent. I liked her much better this way.

She said, "No, but maybe from Clarence. He's vicious."

I bent down and gave him a good neck rub. He slurped my face, and his tail swept the sidewalk clear of any remaining acorns. "Such a brute," I said with a laugh. "His obedience classes are clearly paying off."

"Bribing with c-o-o-k-i-e-s helps."

"I mean, come on. That works with me, too. Cupcakes are even better."

Glinda smiled, but it faded quickly. "I heard about what happened at Ve's. Do you know who the man is?"

"Not officially. We think it's Miles Babbage, Ve's second husband."

With a shocked tone, she said, "Miles Babbage?"

"Do you know of him?"

"I heard the name recently," she said vaguely.

Overhead, leaves rustled noisily in the wind. I fussed with my scarf. "From your mother? Apparently, she knew him. . . ."

"Maybe so," she said noncommittally. "Are you waiting on dental records or DNA for confirmation?"

It was times like this that I questioned whether she had truly changed, because I could tell she knew more than she was letting on.

"We're hoping dental. It's a long shot. Apparently he was a vagabond, but there's some hope he had work done on his teeth since he was often here in the village with the Roving Stones."

"The Stones? Really? Was he a Crafter?"

"Mortal, but he was an expert potter and traveled with the show." If she didn't know her mom had had an affair with Miles, I didn't want to be the one to tell her. "I was just on my way to Third Eye to ask your mom some questions about him."

With a push of a button, she retracted Clarence's leash a little, stopping him from climbing the stairs of the playhouse. He went back to sniffing along the grass edge of the sidewalk. "You're working the case, then?"

Glinda knew all about my job investigating for the Elder, but she didn't know the Elder was my mother. "Yes. I'm hoping Dorothy will talk to me without it being a major ordeal."

Glinda let out a slow hiss of breath. "I wouldn't count on it. It's a good thing you have those acorns."

I wasn't sure they protected against someone who was simply mean and liked to cause trouble. Because as much as I disliked Dorothy, I didn't think she was truly evil.

Well, maybe she was a little evil.

Okay, all right. I was glad to have the acorns in my pocket. It certainly couldn't hurt to have them on me when questioning Dorothy. "Maybe I'll pick up a couple more just to be safe."

Her light eyebrows dipped as she nodded. "Good idea."

Clarence licked my hand. I patted his head. "I saw Starla a little while ago. I heard about your apology."

"It was long overdue. I know the apology can't change what happened, but it needed to be done. I know Starla said she already forgave me, but I came to realize that I also needed to forgive myself. The apology was the first step in that. I'm working on the rest of it."

"Change is hard," I said gently.

"You have no idea. Especially when my mother . . ." She shook her head. "It's just been hard."

She and Dorothy had a strained relationship at best. At worst, I suspected Glinda wanted to wish her mother to Siberia. It would have been a wish I'd have been happy to grant.

I said, "Starla also mentioned you're working for Vince."

Clarence tried eating an acorn, and Glinda pried the now-soggy nut out of his mouth. "No," she said to him sternly. "These aren't for dogs."

Glumly, he stared at her.

I wasn't sure I'd ever be able to say no to his woebegone eyes.

Glinda looked back at me. "Vince is . . . persuasive. I thought it best I take the case rather than someone else."

"Like a mortal?"

"Exactly."

"Have you tried talking him out his ideas that he's a *warlock*?"

She rolled her eyes at the word. "I've tried my best to tone him down. I'm working on filling out his family tree, hoping that'll be enough to appease him. . . ."

Again, her words were oddly stilted. "Have you found anything interesting?"

"Not . . . particularly. I'm still looking."

Yep. She was definitely keeping something from me. I supposed as a PI, she was sworn to keep Vince's confidences unless ordered by a court of law, but I rather hoped she'd share details if they were important to my case . . . and to the Craft.

She added, "There are some empty branches I need to fill in and not really any way to find that information. At least that I've uncovered so far."

Empty branches? I lowered my voice. "Is it possible he *is* a witch?"

"If we know anything about this village, it's that anything's possible around here," she said. "I'll keep trying to steer him away from the possibility that he's a witch, but I have the feeling he's not going to let this go anytime soon."

Seekers were often relentless. Obsessive. I should have known he couldn't keep that side of him tucked away forever. But I'd been hopeful for Starla's sake. So hopeful.

Clarence started tugging his leash. Glinda said, "I should go before he reverts back to old habits and drags me across the green."

"I'll see you and Liam at the housewarming?" I asked.

With apprehension in her eyes, she glanced in the direction of my house. "Are you sure you want us there?"

"I'm sure. Clarence can even come along if he wants." He gave me another kiss.

He was a sweetheart, that dog.

"But—," she started to say.

I cut her off. "No buts. Two o'clock next Saturday."

A bright, beaming smile spread across her face, and she suddenly looked like she was a beatific subject in a Renaissance portrait. I fully expected cherubs to start dropping out of the clouds any second now.

"We'll be there," she said. "But you'll see me before that. I'll be at the auditions tomorrow. Liam's trying out."

"I thought he was more into Shakespeare." His whole family was nutty for old William.

"When *The Sound of Music* is the only play in town, you do what you have to do. I'm actually glad I ran into you. I wanted to ask if you needed extra help with the scenery. If Liam's going to be at the playhouse, I might as well be, too." She grinned. "I'm really handy with power tools."

As a Broomcrafter, she could turn wood into magic. "We'd love to have you. But, fair warning, Starla will be there. If that bothers you . . ."

"Will it bother her?"

"Only one way to know."

She took a deep breath. "Okay. Let's give it a try. If I sense she's not happy I'm there, then I'll back out."

"Sounds fair enough. We're meeting tomorrow at two o'clock. In the scenery shop at the playhouse."

"I'll be there. And just a fair warning for you, Darcy . . ."

I didn't like the warning in her tone. "What?"

"You might want to save a few of those acorns for tomorrow, because my mother will be there, too. She's auditioning as well, hoping to get the role of Maria."

Shock rippled through me on many counts. One, that Dorothy was trying out. Two, that I was destined to spend a significant amount of time with her. And three, that she was trying out for a role that should go to a woman much younger than she was. "Thanks for the tip."

"Forewarned is forearmed." She waved good-bye and wandered off, letting Clarence lead the way.

Wind whipped my dark hair around my face, and I grabbed hold of the wayward locks and tucked them into my coat. The clouds had begun to darken, and I could now smell rain in the air. The village green, which in a few weeks would host the Harvest Festival, was nearly empty. Its paths stood bare except for racing leaves, its benches and picnic areas empty. The day, so full of promise, had taken a sudden turn for the worse, and it seemed everyone had felt the shift in the atmosphere and sought shelter.

Across the empty space, I spied the Gingerbread Shack, Evan Sullivan's bakery. One of his miniature devil's food cupcakes sounded like heaven right about now. I made a mental note to stop there on my way back to Ve's. It was a good time to see if he'd help me out where Archie was concerned as well.

But first I had to see a witch about a weasel.

I hurried along, hoping the rain would hold off while I ran my errands. I could see my first destination ahead, a small brick-faced shop with a vibrant red awning shading its window front and door. Third Eye Optometry.

I paused to admire the display window, which was decorated with three stuffed witch dolls, primitive in design, that sat at a small wooden table adorned with a tea set. All three witches had their own broomsticks and wore long black capes, plain dresses, pointed black hats, and brightly colored glasses. Even the black cat under the table wore glasses. It was adorable, and I recognized the dolls as ones made by the owner of the Spinning Wheel, a witch herself.

Through the glass, I saw Sylar Dewitt tapping away at a computer behind a glass counter display and the hind side of Dorothy as she hurried into a back room. Her blindingly blond hair and exaggerated butt swish were unmistakable.

She'd worked here at Third Eye for years and years, long before I'd moved to the village, long before she married Sylar last year, long before she'd wooed him while he'd been engaged to Aunt Ve. As far as I knew, Dorothy truly loved Sylar, a mortal, but she hadn't told him that she was a Broomcrafter, and I doubted she ever would. She wasn't one to give up any kind of power, magical or not.

Drawing in a deep breath, I pulled open the door and went inside and was immediately grateful for the warmth of the shop. Sylar looked up, and his blue eyes narrowed.

Above his glasses, his bushy white eyebrows dipped low. "Darcy, did you have an appointment?"

"No, no. I actually stopped by to see Dorothy."

Nodding, he said, "She suspected as much when she saw you standing outside." He rested his hands on the upper curve of his round belly. Although he'd always been on the heavy side, he'd gained more weight after marrying Dorothy. An argyle vest was stretched to its limits over his girth.

"Oh?"

"She figured it had something to do with the hulla-balloo at Ve's home earlier today."

I wasn't the least bit surprised that they'd heard the news. By now the whole village knew. Some would re-peat the truth while others would repeat the Salem witch graveyard story Starla had heard. By tomorrow I wouldn't be surprised to hear that it was Jimmy Hoffa's skeleton in Ve's garage.

After clearing his throat, he mimicked Dorothy's voice: "I bet that nosy b—"—he coughed sharply—"*witch* Darcy Merriweather is here to see me."

He suddenly clamped his lips together as though he'd said something he shouldn't have and darted a fearful look over his shoulder.

Clearly he was terrified of Dorothy.

Rightfully so.

She was scary.

I almost gave him one of my acorns but decided I needed to keep them all for myself. Dorothy at least *liked* Sylar.

She hated me.

My left eyebrow rose as I said, "She didn't really say 'witch,' did she, Sylar?"

His chubby cheeks reddened. "I was trying to spare your feelings."

I doubted it. If so, he would have said nothing at all. Dorothy's meanness was rubbing off on him.

Plus, he was probably still angry about losing the village council election to Ve. When she had declared her intent to run for his long-term position of chairman, in one fell swoop she became his adversary and, in turn, so did I. The family ties that bind . . .

"I've known Ve to have a temper," he said, stroking his chin, "but to kill a man?"

I put my hands on my hips. "When has she had a temper?"

He sputtered. "Do you recall the showdown she had on the green with my beloved Dorothy last spring?"

Oh. Yes. There had been that.

It was a miracle there hadn't been bloodshed.

"Ve didn't *kill* anyone," I stated firmly, then glanced toward the back room. "May I talk to Dorothy now?"

The sooner I got this over with, the better. This shop made me uncomfortable. Partly because I'd once broken into it and still felt shards of guilt poking my conscience.

And partly because it *felt* like Dorothy in here. It might be Sylar's shop, but it was her lair. It was as though her disagreeable aura surrounded me, even when she wasn't present. It was unnerving, to say the least.

"Certainly. I'll get her." He strolled toward the doorway at the back of the shop, and I walked over to the display window. What I really wanted was to run through the front door and not look back, but I was pretty sure "chicken" wasn't part of my job description as Craft investigator.

I heard some doors opening and closing from the storage room and figured Dorothy was toying with me, making me wait on purpose.

That was, until I looked out onto the green to see her swishy tush hightailing it down the sidewalk, heading in the opposite direction from where I stood.

I turned and said, "Sylar?"

He stepped out of the back room and wiped his forehead with a tissue. Smoothing his spiky white hair, he said, "Dorothy, uh, seems to have stepped out."

So I'd seen.

"Where'd she go?" I asked.

"I don't dare presume. A woman's mind is a mysterious creature, and Dorothy's is more puzzling than most."

Truer words had never been spoken. I didn't understand why she did half the things she did.

"You don't think she's avoiding me, do you?" I asked, sidling back up to the counter where he stood. It certainly seemed that way to me.

"Dorothy avoids no one."

He had a point, but that didn't explain why Dorothy was practically sprinting down the street in her four-inch heels.

"Besides, why would she?" he added. "What's this about?"

"She probably doesn't want me to ask her about Miles Babbage. Or, more likely, she doesn't want to answer any questions about him."

"Miles Babbage!" he exclaimed. "Is that who Ve knocked off?"

By the twinkle in his eye when he said Miles' name, he'd already known the suspected identity of the skeleton found. He was poking fun at my expense and also testing my patience.

Dorothy was definitely rubbing off on the man.

I did my best to ignore his gibes.

"We don't know for certain it's him, but it's highly likely." I bit my lip, wondering how much Sylar knew of Dorothy's past. Finally, I said, "I heard Dorothy used to know him fairly well. Has she mentioned him?"

"If you're speaking of her romance with the man, it's old news, Darcy."

Relief swept over me. He knew, which meant that maybe he could answer some of my questions. I'd much rather deal with him than Dorothy. "New news, considering the skeleton . . . I'm guessing that whoever put the body in there had some sort of gripe with Ve and wanted her to be blamed for the crime."

"Someone like Dorothy, perhaps?" he said, his displeasure with me filling his eyes.

I shoved my hands into my pockets. "Their discord *is* quite well-known around the village."

"Be that as it may, it's a preposterous supposition that Dorothy was involved in the man's death. Ve certainly had motive enough on her own. You might recall that she has quite the track record for taking the easy way out of relationships."

More poking. Two could play that game. "Well, it's certainly warranted on her part to cut and run if the man had been *cheating.*"

As Sylar had been the week before Ve was to marry him.

Sweat beaded along his hairline as he pressed his hands to his heart. "But for the loving grace of my Dorothy, I could have been that skeleton in Ve's garage . . ."

I couldn't believe he said "loving grace" and "Dorothy" in the same sentence. He wasn't only terrified of her but clearly besotted as well. It was a baffling combination. "Oh please."

Ve killing Sylar would have been an act of mercy.

Because in my opinion, marriage to Dorothy was a fate worse than death.

Sylar folded his arms on top of his stomach bump. "What does all this have to do with you, Darcy? It's a police matter now."

I couldn't tell him the truth about my job, so I improvised. "Ve doesn't deserve consideration as a suspect, so I'm doing everything I can to prove her innocence. Just as she and I once did for you . . ." It wasn't that long ago he'd been a suspect in a homicide as well. I let him stew on that for a moment before I said, "I'll come back later when Dorothy's here."

I was halfway to the front door when he said, "You're barking up the wrong tree, Darcy."

I looked back at him. I thought I spotted a speck of humility in his features. Maybe Dorothy hadn't quite turned him completely wicked just yet. "What tree should I be looking at, then?"

He dabbed his forehead with the tissue again. "Dorothy's relationship with that man was long over by the time he disappeared. She'd reconciled with her husband more than a year before. They'd renewed their vows and had gone on a lengthy second honeymoon around the world. By the time Miles returned to the village, she was four months pregnant with Glinda. She had no interest in Miles' return."

For him to know those kinds of details off the top of his head after thirtyish years told me that he and Dorothy had been discussing this very topic quite recently. Perhaps even today. Perhaps only moments before she sprinted out of here.

I waited for him to go on. He clearly knew something he wanted to tell me.

"When I heard the skeleton in Ve's garage might be Miles Babbage, I was reminded of a fight I'd broken up between Miles and another man in the village. It occurred only moments after the man left this very shop, in fact. It seemed as though he stepped out the door and fists began flying. I checked my records, and sure enough the date confirms it was thirty years ago this very week. It was one of the last times anyone saw him in the village. He married Ve a day later and then disappeared."

"How do you know that about the marriage?" I asked. "I was under the impression that very few knew of the elopement when it happened."

"That's very true. But several months later, Ve's petition for divorce became a matter of public record. Abandonment was listed as the grounds for the dissolution, as was the date of the elopement. It was fairly easy to connect the dots."

That's right. Archie had mentioned that Ve had to put a notice in the paper since Miles wasn't able to be found.

"The divorce notice was all the talk around the village for quite a while. Gossip abounded with theories that Ve and Miles had been drunk as skunks when they eloped, and that once Miles sobered up, he ran for the hills. We all presumed that Miles hadn't returned to the village so he didn't have to face Ve's wrath."

I winced, imagining Ve's embarrassment with the village chatter. I didn't point out that everyone had thought Miles *ran off* and not that Ve killed him. I'd known Sylar's earlier bluster about Ve being capable of murder was just that . . . bluster.

I pressed on. "You said you broke up a fight. Who was Miles fighting with?"

"It was Steve Winstead."

I jerked a thumb over my shoulder, motioning to the shops across the green. "Steve from the Trimmed Wick?"

"Indeed. He didn't own the candle shop back then, however. He was just another starving artist, selling his wares at craft fairs and the like." He jabbed the air like an out-of-shape boxer. "He and Miles were going at it something terrible. The police were called."

"Do you know what they were fighting about?"

"It wasn't a *what*, Darcy. It was a *who*. They were fighting over Penelope."

"Debrowski?" I asked, shocked by the idea that Marcus' mother had been involved with any of this.

"She wasn't married to Oliver at that point, but yes. *That* Penelope."

"Why were they fighting over her? Anything specific?"

He lifted his shoulders in a shrug. "I've no idea . . . but I can imagine."

My mind was spinning. What in the world had Miles been up to? And how did Steve . . . and Penelope . . . and Ve factor into it?

I had a lot of work to do. "Thanks, Sylar."

He tipped his head in acknowledgment and went back to his computer work. As I headed for the door, I tossed him one last look.

Sylar had spun me a nice, tidy story and had given me more leads to follow . . . but I wasn't ready to discount Dorothy's involvement with that skeleton just yet.

Not after the way she'd booked it out of here.

But now I wondered if she was truly running away from me . . . or from her past.

Chapter Seven

Raindrops sprinkled the village as I dashed across the green, debating how in the world to tell Marcus his mother was possibly involved in a murder case.

I wasn't sure, but I knew one thing for certain. That kind of conversation required chocolate. Mini devil's food cupcakes to be exact, and there was no one who made them better than Evan Sullivan. The magic he added to the batter was the secret ingredient that allowed all his treats to deliver an aftertaste of pure contentment.

Contentment sounded really nice right about now.

A cool breeze chased after me as I hurried inside the Gingerbread Shack. I tugged the heavy glass door closed behind me instead of letting it shut on its own. Outside, the low clouds had darkened ominously, and a sudden sense of apprehension sent a shiver through me, leaving me unsettled. As Harper would say, there was bad juju in the air.

Being inside the bakery alleviated that feeling somewhat. How could it not, with its soothing scents of vanilla and chocolate and a hint of hazelnut? I also caught a whiff of nutmeg and apples, most likely from Evan's seasonal apple pies.

The shop was relatively quiet, with only a few tables full of guests. Large framed close-up photos of cake slices hung on the walls, and white beadboard trim lent a homey feel to the space.

Smiling at the young woman behind the counter, I headed straight for the big glass display case at the rear of the shop. She was another new hire. It was just one more sign that after the tragic death of a former employee, Evan was finally starting to live life again instead of letting life live him. He was still dating FBI agent Scott Abramson and had started taking more time off to enjoy other pastimes.

Like directing a play.

He was an accomplished stage manager, but taking on a bigger role at the playhouse meant relinquishing even more control here at the shop. Which he had done, and it was a joy to see.

My gaze skipped over the rows and rows of tiny confections. The bakery specialized in miniature delights, and Evan's creations never ceased to amaze me. Beyond being delicious, they were beautiful.

Cupcakes took up much of the case. Toffee crunch, triple chocolate chunk, mint swirl, white chocolate espresso, to name a few. Each had a thick swirl of frosting, and some had additional toppings such as shaved chocolate, toasted coconut, and jimmies. There were bite-sized cheesecakes, delicate squares of tiramisu nestled in foil liners, brownies, cookies, and tiny pies.

The choices were endless, but when I was stressed-out, I always picked the same thing.

As I ordered a dozen mini devil's food cupcakes and a cup of coffee, Evan stuck his head out of the kitchen.

"I thought I heard you out here." He eyed my order and frowned. "Get your coffee and come back here with me."

"Bossy," I teased.

"It's what I do best." He ducked back into the kitchen.

Smiling, I walked over to the coffee station. I filled my paper cup to the brim, set the lid, and grabbed a sleeve. As I took a sip, the warmth seeped deep into my bones. I spared a glance out the front windows and noticed leaves racing down the road as though trying to leave the village as soon as possible. As if they, too, sensed the bad juju and had implemented an emergency evacuation plan.

Fighting the urge to join them, I headed for the kitchen. Behind a long stainless steel worktable, Evan sat on a stool with a mixing bowl on his lap and a wooden spoon in his gloved hand. Even though he had half a dozen stand mixers, he almost always preferred to mix his batters the old-fashioned way. The chocolate in the bowl was thick and creamy and calling my name. I didn't know what it was, but I wanted to take the spoon from Evan's hand and dig in.

I held out my to-go box. "I'll trade you."

Evan's gaze narrowed. "No way. Do you know how many raw eggs are in here? You'll get salmonella for sure."

It was not the first time he'd warned me of that particular risk. "I'll take the chance."

"No. Eat your cupcakes and tell me more about what happened at Ve's today."

It had been worth a try. Darn him and his health consciousness.

It was warm in the kitchen, so I shrugged out of my coat and sat on a stool on the opposite side of the counter. This small space was a lot like Evan. Neat and tidy and a little bit whimsical. He preferred colorful ceramic mixing bowls to stainless steel, old cooking utensils to new. He often said the vintage items had a magic of their very own. I believed him. "How much do you already know?"

"Starla stopped by a little while ago and filled in most of the blanks. By the way, how about her and Vince?" He grimaced as though stricken by a sudden migraine.

"I know. I feel for her. And him. Mostly her, though. It's a tough situation."

"I thought he had changed," Evan said, shaking his head.

"Maybe he did. Just not enough."

He sighed and stirred the batter with more vigor. "If he hurts her, I'll kill him."

The thought of Vince causing her any pain made my stomach churn. "I'll help."

He gave me a firm nod and a quick smile. "Now that we have that settled, is that skeleton really Ve's ex-husband?"

"We don't know for sure yet, but it looks that way." I moved a large tray of eggs down the counter, set down my pastry box, and took another fortifying sip of coffee. "Miles Babbage."

"Babbage," Evan said, enunciating carefully. "Babbage."

"Do you recognize the name?"

"No," he said. "I just like saying it. Babbage. Babbage. Cabbage. Babbage's cabbages." His voice soared high and dropped low as he kept repeating the name.

I studied him carefully. "Have you been drinking on the job? Making rum balls or something?"

He laughed. "No. It's just an unusual name. I like it."

"Starla thought she'd heard it before. . . ." I bit into one of my cupcakes and waited for the rich chocolate to work its magic. It didn't take long before my stiff muscles relaxed. The bad juju I'd felt only moments ago suddenly seemed as if it were a distant memory.

"Well, I haven't. I'd have remembered that one. *Bab . . . bage*," he growled.

I couldn't help smiling. Because he seemed happy. He *was* happy. Which made me all kinds of happy for him. I'd been so worried about him this past spring.

An oven timer dinged and Evan placed the bowl he'd been stirring on the counter behind him—out of my reach. He knew me well, too. Using an oven mitt, he pulled a batch of fudge cookies from the oven and slid the pan onto a tall cooling rack loaded with similar trays.

His movements were swift, precise. The actions of a man who'd done this a million times before. A long white apron was tied around his waist, covering all but the hem of his jeans, and he had on a pale blue T-shirt that matched his eyes and complemented the ginger tones in his short hair.

He reclaimed the batter he'd been mixing and sat back down. "How's the investigation going so far?"

"It's just started, really. I need to find out more about Miles—his history—and that's going to be challenging. He was essentially a transient with no relatives here in the village. I don't know where he stayed while here or if he had any friends other than the lady kind. After I leave here I'm going to see Pepe and Mrs. P. I can only hope they remember something I can use to fill in some blanks."

The pair of mouse familiars were not only dear

friends but also village historians. If Miles truly was some sort of village Casanova, surely they'd have juicy gossip to share about the man.

I ate another cupcake. "Miles was a ceramic artist and often traveled with the Roving Stones. Since Andreus is supposed to be in the village this weekend visiting Ve, I'm hopeful that he might be a good source, too."

Evan shuddered at the mention of Andreus' name.

I knew the feeling.

"What's with all Miles' lady friends?" Evan asked. "Starla mentioned something about that."

I told him about Ve's description of the lecherous man, then leaned in and wiggled my eyebrows. "I don't know how many girlfriends the man had here in the village, but I heard he had an affair with Dorothy Hansel Dewitt."

He laughed. "Get out!"

"It's apparently true." I relayed what Archie, then Sylar, had told me about the witch.

Evan whistled low. "I can definitely see Dorothy stashing the guy's body in Ve's garage so Ve would get blamed. That kind of move is right up her alley."

I agreed, but after what Sylar had just told me about Dorothy having been long reconciled with her husband and pregnant with Glinda when all this took place, it didn't seem likely. She'd moved on from Miles. Or he from her. I wondered who'd done the breaking up in that situation. . . .

"Then," I added, "Sylar dropped a bombshell about Miles and Steve Winstead fighting in front of Third Eye the day before Ve married Miles. Sylar said the fight was over Marcus' mother, Penelope, who wasn't married to Oliver at the time."

I wondered when she'd met Oliver, because Marcus was in his late twenties. It couldn't have been too long after all this had happened.

Evan stopped stirring. "Wait. What? Miles was fighting over Penelope the day before he married Ve? Why?"

"I don't have a clue, but Ve said she'd had nothing to do with Miles until the day he showed up at As You Wish to hire her. Had never had any dealings with him and knew him only by reputation. They eloped that afternoon."

"You're kidding."

"I wish."

"She married him the day she met him? Why?"

"It's part of the mystery," I said, "since she can't remember much about that weekend at all."

"This is all so bizarre."

I completely agreed as I ate another cupcake. "How well do you know Penelope?"

He tipped his hand from side to side. "Fairly well. She drops in when she's here in the village. She's . . . quirky, a mix of serious and lighthearted. Enjoys art, nature, photography, books. To look at her from afar, you'd automatically think *soft*. Yet . . . I wouldn't cross her. There's something in her eyes, almost a warning. There's steel beneath that softness. What do you think of her?"

"I've never met her."

"That's surprising, considering how close Harper and Marcus are."

"She travels a lot, and apparently she's not a big fan of my family." I explained what Ve had said about Penelope's jealousy.

He banged the spoon on the side of the bowl and grabbed a scraper. "I can't see jealous. Envious, maybe. It probably stings for her to see your family living the kind of lifestyle she wanted and couldn't have because of her parents' interference. It's easier for her peace of mind to keep her distance from all of you."

Leave it to Evan to look at the situation rationally.

"And you're going to meet her tomorrow," he added as he grabbed a brownie pan. "She's in your scenery crew. I thought I told you."

"No, I'd have remembered that."

"Oh. Well. Sorry." He grinned, not looking sorry at all. "She'll be at the scene shop helping paint sets tomorrow afternoon. She and Oliver will be in town until Samhain, so last time she was here she volunteered to help out once she learned I was running things."

Knowing I'd see her tomorrow gave me time to prepare. I'd see what I could find out about her and Miles beforehand, and hopefully she wouldn't mind answering a few questions after the build session.

"Did you talk to Nick about helping to build the sets?" Evan asked.

"He said he would. Between him and Hank Leduc, those are going to be the best sets the playhouse has ever seen."

"Hank?"

I waved a hand. "Long story."

He grabbed my hand and his gaze narrowed on my ring finger. "I don't see anything sparkly yet."

I pulled out of his grip. "What? My personality isn't shining through?"

With a grin, he said, "What's Nick waiting for? We all know he's had the ring for months."

Mimi had apparently let that detail slip to a lot of people. "He must have a plan. I'm patient. I can wait."

"Well, *I'm* running out of patience fast."

"Good thing he's not thinking about marrying you."

He laughed. "Our kids would have been so gorgeous, too. It's a shame."

They would have been. Then I got to thinking about the kids I might have with Nick and my heart went all mushy.

Evan carefully poured his batter into the brownie pan. "And I think the problem is that Nick *doesn't* have a plan."

"What's that mean?"

"Oh, I can see it," he said, leaning the scraper against the side of the bowl. "He's probably trying to plan this big to-do. Fireworks or skywriters or something like that."

I laughed. "Nick's not a skywriter kind of guy, and I wouldn't want him to be."

"*We* know that, but does he? Because he's waited so long, there's this huge buildup happening. He's probably feeling the pressure to do something big and bold. Do you want me to talk to him? I'll talk to him. I'll do it. Tomorrow afternoon, I'll pull him aside, give him a stern talking-to."

I had the feeling he'd been talking to Harper. Laughing, I said, "Settle down, Dad. Nick will ask when he's ready."

"Yeah, well, we'll see."

I was going to have to keep an eye on Evan, make sure he didn't corner Nick tomorrow. I retied the pastry box and was glad I bought a dozen mini cupcakes. There were nine left, and I had the feeling I'd need the leftovers this weekend. "Speaking of tomorrow . . ."

Evan shook the scraper at me. "You're not trying to back out of helping me with those auditions, are you?"

A speck of batter landed on the top of my hand, and I licked it off. "Oh my God. Can I take that pan home with me?"

"Salmonella," he sang.

I frowned. "*Anyway*, no, I'm not canceling. I'll be there. I was thinking you might want additional help."

He eyed me dubiously. "Who are you thinking?"

"Someone with impeccable insight into human

nature, who is knowledgeable about the theater, and who isn't afraid to give brutally honest feedback." I gave him a broad, toothy smile. Batted my eyelashes.

Evan dropped the scraper. "Darcy, you didn't!"

I kept fake smiling.

"Not *Archie*," he said with a groan.

As I slipped into my coat, I said, "Oh, come on. I kind of promised him he could be part of the play in exchange for info about Miles Babbage. He's a tenacious one, that bird."

Evan's face puckered like he smelled something bad. "He's something, all right."

"I think he'd actually be good casting roles."

He grumbled.

"So, will you let him be an assistant casting director? Pretty please? Please, please, please?"

He mumbled under his breath, then said, "Fine. But he'd better keep his ego in check. I make all final decisions."

Archie keeping his ego in check was never going to happen, but I wasn't going to jeopardize this moment. I walked over and kissed Evan's cheek. "Thank you."

He waved a hand. "Yeah, yeah. Now, go before I change my mind."

"I'll tell him you'll pick him up at three thirty," I said, then made a show of sprinting for the door, dropping my empty coffee cup into the trash along the way.

But as I pulled open the front door, and the rain and bitterly cold wind reminded me of the danger in the air, I wanted nothing more than to go back inside and hide.

Chapter Eight

I practically sprinted along the deserted sidewalk, dashing past shop after shop in an effort to stay dry. I slowed only when I reached the Bewitching Boutique, where Pepe and Mrs. P lived in the walls of the sewing room at the rear of the building.

The shop was dark and a CLOSED sign hung askew from a chain on the other side of the door. Cupping my face against the glass, I peered inside, hoping to see any kind of light coming from within. There was nothing. According to the hours stenciled on the display window, Godfrey should be here, as it wasn't even yet noon. I tried knocking, but no one appeared, mouse or man.

Questioning Pepe and Mrs. P was going to have to wait.

Pressing on, I set my sights toward Spellbound, at the end of this stretch of shops. Light shone from the windows above the bookshop, so I suspected Harper had returned from the police station. But as much as I wanted to head straight there, I had another stop to make first.

A moment later, I stood in front of the Trimmed Wick. Here, the lights were on, glowing invitingly like beacons of safety, as the skies outside had turned from a charcoal gray to an inky black.

Inside, Steve Winstead sat at a potter's wheel in a corner of the shop, which some outsiders might find an odd sight in a candle shop, but his specialty was candle-filled pottery. Steve threw, glazed, and fired his own pots, then filled them with his wax creations. It was a popular shop here in the village.

There were several tourists watching his demonstration, and a couple more roaming about the shop. I'd rather question him alone, but I had to make do if I wanted to know why he'd been fighting with Miles Babbage thirty years ago.

The wind practically shoved me inside the shop as I pulled open the door, and everyone's attention turned to me as I made my not so subtle entrance.

Feeling heat rising to my cheeks, I righted myself. I tugged the hem of my coat, tucked my pastry box securely in the crook of my arm, pasted on a smile, and gave a little wave. "Hello."

I received a chorus of friendly hellos from all but one person. His hands covered in oozing clay, Steve remained oddly silent.

In his fifties, he had thinning ash blond hair and keen blue eyes, and he usually had a smile on his face when we ran into each other.

Not today.

He didn't look happy to see me at all.

I tried not to take it personally.

As he finished his demo, I strolled around the small shop, which had a decidedly rustic, cottagelike feel to it. Whitewashed wooden paneling covered the walls, and dark, wide, oak planks covered the floor. A robin's-egg blue weathered sideboard had been transformed into the shop's point-of-sale area, which housed the cash register and several smaller displays. Above it, a trio of glass pendant accent lights that appeared to be hand blown hung from the ceiling, casting wide circles of light across the space. More discreet were the pot lights tucked into the ceiling next to thick wooden beams stained the same color as the flooring.

Despite all the various scents used in candle making, the predominant one I smelled in here was sage, which reminded me that I should probably smudge my house before I slept there, just to chase out any unwanted juju. Aunt Ve was planning to lead a more formal blessing at my housewarming next weekend and had been collecting items for that ritual these past couple of weeks.

The older woman ringing up sales kept giving me the side eye as though she suspected I was going to pinch a pot and dash out. I gave her a smile to try to reassure her that I wasn't a shoplifter and continued to wander around, biding my time.

Steve's colorful pots glowed brightly against the distressed white trestle shelving they sat upon. From tiny petaled votive holders and carved pots to skinny vases, coffee mugs, and chubby birds, there was every shape and size candle imaginable.

Steve was a gifted artist, which made perfect sense, as he was a Manicrafter. I'd learned over the past year that that particular Craft was the most common in the village. The number of Manis far outweighed all others. It was believed by some that Manis had been the original Craft of all witches but had branched over time, creating new varieties. It was an interesting theory, because it would suggest that at some basic level all witches were capable of one another's abilities. I wasn't sure I believed it to be true. If it were, I figured witches would have been granting wishes left and right for generations. But still, I wondered. It was a conversation to have with my mother some other time.

Steve was speaking about using something called a bat to make his work easier, and I half listened as he described the flat disk. He talked easily, knowledgeably. He came from a long line of artisans, but it was his sister's family I knew well. The Chadwicks. Cora Chadwick had once been Starla's mother-in-law (and was currently Glinda's potential one). She and her husband, George, owned Wickedly Creative, an art studio here in the village, where her two surviving sons, Will and Liam, both worked. I wished I was more comfortable around the family, because I'd love to take classes at the studio. But after what had happened last winter, I wasn't sure I ever would be. Oh, we were friendly enough, but there was an awkwardness to every meeting.

Time healed, yes, but there was no set date as to when that process would be complete, when I could look back on what had happened with a twinge rather than an ache.

On a tiered table by the door, handwoven baskets held cellophane-wrapped scented wax spheres in varying shapes and styles. The beautiful creations released their fragrance without melting, rather like a decorative a wax sachet. I was mentally making a shopping list as I waited for Steve to get a free moment. I could easily imagine a family of bird candles and a set of bird's-egg wax spheres on those empty shelves under the stairs. . . .

"I'm guessing you're here to see me."

I jumped, nearly dropping the sphere I'd been holding. I carefully set it back in its basket, and I swore the woman behind the counter breathed a sigh of relief.

Steve stood at my elbow, wiping clean wet hands on a tea towel. I'd been so lost in thoughts of decorating my house that I hadn't noticed his demonstration had ended. On a table near his potter's wheel sat a freshly crafted cup with horizontal ridges and an overexaggerated lip, ready for drying. I knew from a pottery class I'd taken back in Ohio that, depending on how fast Steve worked, it could be a week or so before the cup would be ready to fill with wax.

"I am." There was no point in beating around the bush. He knew who I was and that I worked for the Elder when crime affected Crafters in the village. "It's about Miles Babbage."

"I figured you'd be by at some point. I just didn't expect it to be so soon." He motioned with his jaw to follow him. "We can talk out back."

He led the way down a short hallway that had an emergency exit door at the far end, and I realized this shop had an almost identical footprint to that of the bookshop, just smaller in scale. We passed a small restroom, an office, and a storage room before veering into a tiny windowless break room with an even tinier kitchenette. Steve held out a tall chair at a square pub table, and I set my pastry box on the tabletop and sat.

"Coffee? Tea?" he asked after closing the door tightly.

Trying not to feel claustrophobic, I said, "No, thanks."

He sat and fixed his gaze on mine. "How did you connect me to Miles so quickly?"

"Sylar Dewitt."

Steve leaned back and shook his head. "Why were you even talking to Sylar? I thought he was persona non grata after the electi— Oh, wait. Dorothy. You went looking for Dorothy."

"Yes." I didn't relay that I hadn't actually spoken to Dorothy at all. Sylar had spilled all these particular beans.

He hooked his elbow over the back of his chair. "She's a good place to start, considering the affair. Did she reveal anything interesting?"

I was beginning to wonder who was questioning whom. I didn't answer, and instead asked, "How did you know Miles?"

Specks of clay had dried on his cheeks, but he didn't seem to notice. Probably a hazard of the trade. Crow's-feet branched out from the corners of his eyes as he frowned and held up his hands. "Potting."

The scent of coffee lingered in the air. It was a smell I normally loved, but in this tight space it quickly grew overwhelming. "Were you ever a part of the Roving Stones?"

"No. I prefer to have roots. A traveling lifestyle most definitely is not for me. Miles was a familiar face at Wickedly Creative when he was in town. Artists have always been drawn to the place."

"It was open back then?"

"Sure was. It was nothing like how fancy it is now. It was just an old dairy barn converted into studio space, created mostly out of hopes and dreams."

If anyone else had uttered that line, I would have thought it incredibly cheesy, and though it still was, Steve said it with such earnestness that I could almost feel the hopes and dreams he'd had as a twentysomething.

"My dream was to eventually open this shop. George and I built a kiln behind Wickedly Creative, and naturally I spent a lot of time there as I created stock to sell at craft fairs and flea markets before I was able to save enough to buy this space."

"How long has this place been open?"

"Twenty-five years, and the fates willing, twenty-five more . . ."

"Not planning on retiring, then?"

He shook his head. "Not until the day when I can no longer dig a hole into a creek bed and pull out magic."

His devotion was endearing. "You dig your own clay?"

"Darcy," he said solemnly, "you can't buy that kind of enchantment."

Studying him, I dropped my voice. "You mean . . . literally enchanted?"

I was baffled at how clay could be magical, but then I thought about healing mud baths, which had been around for generations.

"There's a reason why when my candles are burned, they provide a feeling of peace and tranquility. The heat from the flame warms the pottery, which releases the magic."

This village never ceased to amaze me. "Where's this creek? Here in the village?"

"It is, but that's all I'll say. Only I know its exact location. . . . Well"—anger flashed in his eyes—"and one other person knew."

I could guess by his tone. "Miles?"

"He followed me into the woods one day, curious about my clay source. He'd been fascinated by my pieces. I had to commission a spell over the creek to protect my source from him, and just for added measure, I memory-cleansed him, too, so he didn't remember the location. That kind of magic could be dangerous in the hands of someone who doesn't know how to use it properly. Someone who might use it for their own selfish purposes."

From what I'd learned of Miles so far, that description could fit him. "Did you two get along otherwise?"

He shifted his weight, crossed his arms. "Otherwise, we didn't *not* get along."

"You were civil?" I deciphered.

"I tolerated him to keep the peace at the studio."

"Did you know much about him? Where he was from? His family life? That kind of thing?"

"He came from somewhere in Maine, was an only child. His mother died when he was quite young. His dad traveled around the country charming women to keep him and Miles housed and fed and clothed. It became a game of sorts. A con. Apparently the young-single-dad angle pays out big. And not that he ever out-and-out said so, but I had the feeling Miles was often lost in the shuffle. Neglected even. I asked him about his broken nose once, and all he said was that his father hadn't believed in verbal punishments."

In one swift moment, I felt an overwhelming surge of sympathy for Miles Babbage. For the little boy he had been. For the man he had become.

Broken. Haunted.

His early years certainly explained some of Miles' womanizing tendencies. Not only had he probably learned his lothario ways from his father, but I suspected that a part of his love-'em-and-leave-'em lifestyle was a form of control. He'd probably had no say-so as a child and was a man intent on being in charge of his own destiny.

Steve added, "Cora and George might know more about him, since they spent more time with him at the studio."

Maybe so, but that meant I'd have to go see Cora and George. I didn't particularly want to do that if I didn't have to.

I pressed on. "What were you and Miles fighting about in front of Third Eye?"

"What did Sylar tell you?" he asked, trying once again to turn the tables.

"Why don't you tell me your side?"

He shoved his hands into his hair and stared into the distance, at nothing in particular. "He came back."

"Miles . . . ?"

Giving an affirmative nod, he said, "He'd been gone . . . a year. It was his longest absence, and we all made up stories about why he hadn't returned. That some jealous husband finally did him in. Or he finally snagged a sugar mama with a bottomless purse. Or even that he got hit hitchhiking. Or attacked by bears or a swarm of killer bees. Literally hundreds of theories, each more outlandish than the last. Then one day, he's here. Back in the village. And he's not only here; he's on the prowl."

"Looking for Dorothy?" I asked. "To rekindle that relationship?"

He shook his head. "She was happily back with her husband at that point. Pregnant, I think, too."

It was what Sylar had said as well.

"Miles showed up at the studio. Penelope was there, painting. . . ."

It didn't surprise me in the least that she'd been there. Not after Ve's "free-spirit" comment. Most Colorcrafters were involved in the arts in one way or another.

"She was . . . there with me."

There was something in his voice, something that hinted at a wound so deep that it hadn't quite healed. "Were you and Penelope . . . ?"

His fists flexed, squeezed tight again. "We'd been dating, though she was also seeing Dreadfully Dull Debrowski—that's what I jokingly called him—at the same time to appease her parents."

Dreadfully Dull Debrowski. Wait till I told Harper.

He went on. "They were the strict type who wanted her to obey their every command."

I recalled that Ve had said they made Penelope join the law firm . . . or risk being cut off. It seemed so harsh to me. I couldn't imagine ever doing that to my child.

"They didn't like her dating me. Didn't think I was

stable enough, that I could never provide for her if I 'played in the mud' for a living. They wanted her to marry Debrowski. He was a lawyer at their law firm and checked every box for quality husband material. Except one issue."

"What's that?"

"She didn't love him."

"Did she love you?"

"I thought so. . . ."

It was almost as though I could hear his deep wound reopening, tearing him apart from the inside out.

Voices floated down the hall as customers came to and went from the shop. His business was steady. It could be because of the magical clay, but I had the feeling it had a lot to do with the man sitting in front of me and the magic he'd worked making his creations. I'd buy his pieces even if I never burned a single candle. His art was beautiful.

"I thought so," he repeated. "Until Miles waltzed into the picture. Penelope was beautiful and rich. I suspect it was only the rich part that he cared about. They'd dated briefly about a year and a half or so before that, but he dropped her to focus on Dorothy Hansel, who'd been even richer. But that fateful day at Wickedly Creative, Dorothy was out of the picture, and Miles turned his charms on Penelope once again. She was instantly smitten. Within a couple of days, she dumped both me and Dreadfully Dull and told me that she was planning to run off and elope with Miles that weekend."

"Wow."

"Yeah. She was willing to walk away from everything for him. This village, her parents, her everything."

Her roots.

"So when I bumped into Miles outside Third Eye that day and saw his smug smile . . . I couldn't walk away." He clenched his fists tighter. "And I may not have won the war that day, but I won the battle."

"How so?"

There was a mischievous glint in his eye when he said, "Penelope's parents caught wind of the fight, and that we'd been fighting over *her*. All hell broke loose. She was forbidden to see Miles and whisked immediately away to a relative's house down on Cape Cod. The next day, Miles married Ve, then disappeared again." The glint faded into dark shadows. "The next month, Penelope married Dreadfully Dull."

"I'm sorry," I said quietly.

"Yeah, well, we all have our heartaches."

It was true, but most didn't carry them around, letting them bleed for thirty years.

"I do my best to keep my distance from her. She seems happy enough," he went on. "It's not the way I wanted my happily ever after to end, but it helps. A little. I'm glad she's happy. I just wanted her to be happy with me."

I was feeling like a sap as he spoke, my chest aching for lost loves. I stood up, picked up my pastry box. "I should go. Thanks for talking to me."

He said, "Part of me always expected him to show up again one day. . . . I just never guessed it would be quite this way."

There was something in his tone. Something that hinted he wasn't telling me the whole truth.

I reached for the door handle. "Just to be clear, you didn't kill him, did you?"

Shaking his head, he said, "I'm not grieving the loss, however."

"Do you have any ideas who might have wanted him dead?"

His eyebrows furrowed. "No."

Again I sensed he was lying. "No one?"

"Nope."

He was definitely lying. But why?

We headed down the hall. "I'm just sorry Ve got dragged into all this. She's a good woman."

"That she is," I said.

He showed me to the front door, but on the way out he handed me a gorgeous pottery candle in the shape of a stubby wide-mouthed vase. Glazed a creamy yellow and white, it had a small white ceramic bird perched on its rim. "A little magic for your new house."

It was perfect. "Thanks, Steve."

"Anytime."

It was still raining when I headed back outside. As I set off toward Spellbound, my mind whirled.

Roots, Steve had said.

Was that why he'd lied to me?

Because he was protecting *his* roots, meaning his shop, his livelihood, his magical clay source?

Or the roots of someone he loved . . . ?

Chapter Nine

I rushed into Spellbound, so intent on heading straight upstairs to see if Harper was home that I took only a moment to wave to Angela Curtis before zipping past her. She was busy anyhow, conversing with a pair of customers, so I hoped she'd excuse my rudeness.

My gaze was firmly set on the back of the shop and the adjoining door that partitioned this retail space from a vestibule and staircase that led up to Harper's apartment when Angela called out, stopping me.

"Darcy! Harper's not up there."

In her mid-forties, Angela stood a bit shorter than my height of five foot seven and had razor-cut dark brown hair that skimmed her shoulders. In recent months she'd gone from part-time to full-time status here at the shop. She'd been an invaluable help to Harper.

Groaning, I reversed course. "Have you heard from her? I thought she'd be back by—"

I snapped my mouth closed, because it was then that I saw to whom Angela had been speaking.

Penelope and Oliver Debrowski.

Oh dear.

"Darcy." Penelope's thin smile didn't quite reach her eyes. She released her husband's hand, which she had been holding tightly, and stretched her own toward me for a handshake. "It's nice to finally meet you."

Angela threw me a horrified glance. "I'm so sorry. I didn't realize you hadn't met yet. Darcy, this is Penelope and Oliver Debrowski. Marcus' *parents*," she added. "Penelope and Oliver, this is Darcy Merriweather."

"No apology necessary, Angela. We've seen each other from afar." Oliver stuck out his hand as well. "But we have not had the chance to meet face-to-face."

I set the pastry box on the counter and shook both their hands. Penelope's was ice-cold and bony, while Oliver's was warm and enveloping. "Nice to meet you both."

Oliver's gaze dropped to the candle gripped in my other hand, and the corners of his mouth tightened. Penelope saw it the candle as well, and she swallowed hard before looking up again. She leaned in to her husband, and he wrapped a protective arm around her.

Tension bloomed in the air, thick and palpable.

Angela looked at me. It was easy to see the concern in her eyes. I gave her a reassuring half smile. I faced Penelope and Oliver, cleared my throat, and said, "I thought you two weren't returning to the village until tomorrow morning." At least that's what Harper had said this morning.

A morning that was feeling like a lifetime ago.

"Our plans changed unexpectedly." Oliver's voice was deep and monotone. "We arrived not too long ago."

I suspected some would find the nickname Dreadfully Dull accurate. My first impression was that he wasn't so much *dull* as socially uncomfortable. And perhaps a bit stodgy. He kept looking at the door as though wanting to leave immediately.

I wanted the same.

"We've come here for the same reason as you have, Darcy," Penelope explained. "We're looking for Harper."

Penelope was tall and lithe, and her son, Marcus, favored her quite a bit. They had the same light brown hair, though hers had copper highlights, and the same peridot green eyes. She wore a billowy floor-length black, orange, and white skirt, printed to look like the wings of a monarch butterfly. With it, she wore a starched white shirt with a generous collar left open at the neck. A black capelet coat was thrown over one shoulder. Beaded onyx chandelier earrings brushed her collarbones, and she wore multiple bracelets on each arm, but no necklace.

I suspected the outfit was a visual representation of the battle within her between her two Crafts. A beautiful war between the creative and conservative. By appearances, it seemed to me the artist within her was proving to be the stronger opponent.

"Technically," Oliver cut in, "we're looking for Marcus. He's not answering his cell phone. Our assumption is that he's with Harper."

Tall and thick waisted, Oliver appeared to be a clean-cut, type A kind of man. His dark hair was cut just so, his beard immaculately groomed. Dark blue intelligent eyes surveyed the surroundings from beneath trimmed eyebrows. His necktie was perfectly knotted, and his suit fit so impeccably I had the feeling it had been tailored by Godfrey.

To me, he seemed the type to floss his teeth twice a

day, pay his taxes ahead of time, and go to bed exactly at ten every night after checking every door and window to ensure all had been locked.

I rather liked that about him.

I appreciated routines and order and imagined he did as well. I couldn't say I'd have matched him with Penelope, but after thirty years of marriage she had obviously made the right choice among the suitors who'd been pursuing her. I had to remember that sometimes opposites attracted. . . .

"Marcus *always* seems to be with Harper," Penelope said by way of explanation.

"That's love for you," Angela said brightly.

The Debrowskis gave her matching grim smiles.

"Yes," Oliver murmured.

I supposed I should be grateful these two weren't trying to break up Harper and Marcus, but I wished they'd welcome Harper's presence in their son's life.

By their looks of utter dismay, that wish wasn't likely to be granted.

It confused me that after the way Penelope's parents had intervened in her love life, she wouldn't openly support the relationship. Marcus was happy with Harper. He loved her. She loved him. They were a happily ever after away from a fairy-tale ending.

"Yes, *love*," Penelope added faintly.

Angela shot me a panicky glance, then hooked a thumb over her shoulder. "I'm—I'm just going to check on . . . something. Holler if you need me, Darcy."

I watched her fast-walk across the store, creating as much distance between herself and this uncomfortable situation as possible. I wished I could do the same.

Penelope lifted an eyebrow and cast a glance around the store. "Your sister has a lovely shop."

"Yes." She truly did. It was a labor of love. Owning

this shop had brought Harper out of her somewhat re-
clusive shell. She'd come to love the village and its people as much as she did the books housed inside the
store. Business was booming. Right now, Angela was
her only full-time employee, and Mimi was a part-timer.
Between the three of them, they kept the store hum-
ming, though I knew Harper was starting to think about
hiring more help.

Penelope added, "You did the artwork in the children's area, yes?"

I wasn't sure why she was so chitchatty with me.
"I did."

After buying the shop, Harper had redecorated it
with a Van Gogh *Starry Night* theme. The walls were
painted a vivid blue with swirls of gold and white. From
the ceiling, delicate glass stars hung from clear string.
When the shop lights hit the glass, it appeared as though
the stars were twinkling. Nick had built her several
birch-branch bookcases, and Harper had installed a
"spooky forest" wall with a dozen tall black bookshelves artfully crafted to resemble Tim Burton–style
trees. The spiraling branches of those trees intertwined
with one another and spread across the ceiling. Another
wall used handcrafted ironwork vines to hold books at
unique angles, which wasn't the most practical bookcase, but it was visually stunning.

It was all wonderful, but my favorite spot was the
children's nook, and not only because it had been my
design. I simply adored seeing little readers enraptured
by the colorful space.

Oliver said, "The cushioned toadstools are a nice
touch."

His tone was so dry I wasn't sure if he was being
sarcastic, but after a moment, I realized that he was
giving me a true compliment. My first impression of

him had been correct—his social skills were lacking. "Thanks. I think so, too."

In the nook, I had created a forest mural alive with fairies and elves. Some were unmistakable amid the wooded realm, but most were tucked within the artwork, just waiting for a child to discover all the hiding spots of the magical beings. The toadstools provided comfy child-sized seating for those who wanted to linger over a book or get lost in the magic of the mural.

"I heard you paint as well," I said to Penelope. "Evan Sullivan said you're helping with sets for the play?"

Oliver let out a bit of a huff, but Penelope smiled at him and patted his hand. "I dabble more than paint these days. I enjoy it too much to give it up, though I probably should, which is why I signed up to help paint scenery."

I tried to imagine a Colorcrafter denying her creative pull and couldn't fathom it. If Penelope didn't "dabble," she'd probably go stir-crazy.

"I've even managed to convince Oliver to volunteer as well," she added.

"Painting?" I asked. He seemed the type to freak out about paint under his fingernails, never mind on his clothes.

"Set building." It was said with a roll of his eyes before he looked upon his wife with adoration. "It is a testament to my love of this woman that I agreed at all."

He smiled at her and for a moment their gazes held.

She might not have loved him once, but she certainly did now. There was no denying the devotion in her eyes.

For some reason, it only made me feel worse for Steve Winstead.

And Harper. If nothing else, they should like her because she looked at Marcus the same way they gazed at each other.

Oliver checked his watch. "We should go. Perhaps

Marcus has returned to his office. Darcy, if you see him, will you tell him to call us? It is quite important."

"Sure." I decided to test the waters, but I had to be careful. As much as I wanted information about Penelope and Miles' relationship, I had to keep in mind that these people standing in front of me might be Harper's in-laws one day. Finally, I said, "The last I heard Marcus and Harper were at the police station with my aunt Ve, so you might want to check there first. I'm not sure if you know that a skeleton was found in her garage this morning."

Both nodded, but neither said a word about Miles or any kind of relationship Penelope might have had with the man.

"We should go," Penelope said abruptly.

Oliver nodded. With hasty good-byes, they rushed out of the shop. He sheltered her with his body as they headed into the rain.

As I watched them get into a fancy sedan parked down the road, it was clear I'd struck a nerve with Marcus' mother when I mentioned the skeleton.

Angela came and stood next to me as soon as the two left the shop. "What was all that tension about? I was drowning in it."

"They don't like Harper."

Her eyes widened. "What? Why?"

Angela and her partner, Harmony Atchison, who owned the Pixie Cottage, had become good friends. At one time I suspected Harmony was a witch, but now I believed the couple—and Angela's daughter, Colleen— were mortals.

Angela had a fondness for literary-quote T-shirts, and today she wore one printed with the line IN A HOLE IN THE GROUND THERE LIVED A HOBBIT.

"I think they'd prefer Marcus to marry someone with a law degree."

"I see," she said icily. "It seems to me that *their* degrees certainly didn't help them, because clearly they're idiots."

I smiled and grabbed my cupcakes. Since Harper wasn't here, I'd head back to Ve's and try to make sense of the morning. "Clearly."

"Let me guess," Angela said, eyeing the Gingerbread Shack box. "Devil's food cupcakes."

"A dozen of them," I said, nodding. "Or, there was a dozen . . . before I ate three of them. It's been quite the day already."

"I'd have bought two dozen if I were you. I've been hearing the rumors all morning about Ve and that skeleton. Harper got back fifteen minutes ago from the police station, but she went straight upstairs before I could get any real scoop."

"Wait. What? She's here?"

Angela laughed. "Yeah, she saw Penelope and Oliver parking their car and went running. Told me to tell them she wasn't here. Now I understand why."

I didn't blame my sister in the least.

Angela straightened a pile of books. "How's Ve doing? I hated hearing she was being questioned."

I leaned on the counter and watched a toddler wobble about the children's area, her chubby arms full of board books. "Confused. We all are."

"Understandable." She tucked a lock of hair behind her ear. "For Miles Babbage to show up after all these years . . . And the way he did? It's shocking."

I straightened. "Did you know Miles?"

A sheepish look crossed her face. "Kind of."

"You were what, thirteen, back then? Fourteen?"

"Fourteen," she said. "And best friends with a sixteen-year-old girl who found him utterly charming." She rolled her eyes at that. "She'd drag me to the Roving Stones fairs to see him every time he was in town."

"You didn't find him charming?"

"He wasn't my type, if you know what I mean. But . . ." Her voice trailed off.

"What?"

"There was something about him. I mean, it was strange. Because you'd approach him thinking he was just an everyday, average kind of guy, but then he'd talk. . . . And within minutes, you'd start to think that he was the best thing that ever happened to the village. My friend threw herself at him."

It was as Ve had described, that Pied Piper mentality. "Did he take her up on it?"

It was a nauseating thought. After all, Mimi was just a couple of years younger than that girl had been.

"To his credit, no. Not even when she snuck out to where he was staying in the middle of the night, intent on seducing the man . . ."

Horrified at what she was saying, I held up a hand. "She did not."

"Oh, she did. But every time she did it, he'd round her up and walk her home. She eagerly awaited his visits to the village. It about killed her the time he stayed away for a year. No one knew about his marriage—and divorce—to Ve until long after the fact. We all thought Miles had left as usual . . . and simply decided not to come back."

I'd heard several mentions that Miles had been gone from the village for a year before his return to the village the weekend he and Ve eloped. Where had he been during that time? Why had he stayed away so long? Everyone I'd spoken to thought the length of absence was unusual.

I said, "You mentioned your friend went out to where Miles had been staying. . . . Do you happen to know where that was? A motel? A campground?"

"Actually, whenever he was in the village, he always

stayed with the Chadwicks. In one of the outbuildings at Wickedly Creative."

Steve had neglected to mention that little detail to me when he suggested I speak to George and Cora. And no matter how awkward it was bound to be, I saw a trip to Wickedly Creative in my future. I would rather not go alone, simply for peace of mind. I needed reinforcements. The kind that would be able to get George and Cora to talk openly about Miles Babbage.

Fortunately, I knew just the witch to call.

Chapter Ten

Harper pulled open the door at the top of the wooden steps before I could even knock. She grabbed my arm and dragged me inside. Working quickly and efficiently, she slammed the door, spun the handle lock, turned the dead bolt, and slid the security chain. "They're not following you, are they?"

"Who?"

"Marcus' parents."

"No. The last I saw of them, they were in their car. They're off to look for Marcus."

They wouldn't find him.

I knew this because he was sitting on Harper's sofa. He must have come in the back door, since Angela hadn't mentioned his being here. He gave me a wave, and I smiled back since my hands were full.

Harper slumped against the door with relief. "Oh thank goodness."

Wind shook the rain-spattered windows. A big storm was brewing. "If you discount their dislike of our family, they're not that bad. I just met them downstairs."

"Not that bad? Oh, okay." She crossed her arms with a huff. "I suppose you think Stalin was a humanitarian."

She was speaking as though their son wasn't sitting on her couch, a pen in one hand as he wrote on a yellow notepad. Marcus looked up while he rubbed the chin of a very chubby orange tabby. Pie, the cat, had his head slightly raised to allow better access to one of his favorite scratching spots.

He said, "A Stalin comparison is a bit much, but they *can* be intense." His green eyes held a mischievous spark from behind a pair of dark-rimmed glasses.

"Especially when they don't like you," Harper added.

For a one-bedroom apartment it was spacious. Both the living room and kitchen had more than enough space for one. Or two.

It hadn't escaped my notice that over the past few months, Marcus had been gradually moving in here. I couldn't recall the last time he'd spent a night at his own place, a town house a few streets down.

Bright blue paint filled the living room with warmth and energy, and bookshelves lined two walls, making the room feel more like a library. Harper's taste wasn't eclectic just when it came to books, but also with her choices in decor. Shabby mixed with chic, traditional with modern, vintage with brand-new.

Her living room set didn't match in the least, with one sofa being a seventies-era gold monstrosity; the other, where Marcus sat, was a contemporary sleek faux-leather design.

He rolled his head as though his neck muscles had tensed. "They just need to get to know you better, Harper. They don't trust easily."

"They've had time," she argued.

"Not really." His voice was laced with patience. "With their travels, they barely know you."

It sounded to my ears as though they'd had this conversation many times.

Harper lifted an eyebrow, turned to me, and said, "Never mind that Penelope has never been fond of our family; she and Oliver really don't like that I have a police record."

Harper had been arrested for stealing Missy back when we lived in Ohio. It was a long story about pet mills, an inhumane pet shop, and activist Harper taking a stand. Her arrest had shed light on the horrible situation, which eventually shut down all the cruel operations. We got to keep the dog. Missy was short for Miss Demeanor.

I couldn't help smiling. "Well, *technically*, neither do I." No, I didn't particularly like that Harper had gotten arrested, but I had been proud of her for standing her principled ground.

She pushed away from the door. "This isn't funny. They don't care that I had my reasons. Valid reasons, I might add. To them, I'm nothing but a lawbreaker."

I studied my sister. This wasn't her usual demeanor. She was a go-get-'em, take-no-prisoners kind of woman. She blazed her own trails, caring little what others thought of her, and focused instead on how she felt about *herself*.

Penelope and Oliver had rattled her.

Hard.

I handed her the pastry box. "Eat one of these."

She sniffed it. "Devil's food?"

"Of course."

She hugged the box. "I'm not giving any back."

By the wild look in her eye, I could tell she needed the nine remaining mini cupcakes more than I did. "Keep them. I know where to get more."

I shrugged out of my coat and sat on the gold sofa. The chunky wooden coffee table between the two couches was completely covered in old books, stacked four or five high. There were more books on the floor. I picked one up. It was a witchcraft spell book. I peeked at the publication date: 1896. I checked another and another. They were all about witchcraft in one way or another.

"A little light reading?" I asked her.

She already had a cupcake in hand. "What can I say? It's fascinating."

The bookstore had been opened originally by a family of Spellcrafters. Last June, Harper had found a veritable treasure trove of witchcraft history hidden in the basement, left behind—or abandoned—by those who'd collected the books.

Harper picked up a book from the stack. "Did you know there's a spell that will dust your house for you?"

I looked for any dust bunnies in her apartment—saw none. "Have you tried it out?"

"No, of course not. You know how I feel. . . ."

I knew how she *said* she felt about witchcraft. She'd always been wary of her powers and opted not to use them. But by the looks of all these books . . . I believed that she would come around eventually.

"But *you* should try it, Darcy. Imagine never having to dust again. I'll loan you the book." She held the hardcover out to me.

Loan, not give.

The witch in Harper definitely wasn't as buried as she liked to think. I took the book, loving the feel of the worn cover. "Thanks."

I looked over at Marcus. "Your parents are trying to get in touch with you."

"I know. I've been screening my calls," he said. "They've left a dozen messages on my phone."

"They want him to drop Ve's case." Harper peeled a wrapper from another cupcake. "They're insisting he walk away and let someone else handle it. Can you believe that?"

Actually, considering what I had learned today, I could. I still hadn't formulated any good way to break the news to Marcus that his mother had been involved with Miles, so instead I asked, "How'd it go this morning at the police station? How's Ve?"

"Ve is oddly calm." There was a twinkle in Marcus' eyes when he added, "A lot calmer than Harper is about my parents."

I glanced up at Harper. Her cheeks were pouched, full of cupcake. Licking her fingers, she rolled her eyes at him and dropped down next to me, still hugging the Gingerbread Shack box.

Marcus made another note on the legal pad, then said, "The questioning was fairly basic, considering the skeleton has yet to be identified. Nick worked on the theory that it is Miles and spent most of the time trying to fact gather. Ve didn't know much about Miles at all, so the conversation went nowhere fast. We're all in legal limbo until we get an identification and a cause of death from the medical examiner's office."

Hope stirred. "So that means she's not going to be charged?"

"Not right now, at least. We have the added benefit of Nick being in charge of the case. He'll take his time, making sure he has an abundance of evidence before taking the matter to the DA. You know the last thing he wants to do is arrest your aunt."

He'd do it, though, if he had to. And I couldn't hold it against him. It was his job. From an integrity standpoint, he bent the rules more than he liked in order to accommodate the Craft in a mortal workplace. But when push came to shove, he was a good cop and took his job very seriously.

Harper licked the cream from the top of a cupcake and bumped me with her elbow. "How'd your morning go? Did you learn anything about Miles Babbage?"

My stomach rolled. "Yeah, some."

"Like what?" she pressed.

"He's from Maine and was an only chi—"

I stopped talking, and we all looked upward at the ceiling as curious sounds floated downward. Footsteps. Tiny footsteps.

There was laughter in his voice as Marcus said, "'And then, in a twinkling, I heard on the roof the prancing and pawing of each little hoof.'"

I glanced his way and could easily imagine him sitting in a big chair by a fireplace where three stockings had been hung with care, reading *'Twas the Night Before Christmas* to a little girl who looked a lot like Harper.

My chest tightened a little as I slid a look Harper's way. She was smiling at him, her heart in her eyes, and I had to wonder if she'd pictured the same scene I had.

As the noise above our heads continued, Pie lumbered to his feet. His tail started swishing from side to side in anticipation of the visitors.

"Hello-o-o-o," a brash female voice called out. It was followed by a knocking sound near the ceiling light. "Anyone home?"

"We're here!" Harper answered. "Come on in."

The rustle of tiny feet carried across the ceiling; then the sound faded. A moment later, one of the baseboards popped loose near the kitchen doorway and two mice wiggled through the narrow opening.

One was brown, a rotund little fella with round eyeglasses. He wore a red vest that had three gold buttons. Its fabric strained ever so slightly over his pudgy stomach. The other mouse was pure white with fur that spiked stylishly between her ears. She wore a sleeveless pink velour dress that hung to the tops of her feet.

They were Pepe and Mrs. P, mouse familiars. Originally from France, Pepe was a Cloakcrafter, a master tailor, and had been a familiar for a couple of hundred years. Mrs. Eugenia Pennywhistle, known affectionately as Mrs. P, originally hailed from the village and had died last January, while in her eighties. She'd been a Vaporcrafter familiar for only ten months.

I considered both of them family.

Pie leaped off the couch, and whiplash-fast Marcus scooped him up again. He cuddled the cat like a baby and Pie settled right down.

Marcus had an uncanny way with cats.

"Has the wicked witch blown by yet?" Mrs. P asked as she scampered over to the gold sofa and climbed up the arm. Her delightful cackling laughter filled the air.

The sound always reminded me of Phyllis Diller's trademark laugh. It was infectious in nature, and I couldn't help smiling at the sound of it.

Pepe followed closely behind her. "By wicked witch, Eugenia is referring to Dorothy Hansel Dewitt. She was raging mightier than dear old Mère Nature when she left the police station only moments ago."

Mère Nature. Mother Nature. One of the things I adored most about Pepe was his French accent and the way he could manipulate its tone from haughty to tender with the barest change of inflections.

With all the big happenings taking place in the village today, I should have known Pepe and Mrs. P wouldn't have remained at the Bewitching Boutique, twiddling their thumbs. They weren't ones to often let the village gossip come to them. They went to it. Clearly, they'd been putting their stellar snooping skills to use at the police station.

They sat on the arm of the sofa, close to Harper's elbow, as I asked, "Was Dorothy at the police station to confess her affair with Miles Babbage?"

A bit of cupcake fell from Harper's mouth as it gaped open. "Her *what*?"

Marcus scribbled like crazy as I told them what I knew of Dorothy's affair with Miles—and how she'd run out of Third Eye earlier.

"Well, I'll be. That hussy!" Mrs. P exclaimed as her tail curved behind her.

"You didn't know?" I questioned. It seemed to me she and Pepe knew everything that happened in this village.

"No. This happened before I moved back to the village. Hot dog!" she exclaimed, rubbing her tiny paws together. "I love a good scandal."

Mrs. P had spent a good chunk of her life living away from the village, after her first husband disavowed his powers and moved his family out of town. They had eventually divorced, and an unfortunate set of circumstances led to an estrangement from her daughter. And, as a consequence, her granddaughter. It had been a troubling family situation, and unfortunately it was one that did not have a happy ending.

"I fully expected Dorothy to confess the acquaintance," Pepe said, picking up the thread of the conversation, "but *non*, it was not to be. She said nothing of the affair at all."

With his little feet crossed at the ankles, he sat close to Mrs. P, their arms touching. They weren't technically married, but that label mattered to no one. For all intents and purposes they considered themselves husband and wife.

I shifted sideways to better face the mouse duo. "You knew of the affair, Pepe?"

"Of course," he replied. "It was the talk of the village at the time. Of how Dorothy abandoned the honorable Joel Hansel and ran off with the village scoundrel. *Quelle horreur!*"

Honorable? It wasn't a word I associated with Dorothy in any way, shape, or form, so I was having trouble imagining she'd married a good, decent man. Or rather, that he'd married *her*.

"Joel was a lovely man," Mrs. P added. "Such a talented furniture maker. He brought out the best in Dorothy, which was a marvel, considering her acidic personality."

"Where is Joel Hansel now?" Harper asked.

Marcus jotted more notes. I assumed he had just added the man to his suspect list. As had I. I wanted to know the answer to the question as well. I knew nothing of Dorothy's first husband, the man who was Glinda's father.

Mrs. P's cheeks were a rosy red, thanks to a generous application of rouge. Her love of cosmetics hadn't wavered, even after she'd become a mouse. She said, "Long dead. Fifteen, twenty years now?" She glanced at Pepe for confirmation.

Pepe smoothed his Dalí mustache, which had been created by twirling his whiskers. "Twenty. Marriage to Dorothy tends to shorten a man's life span considerably."

I suddenly had an aching compassion for Glinda's loss. She'd been only nine or ten years old when her father passed. I knew she and her mother had a contentious relationship and wondered if her father's early death had contributed to that dynamic.

Marcus set down his pen and asked, "What happened to him?" Pie had nestled contentedly next to him but kept a diligent eye on Mrs. P and Pepe.

"Heart attack," Pepe answered.

Mrs. P added, "Dorothy's second husband died of a heart attack as well, if I recall correctly, not too long after they divorced."

I never knew that man, either, but I did know he'd been a mortal and that Dorothy and he had adopted a daughter together. Now in her twenties, Zoey Wilkins was currently in prison on kidnapping and attempted murder charges. Technically, she should have faced an additional charge of murder, but her own husband had fallen on the sword for her. . . .

Honestly, the whole family was a mess. No wonder Glinda was as troubled as she was.

"Two heart attacks? Sounds suspicious to mé," Harper pointed out. "Someone should probably warn Sylar."

Pepe's mustache twitched. "It was suspicious to everyone in the village as well. Alas, completed autopsies proved the men died of natural causes."

I was also suddenly worried about Sylar. He'd gained a lot of weight since marrying Dorothy. That couldn't be good for his heart. I looked at Pepe. "Were Dorothy's first two husbands overweight?"

"Not until they married Dorothy," he said with a chuckle. Pepe twirled his mustache. "After their yearlong second honeymoon, Joel returned a good fifty pounds heavier. He was nearly unrecognizable."

"A year?" Harper said, her eyes wide.

"*Oui*. It was a trip around the world. They left no corner of the earth unexplored."

"Still," Harper pressed. "A year?"

Pepe said, "It was believed they anticipated the distance from the village and the length of time would continue to heal the wounds to the marriage incurred by Dorothy's affair." He gave a curt nod. "As they returned a couple obviously in love, it proved to be a therapeutic journey."

"How long were they back in the village before Miles returned?" I asked.

Scratching his chin, he pursed his lips. "It was springtime when Dorothy and Joel returned from their extended honeymoon, so they'd been back to the village five or six months by the time Miles surfaced from his sabbatical the following October."

"Do you know why *he'd* been gone for nearly a year?" I asked.

He pushed his glasses up his nose and shook his head. *"Non."*

Mrs. P *tsk*ed. "I imagine his return tested the Hansels' marriage a second time."

I nodded. "From everything I've heard today, Dorothy was fully committed to Joel when Miles came back. But we all know Dorothy's a good actress."

I did some mental math. Between her second honeymoon and Miles' yearlong absence, it would have been around eighteen months since Dorothy had last seen Miles. Eighteen months in which she supposedly fell in love with her husband all over again.

But I wasn't sure I bought that. After all, this was Dorothy we were talking about.

I went on. "She *could have* seen Miles when he came back to the village. They *could have* reconciled. She *could have* killed him. Dorothy's a smart witch. If she wanted to have another affair . . . or get away with murder, she could."

Marcus tapped his chin with the pen. "Do you think Dorothy is *truly* capable of murder?"

"Absolutely!" Mrs. P said.

The rest of us nodded. Great, big, overexaggerated nods.

Marcus went back to writing.

"So why, then, was Dorothy at the police station?" Harper asked our little friends.

"She was in a snit about Nick," Mrs. P said. "A great, big snit."

I straightened, suddenly defensive. "Nick? Why?"

It was Pepe who answered first. "Dorothy demanded Nick's removal from the case. She claims he's too personally involved in the matter and cannot possibly remain impartial since Ve is involved, and she is his *girlfriend's* aunt."

Both looked at my ring finger and sighed loudly. I was grateful neither pointed out that Nick still hadn't popped the question. Maybe Evan was right. . . . Perhaps the pressure was getting to Nick. It was starting to get to me, and I wasn't even the one doing the asking.

Mrs. P laughed. "But ha! The joke is on Dorothy. At least for the time being."

"How so?" Marcus asked.

Pepe said, "As Nick is chief of police, in order to remove him from the case Dorothy needs approval from the village council chairwoman."

Harper smiled broadly. "That's Ve!"

"Oui." Pepe nodded with a grin of his own. "Dorothy was in quite the fury when informed. She must now request a special convocation with the council as a whole for approval. It will take weeks to schedule a meeting as such."

"Dorothy ranted and raved like a lunatic," Mrs. P said, gesturing far and wide with her tiny paws. "Well, an even greater lunatic than normal. I've never seen her in such a state. It was highly entertaining."

Harper drew her legs beneath her. "But why? If she had nothing to do with Miles' death, why is she so invested in this case? Why would she care if Nick investigates? For that matter"—she looked at Marcus—"why do your parents care if you represent Ve? I keep feeling like there's something bigger going on."

Because there was. Exactly how much wasn't yet clear, and with its being a cold case, I wondered if we'd ever know the whole truth of what had happened to Miles Babbage.

"Penelope and Oliver? They want you off the case?" Mrs. P questioned Marcus. "Why?"

Marcus shrugged. "I don't know, but I'm not going to leave Ve high and dry, no matter what their argument. And I'm quite frankly relieved to have Dorothy as a possible suspect. The more, the merrier, as far as I'm concerned. It can only help Ve's case."

My palms had dampened. "Actually, from my investigations this morning I can shed some light on the situation. . . ."

As I glanced around, I caught Pepe's watchful, supportive gaze. I had the feeling he knew all about Penelope's involvement with Miles and guessed what I was about to say.

"About?" Harper asked.

My stomach ached. "Penelope and Oliver."

Marcus, who had been writing, set his pen down. "My parents? Did they tell you something while you were downstairs with them?"

I clenched my hands, unclenched them. "No, not them so much as Sylar . . . and then Steve Winstead."

Marcus took off his glasses, rubbed his eyes. "Sylar? Steve? You lost me."

I glanced at Harper, then back at Marcus, then back at her again. I took a deep breath. "Maybe you should call your parents. It might be best if you heard this from them. It's why they want you off the case."

"Oh no," Harper said, sitting up straight. She poked a finger my way. "You need to tell us right now. Right. Now."

"Just say it, Darcy," Marcus said stonily. He put his glasses back on and stared at me.

I just had to spit it out, because there was really no other way. In one big breath I said, "A month before your mother married your father, she had a whirlwind relationship with Miles. They were supposed to run off and elope the same weekend he ended up marrying Ve."

There was a moment of stunned silence before Marcus blurted, "My mother? With Miles Babbage? You're joking."

"Not joking," I said, wishing I were.

"Miles . . . Babbage?" he repeated.

I nodded.

He said, "No. No way."

"Oui," Pepe confirmed solemnly. "It's true."

Harper's and Mrs. P's mouths dropped open.

Marcus just kept shaking his head. Pie tapped his arm with a paw as though sensing something was seriously wrong.

"I don't understand it, either," I said, wishing more than anything that I did. "But Ve mentioned that women tended to flock to him. I'm sure she told you the same thing."

"She did," Marcus confirmed. "But I never dreamed one of those women would be my mother. My intelligent, well-educated, elegant mother hooking up with a homeless gigolo? It's baffling."

"What about *Ve*?" Harper said to him, her words sharp. Scooting to the edge of the couch, she added, "She somehow ended up *married* to the man!"

Her body language made it clear that he best not be implying anything untoward about our aunt's intelligence, education, and elegance.

Marcus opened his mouth, then snapped his lips together. If he'd been contemplating mentioning Ve's colorful and varied dating history, he'd been wise to keep his mouth shut.

I intervened before they started bickering. "Ve has made it clear she didn't even know Miles Babbage other than by reputation and wouldn't have married him under normal circumstances. That's what's important here and now."

Harper shot me a dismayed look, and I realized she was itching for a fight. I blamed Penelope and Oliver's influence on her current state of mind.

After a moment, Marcus said, "It's just a ludicrous notion. I can't comprehend it."

Harper relaxed out of fight mode and settled back against the couch and nodded.

Pepe cleared his throat. "I dare not presume to know what possessed the women in this village to collectively lose their minds when Miles was near. After much thought on the matter following Ve's marriage to the man, I will venture the theory that it was not a *natural* attraction per se."

Rain pelted the windows as we let his words sink in.

"A supernatural one, then," Harper speculated after a moment. "The Craft, somehow?"

"Non," he said. *"Impossible.* Miles was a mortal."

We knew all this. I tried to think of other variations of magic. Like sorcery. It had been on my mind since Starla brought it up. "What about sorcery?"

Mrs. P gasped. "Heaven forbid!"

"I think not," Pepe said with a shake of his head. "Miles was not so intelligent as such. Sorcery requires a great deal of learning."

"But what else—" I cut myself off. I already knew the answer. "An amulet."

"Oui." He nodded. "One must consider the company Miles kept."

I said, "The Roving Stones."

Pepe nodded again.

Of course. The rock and mineral group was infamous for its dealings with charms and amulets. Both of which were in a magical category of their own with few to no rules or regulations to follow, especially if used by a mortal.

I recalled the photo Ve had shown us that morning. "Miles was wearing a pendant of some sort in his and Ve's wedding picture. It hung from what looked like a leather cord."

One could buy any amulet under the sun at one of the Roving Stones fairs, most harmless and not charmed in the least. The amulet Miles used had to have been extremely powerful to produce the effect it had among village women. There were only a few who could create those kinds of amulets. All were Charmcrafters.

At that moment, I couldn't have been more grateful that Andreus Woodshall was returning to the village this weekend. As a Charmcrafter and the director of the Roving Stones, he could be the only one who'd know exactly what kind of magic that amulet had possessed.

Harper asked Pepe, "Do you think it was a seduction amulet of some sort?"

"Without any doubt," he replied.

Marcus groaned as though he was in pain.

I asked Pepe, "Did you ever mention your amulet theory to Ve?"

"*Non.* It came to me long after the accursed marriage took place; therefore, it seemed a moot point. Miles had already disappeared, and Ve didn't care to speak of what had happened. She'd told only a trusted few the true story of not being able to recall the wedding at all. I certainly didn't want to upset her any further. What was done was done."

What was done was done.

Yet it wasn't quite done, was it? Not anymore.

"An amulet at least makes sense," Marcus said, shuddering. "My mother wouldn't have . . . I don't even like thinking about it. But what is this about Sylar and Steve? What do they have to do with anything?"

I fidgeted as I blurted out the whole story. By the time I was done (out of mercy, I left out his father's nickname during the retelling), Marcus had dropped his head against the back of the couch and stared, without blinking, at the ceiling.

The rest of us shared furtive glances, not sure what to say to console him.

Finally, he said, "This certainly mucks things up, doesn't it?"

"The muckiest," Mrs. P said.

Harper went and sat next to him. She held out the Gingerbread Shack box. "Cupcake?"

That was a display of true love if I ever saw one.

Marcus shook his head and smiled at her. "No, you keep them. But I should go talk to my parents. Hear their side."

Harper kept her gaze steady on his. "I'm sure they're not involved at all with what happened."

It was a bigger display of love than the cupcakes, considering how she felt about his parents.

"Me, too," he said. "But it'll be good to clear the air."

A quick kiss and rushed good-byes later, and he was out the door.

Harper stared at the door for a moment before she went to the window.

Mrs. P looked at Pepe, who looked at me.

"It'll all be fine," Mrs. P said brightly. "This will all pass over in a blink, and we'll move on to happier things. Like Darcy getting married! You know, if she ever gets engaged."

So much for not bringing it up. I threw her a quelling look.

"Perhaps, my love, it is time to bid our adieu," Pepe said quickly.

Mrs. P nodded, then blew kisses before she and Pepe made a mad dash for the baseboard portal.

After they were gone, I went to the window and put my arm around Harper. She rested her head on my shoulder as she watched Marcus trot across the village green.

"Are you okay?" I asked. "You're not yourself."

"There's something in the air, something dark and dangerous."

The juju. I wasn't surprised she felt it, too. She was often the first to notice its presence. "It'll pass. It always does."

She looked at me, her eyes full of turmoil. "But what damage will it do in the meantime?"

I didn't have an answer for that, but as beads of rain slid down the windowpane like teardrops, I feared the worst was yet to come.

Chapter Eleven

Not ten minutes later, some of *the worst* made itself known as I headed toward Ve's, taking advantage of a slight break in the rain. The downpour had subsided, and sprinkles fell gently from clouds that still hung low in the steely sky. I gripped my pottery candle tightly to keep it from sliding out of my slippery hands. I'd forgotten the spell book at Harper's and made a mental note to call her about it later.

My shoes were soaked through, and my poor wool coat smelled like Missy when she came in from the rain.

It was unpleasant, to say the least.

I'd just crossed the street onto the green, and I'd been thinking about Miles using a charmed amulet and about Harper—worrying, really—when I heard the *click-clack* of high heels striking cobblestone. I glanced over my shoulder and noticed a woman power-walking in the same direction I was.

Even though her face was hidden by a big umbrella, Dorothy Hansel Dewitt's form was unmistakable. Her burnt orange A-line skirt swished left and right with each step she took, and her big bosom bounced in a tight scooped-neck black sweater, making her look a little like a risqué Halloween decoration.

She hadn't seen me.

I debated whether to make a break for it or stay right where I was so I could ask her a few questions.

It had been a long day.

A really long day.

My nerves were raw, and I didn't know if I had the wherewithal to deal with Dorothy right now.

Which was why I decided to run.

My self-preservation instincts ran deep.

No sooner had I made the decision than the umbrella came up. Dorothy's eyes met mine, flared.

I was a little relieved that she appeared to be as horrified to see me as I was to see her. Her gaze darted about as if she was planning her own escape.

My escape plan had just been foiled. My chance to run had passed the moment she spotted me. With a weary sigh, I gave in and fully turned to face her. It was best to get this conversation over with.

She must have come to the same conclusion, because her apple red lips curled into a sneer. Cocking a curvy hip, she closed the umbrella.

We stood ten feet apart, and suddenly I felt like a gunslinger at the O.K. Corral as we stared each other down.

"You," she said, pointing the tip of the umbrella at me, "need to mind your own damned business."

At some point during the day, she'd been caught in the rain. Her normally voluminous white blond hair hung flat and limp against her head and shoulders.

Black eyeliner and mascara had smeared, creating a raccoonish effect around her eyes, and her foundation had crackled.

She obviously hadn't passed a mirror lately, or she would have stuck her head beneath that umbrella and not popped it out again until her makeup had been fixed. Dorothy didn't like to look anything but put together.

Right now she appeared to be falling apart. It was a look I'd never witnessed before.

Something had clearly rattled her as well.

There was a lot of that going on in the village today.

I took a step toward her. "I could say the same for you. Throwing a fit to get Nick pulled off this case. Why could that be?" I tapped my chin and looked upward as though in deep thought. *"Hmm."*

She took two steps toward me. *Click-clack.* Her pointy jaw lifted. Her voice was ice-cold. "What are you trying to say, Darcy?"

I took another step. "I'm saying that maybe you have something to hide where Miles Babbage is concerned and don't want Nick uncovering what it is. Like your affair with Miles? From what I heard, you neglected to mention that little piece of information to the police when you were trying to get Nick yanked off the case."

Raccoon eyes narrowed into thin slits. She took two more steps toward me, putting us nearly eye to eye, thanks to those four-inch heels she wore.

Venom dripped in her voice as she said, "Nick shouldn't be on the case. We all know he'll give Ve a free pass. She shouldn't be able to get away with murder just because of who *he* is sleeping with."

I clutched my candle more tightly. "You know Nick better than that, which only makes me more convinced *you're* hiding something. And we both know Ve didn't kill anyone."

She pressed a hand to her bosom and smiled, a thin, smug smile. "*I* don't know anything of the sort, and you can't possibly, either. Everyone has their secrets."

"And what about you, Dorothy? Your secrets? Did you happen to see Miles the weekend he went missing?"

A visible shudder went through her, and I wasn't sure if it came from the cold, raw weather or the mention of Miles.

I added, "Did you try to rekindle an old flame that fateful weekend and kill the man when he wasn't interested? We all know how well you take rejection. I'm surprised the skeleton wasn't *charred*."

"You don't know what you're talking about. As usual. And you're lucky *you're* not charred," she sniped.

I sniped back. "It's certainly not from your lack of trying, is it?"

"Darcy," she said smugly, "you and I both know that I hadn't been truly trying. If I had been, you would not be standing here."

She made an excellent point.

She said, "This matter is none of your business. None at all."

"You and I both know it is, don't we? The Craft is involved in what happened to Miles; therefore, I am involved."

She knew I was a Craft investigator and that asking her these questions was my job.

She must have suddenly realized that it was in her best interest to deal with me rather than the Elder, because she said, "Fine. Let's get this over with, shall we? It is a matter of fact that I did not see Miles at all when he returned to the village, and I had no desire to do so. Never mind that my little dalliance with him was long over—which I had ended, by the way—I was terribly ill during my pregnancy and rarely left the house."

She was a seasoned liar, and I couldn't tell if she was spouting the truth or lying through her teeth. From what I'd learned, Miles hadn't been in the village long before he disappeared—only a few days—and it was entirely plausible that she hadn't run into him.

I wasn't quite ready to rule her out, but I wanted more information. "What about Joel? Did he pay Miles a visit? Dish out a little retribution for Miles' role in your affair?"

Anger flared in her eyes. "If Joel had seen him, Miles would have been strung up right here on the village green, not tucked away all nice and tidy inside a garage for decades. It would have served Miles right, too. Joel had warned him not to return."

"Warned him? After the affair?"

"Yes," she said through clenched teeth. "And Miles promised to comply."

The warning was most likely the reason why Miles had stayed away so long. But no. That wasn't quite right. The affair had ended more than a year and a half before he'd gone missing. He'd returned to the village at least once before his final visit—a year before he'd gone missing. . . . Then I recalled that Ve and Joel were out of the country during that time. Miles had probably figured it was safe to pop in while they were gone.

And it had been. That time . . .

I didn't know if Dorothy was aware that Miles had been in the village while she was on her second honeymoon and figured it didn't much matter. All that truly counted was the final time he'd returned. "But Miles did come back . . . and apparently died that very weekend."

"Fortunately for the sake of my husband's freedom,

he was out of the country at the time at a furniture exposition in Austria."

There had to be a way to verify that, but I'd leave it to Nick. If Joel had been out of the country, Miles had probably figured he was safe to return once again. But how had he known the man wouldn't be here? "Was Joel's trip well publicized?"

She frowned as though wondering why I was asking but said, "Yes. The *Globe* picked up an article the *Toil and Trouble* had done about him selling his woodcrafts to overseas markets. Why?"

I shrugged.

Her gaze narrowed. "You think Miles saw the article and *that* was why he returned? Because Joel wasn't here?"

Dorothy was many things, but dumb wasn't one of them.

"It's possible."

Angrily, she said, "No, not *possible*. Probable. Damn him."

It was then that I realized she hated Miles Babbage. Truly loathed the man. It was evident in the derision of her tone, her fiery gaze, the set of her jaw.

She shifted her weight, cocking the other hip. "Miles got what was coming to him, nonetheless, thanks to Ve. We should throw her a party before she goes to prison."

"Ve didn't kill him," I said through clenched teeth.

"Why? Because she *said* she didn't? She can't remember that weekend at all, so how does she know she didn't kill the man? Did you consider that in your *investigations*?"

I felt a pinprick of fear pierce my heart. I hadn't considered it, but given the circumstances, it was entirely possible. . . . Ve hadn't liked Miles. And he'd tricked her by using an amulet. Maybe she'd found out? It could have been self-defense. . . .

But no.

No!

I wouldn't let Dorothy do this to me.

She was simply deflecting, trying to redirect my investigations away from her. . . .

"You're trying too hard," I said to her as the sprinkles turned into a steady rain once again. "First with Nick, now with Ve. And it makes me wonder why. What are you hiding, Dorothy?"

"I'm not hiding a thing. My life is an open book, as you're well aware since you already knew about the affair. . . . Let me ask you this. Have you uncovered that Penelope Debrowski had a torrid relationship with Miles?"

I was glad Marcus hadn't heard the word "torrid" used in tandem with his mother's name. He might have needed a memory cleanse.

"Yes, which I'm sure you already know, as you instructed Sylar to mention it to me."

She smiled. "You're a smart cookie, Darcy. Too smart not to see what's in front of your own eyes."

"You, as a killer? Oh, I see that fairly easily."

"No, though *you're* pressing your luck on that front." She cast a glance at the bookshop. "Sometimes the most visible things are the most hidden." Her voice rose, turning sickly sweet. "Like, oh, the shape of Marcus' eyes. His height, his thin stature . . . They remind me of another man. A man who isn't Oliver. You should be investigating *that*. Not me."

I suddenly did some mental math, and unless Penelope had had the longest pregnancy in history, the dates didn't add up. "Good try, Dorothy. Marcus turned twenty-nine at the end of August."

She raised a dubious eyebrow. "Are you certain about that?"

Her needling tone suggested that I was wrong and she was giving me the chance to correct myself. "What's that mean? Of course I am."

"If you can't see the ease with which a Lawcrafter could alter a birth certificate, that's your problem, not mine." She snorted derisively, then muttered under her breath, "Some investigator you are."

Now that she had planted the seed, I recalculated my mental math. If Marcus had been conceived the same week Miles had disappeared, then a normal pregnancy would place his due date at the end of June or the beginning of July. Definitely not August. However, Dorothy was right about Lawcrafters. It would be extremely easy for them to doctor a legal document.

Had Penelope and/or Oliver changed Marcus' birth certificate to make it appear as though he'd been conceived after Penelope married Oliver?

I couldn't rule it out; that was for sure.

Oh boy.

Then I glanced at Dorothy. She was smiling like she'd just given me the biggest scoop since Watergate. But the smile didn't quite reach her blue eyes. No, there was no joy in her gaze at all. Instead, I saw another emotion altogether.

Whether it was true or not, the Marcus tip had been another deflection. I would have to look into it further; however, the tip itself changed nothing about my interest in *Dorothy*.

She talked a pretty game. A pretty game that I suspected hid ugly truths. I pushed wet hair off my face and said, "Be that as it may, you're still not telling me everything."

"As I said, my life is an open book. You're wasting your time with me. I didn't kill Miles."

I took a step closer to her. "You can tell me you're not hiding anything until you're blue in the face. You can run away from me when you see me coming, and you can maybe even get Nick to stop investigating. But I'm not going to stop until I figure out the whole truth of what happened to Miles that weekend. And my instincts tell me it involves you somehow."

Rain dripped down her face as it hardened with hatred. "Listen to me, Darcy Merriweather. You might think you have some power in this village, thanks to mommy dearest, but you don't. You hear me? You need to stay out of matters that don't concern you. I told you I didn't kill him, and I didn't. That's that."

Mommy dearest. It was clear she knew who the Elder was. . . .

But if she'd meant to bring up my mother as some sort of veiled threat, then her plan had backfired. The mention of my mother had only served to bolster my courage.

"Not quite," I said. "You'll have to forgive me for not taking your word for *anything*."

Sharply, she said, "You need to keep in mind that witches who play with fire get burned."

That had definitely been a threat, considering Dorothy's firebug nature. I closed what little distance remained between us and said, "I told you, I'm not stopping. Because I see it in your eyes. I practically smell it coming off you in waves. Fear. Why, Dorothy? Why are you so scared?"

She gave me a shove, and my arms flew out so I could keep my balance. The candle went flying and crashed on the cobblestone pathway, breaking into pieces. The tiny ceramic bird popped off and rolled away.

"Darcy!" someone yelled.

Dorothy and I both turned. It was Mimi, and she wasn't alone. Andreus Woodshall stood next to her, holding an umbrella over her head as they rushed toward us.

Dorothy turned back to me. "Stay out of my way, Darcy," she said, moving past me. "And maybe I'll stay out of yours."

Striding off, she took a moment to stomp the ceramic bird and then kept going, her *click-clack, click-clack* sounding like gunfire.

A moment later, Mimi threw her arms around me and held on tight. "Are you okay?"

Andreus lifted a dark eyebrow and humor laced his words as he said, "I see nothing much has changed since the last time I was in the village."

"What are you doing out of school?" I asked Mimi as we crouched low, cleaning up the candle mess. Rain came down in sheets, and I was soaked to the bone, despite Andreus' best attempts to keep both Mimi and me dry with his umbrella. By my calculations, Mimi had another hour or so left of classes.

"I heard a rumor that something happened at Ve's, so I, uh, left. . . ."

Left? Skipped out was more accurate. "Mimi . . ."

"Don't 'Mimi' me," she said, sounding a lot like Harper. "I couldn't just stay there after hearing that." She shrugged. "It's no big deal."

Discussing the big deal of it all could wait until later.

"I came across her shortly after the little felon made her escape," Andreus said, tossing a chunk of candle into a nearby trash bin.

Mimi threw him an exasperated look, so funny that it made me smile. After what had happened with Dorothy, I was glad Mimi was here. Andreus, too, and that was saying something.

However, I wasn't entirely sure he would have been

on my side if I'd gotten into a knock-down, drag-out fight with Dorothy. He was a family friend of Dorothy's and he was Glinda's godfather.

As I've mentioned, he was a complicated man.

"What?" Andreus said to her with a grin. "It's true."

Despite the gloominess of the afternoon, there must have been enough ambient light to keep his dark, Dracula-ish countenance at bay. Sometimes when in shadows, his face morphed into something that could cause nightmares. It was an ability he knew he possessed, and he used it to his benefit when needed. His normal, everyday face was quite handsome. He was nearing fifty, his black hair had started to silver, and his dark eyes and swarthy skin tone had always reminded me of a silver-screen star from days of old. Aunt Ve had started dating him last spring. She didn't mind a bit that she was more than a decade older than he was and welcomed any and all cougar references.

I glanced at Mimi. "We would have come to get you if it was something serious. You know that, right?"

"Don't you think Aunt Ve murdering someone is serious?" she asked, her brown eyes wide with earnestness. Her dark curls had spiraled out of control with the moisture in the air. At thirteen her baby face was giving way to that of a young woman, slimming out and lengthening.

I sighed. "She didn't murder anyone."

"Yet," Andreus added drolly.

"Not helping." I tossed the last of the candle into the trash.

Andreus adjusted the umbrella as the wind shifted. "Dorothy should count herself lucky Ve didn't witness what Mimi and I came upon, or I fear she'd have gone the way of the skeleton I've been hearing about so much. What sparked this particular altercation?"

"Secrets," I said, standing up. I gave them both a quick rundown of what had been happening as we headed off to Ve's house. I didn't mention Dorothy's suggestion that Marcus might not be Oliver's son. I wanted to look into that a bit further before I put that information out into the village.

"Hey, look!" Mimi ducked out from under the umbrella. She stooped and picked up something from the grass.

It was the ceramic bird. Intact. It had somehow survived Dorothy's stiletto.

Mimi held it out me, and as I closed my hand around it, I smiled. I hoped Dorothy had hurt her foot trying to break the piece. Served her right.

"How's Aunt Ve doing?" Mimi asked as we pressed on. "I mean, is she okay?"

"She's confused," I said. "A little bit quiet. I think she's just processing and is trying to figure out *why* it happened. We all are."

"Poor Aunt Ve," Mimi murmured.

As we headed through the side gate at Ve's, I noticed Archie's cage was empty . . . and also that there was music in the air. Something bright and lively. Latin.

"Do you hear that?" I asked.

Mimi nodded.

Andreus looked toward the house and said, "Sounds like it's coming from inside."

As we hurried up the back steps, the music grew louder. I also picked up the sound of laughter coming from within. Missy ran to greet us in the mudroom, and Mimi scooped her up. Missy adored Mimi. The feeling was quite mutual.

We followed the music to the family room. All the furniture had been pushed back against the walls, and the area rug rolled up.

Aunt Ve and Godfrey were in the middle of an elaborate salsa dance, laughing as they twirled around. They didn't notice us at all, lost in their own little world.

Dripping rainwater onto the wooden floor, I walked over to the stereo and clicked off the music. The two froze, midstep.

Andreus looked on with an amused expression. "Ah yes, poor Auntie Ve."

Chapter Twelve

"Absolutely not," Ve said adamantly to me as she danced across the kitchen, shimmying and swaying. She was gathering ingredients to bake cookies.

No doubt about it. In times of stress and strife, the women in my family took to baked goods like warriors to a battlefield. I tended to head straight to the Gingerbread Shack for my weapons of choice, but Aunt Ve liked to make her own sweet munitions.

I'd taken a quick hot shower and rummaged through the lone box of clothes that remained upstairs in my room to find something to wear. It had been slim pickings: a pair of old sweatpants and a T-shirt I used when I oil painted. My wet hair was pulled back into a long braid, and I sat barefoot at the kitchen peninsula with a crocheted blanket tossed over my shoulders. Annie was warming my lap and kept looking at me with her big amber eyes as though wondering why I smelled so odd.

The scent of oil paint and thinner tended to cling to fabrics, even after washing.

The salsa music had been turned back on, albeit at a much lower volume. Godfrey was giving Mimi a lesson in the family room, while I tried to talk some sense into my aunt. "But—"

Ve shook a finger at me. "No 'buts.' I don't need you to babysit me. I have Andreus for that."

I had just told her that I wanted to stay another night or two here at her house, and she'd shot my offer down before I even finished my sentence.

"It's a full-time job indeed," Andreus said as he used some fancy foot moves of his own to pass by her on the way to the sink.

He looked perfectly at home here as he went about making a pot of coffee.

I rather wished it were a vat.

"I expect compensation," he added as he suddenly pulled Ve into his arms and dipped her low to nuzzle her neck.

She giggled and pressed her hands to his chest. "I know just the thing."

"Hello!" I waved like I was motioning a jetliner to its gate. "I'm sitting right here. And I'm going to need a serving of memory cleanse with my coffee."

"Oh, you." Ve waved a dismissive hand in my direction. She'd changed out of her overalls into a pair of black leggings, a turquoise tank top, and a gray belted cable-knit cardigan sweater that hung to midthigh.

Her attitude sure had shifted since this morning. Dancing with Godfrey, flirting with Andreus . . . "Has Cherise been by?"

It seemed to me that Ve was under the influence of

a calming spell of some sort. With a touch of her fingertip, Curecrafter Cherise Goodwin could eliminate stress, replacing it with just this kind of contentment.

Only the cookie making hinted at any lingering anxiety lurking under the happy facade as Ve grabbed a carton of eggs from the fridge. "No, why?"

I rubbed Annie's silky ears, and her purrs rumbled against my sternum. "You're much too cheerful for someone who spent the morning at the police station."

"I'm just relieved, Darcy. Miles is never coming back. For thirty years I've dreaded the day he'd show up on my doorstep once again. It's like a weight has been lifted from my soul." She tossed her arms in the air, executed a pirouette, then laughed. "This might be the happiest day of my life."

"Now, now!" Godfrey exclaimed as he strolled into the kitchen. "Wasn't that the day you divorced me? I recall those precise words coming from your mouth. . . ."

He wiped his damp brow with a handkerchief, then tucked it into his pants pocket as he headed for the fridge and a pitcher of water. Mimi followed behind him, her cheeks rosy as she cradled Missy in her arms. She set the dog on the floor and sat on the stool next to mine. Missy trotted to her dog bed and settled in as though she'd had enough excitement for the day. She and Tilda both. The fussy feline had been MIA since the music had restarted. She'd never been a big fan of the stereo in general.

Ve patted Godfrey's flushed face as she said, "That *was* a lovely day, wasn't it?"

Godfrey was dressed casually. Well, casual for him. He wore a pair of soft gray dress pants and a coral cashmere zipper sweater. No tie. There were only a handful of times I'd ever seen him without one.

He'd been on a diet since June, and the results showed. Not only in the diminishment of his Santa-like belly, but also in the narrowing of his face. No jowls jiggled under his white beard. His perfectly groomed eyebrows wiggled. "The best."

Frowning in confusion, Mimi glanced at me. "I don't get it."

I put my arm around her. "I think what happened is that they were able to save their friendship because they got a divorce. Now they're best friends."

Ve cracked an egg. "Exactly. We'd both be in an asylum if we'd stayed married."

"Straitjackets for both of us," Godfrey agreed, sliding a glass of water over to Mimi. "And you know how I feel about institutional wear." He shuddered, then suddenly started sniffing the air. "What is that malodor?"

Mimi surreptitiously sniffed her armpits, then let out a breath of relief.

I smiled until Godfrey followed his nose into the mudroom. "Gah!" In the doorway, he held my coat with two fingers and made loud gagging noises. "I've found the culprit."

"Sorry," I said. "I didn't know it was supposed to rain today."

Ve held her nose closed. "Take it away!"

Missy whimpered.

Godfrey said, "I'll care of this."

The last time he'd "taken care of something," I'd lost one of my favorite pairs of jeans. I loved that coat. "Wait—what are you going to—?"

He swung his right arm far and wide, then shot his fingers out like he was flicking water. In an instant, my coat went from a stinking-wet mess to looking like it had just returned from the dry cleaners.

He smiled and patted it. "There. That's better."

Ve let go of her nose. "Wool, Darcy dear, is never a good idea in the rain."

I didn't bother to protest again that I hadn't known

the weather was going to turn on me. Instead, I said, "Thank you, Godfrey."

"Oh, trust me. It was my pleasure." He sat on the other side of me and picked up my left hand. He *tsk*ed and let it fall again. "Do I need to have a word with the young man?"

"Yes!" Mimi said, pushing her glass aside so she could lean forward. "Will you? Dad's forbidden me from talking about it anymore."

"No!" I said at the same time. "He'll ask when he's ready."

Under her breath, Ve said, "He's sure taking his sweet time."

Mimi said, "I know, right? It's killing me. I'm dying." She melted onto the countertop.

Andreus handed me a mug of coffee. "Careful, now. It's hot."

I thanked him and wrapped my hands around the mug. "Don't make me ban all of you from talking about it, too," I said, giving them all a stare down.

Andreus chuckled. "This reminds me. I have something for you, Darcy."

"For me?"

"For your basket," he clarified.

For weeks now Ve had been collecting trinkets inside a decorative basket made from a hollowed gourd. It was for my house blessing. By tradition, the objects should be placed in a box and buried by the front door to bring specific blessings to those who dwelled within, but that was impossible due to the construction of my front porch, so we were going to do the next best thing. The beautiful painted gourd would have a place of honor on a table next to my front door.

Already inside the unusual container were a whole nutmeg and oak bark for luck; a penny for wealth; a dried daisy for love; a fuchsia-colored witch bottle filled with herbs, sea salt, needles, three nails, and berries, and sealed with wax; and a cherry pit for hospitality. Written best wishes from our friends would be collected at the housewarming party, rolled into a tight scroll, and tied with a twig of rosemary before being added to the basket as well.

"Aw," Ve purred. "That's nice of you, Andreus. Isn't he nice?" For confirmation, she glanced at me, Godfrey, and Mimi as Andreus rummaged around in his weekend bag, which sat next to the back staircase.

Saying nothing, Godfrey stared at his fingers. Mimi nodded.

"Very nice," I said. Because it was. That didn't mean Andreus couldn't turn scary at the drop of a hat, however. It was all part and parcel of his ambiguous nature. Good, evil. Good, evil.

Today, he was good.

And I was grateful.

Andreus came to stand at the end of the peninsula, a velvet pouch in hand. He shook loose its contents. "For the home's happiness, love, peace, and protection, a perfect pearl."

He held up the stunning gem, then handed it to me. It was gorgeous, a lustrous white with a hint of pink. "Thank you so much. It's beautiful, both the pearl and its blessing."

He bowed. "A pleasure."

"Looks fake to me," Godfrey said, cracking a smile.

Andreus rolled his eyes and headed back to the coffeepot.

"Can I see?" Mimi asked.

I handed it to her. She oohed and aahed over it. "It's so pretty."

"A perfect addition to the basket." Ve also mixed

her cookie batter by hand. She dumped in a whole bag of chocolate chips. "We should be drinking champagne. It's a wonderful day."

Andreus stood next to her, leaning a hip against the countertop. He wore black gabardine slacks and a black turtleneck. "I'd be more inclined to celebrate if we knew what Miles Babbage was doing in your garage."

Mimi reluctantly handed the pearl back to me. She said, "Did you know him, Andreus?"

I put the pearl back into its velvet pouch. I'd add it to the gourd basket before I left.

Left.

I ignored the way my stomach ached at the thought and tried to focus on Andreus' answer. I hadn't yet had a chance to delve into a conversation about today's investigations and was a bit surprised Ve hadn't asked.

He said, "I never met the man. I knew of him from reputation only."

Ve stopped stirring. "You didn't know him? How is that possible?"

Andreus smiled. "I was sowing wild oats in Europe during the years Miles was part of the Roving Stones. Word of him still reached me via other Charmcrafter friends who were in the group, but no, I never had the chance to meet him face-to-face."

"Count yourself lucky," Ve said as she used two teaspoons to transfer cookie dough from the bowl to a baking sheet lined with parchment paper.

Annie hopped off my lap and went to curl up with Missy. The two got along for the most part—except when Annie tried to groom the little dog. I went into the family room and came back with Ve's wedding photo. "Did those rumors include any information that Miles was using a seduction amulet to attract women in the village?" I asked Andreus, handing him the picture.

Ve's mouth gaped open. "He was *what*?"

"That necklace . . . ," I said, pointing to the leather choker around Miles' neck.

Godfrey picked up the cookie-dough bowl and set it down between him and Mimi. He handed her one of the two spoons Ve had been using, and they dug in.

Evan would have a fit if he saw them.

Cherise would have lectured Godfrey about his diet.

I, however, wanted to join them.

Ve grabbed the photo. "That no-good son of a—"

Andreus cut off Ve's outburst. "Back then there was much speculation among the few Charmcrafters in the Roving Stones that Miles was wearing some sort of allurement amulet, but no one knew how he could have acquired such a powerful piece."

"He didn't get it from one of the Stones?" I asked.

"No," Andreus said. "It's why I heard about the pendant at all—the Charmcrafting community is a small one. For me to hear of Miles while in Europe meant that the Charmcrafters in the Stones were casting nets far and wide to learn the amulet's origin. None of the Charmcrafters knew who could have made it, and Miles was proprietary. He wouldn't allow any of those who asked to view the pendant to get an up-close look. Holding it would have been the only way to know for certain that the piece was charmed."

"He's lucky he's dead," Ve stated, still staring at the picture.

Andreus smiled at her, then said to us, "Miles was a mortal, so it would not have been a Crafter's first thought that he'd be using magic on them. The amulet looked much like a normal pendant anyone would wear. A simple circle, as you can see. Of the Charmcrafters in the Stones at that time, none were from the Enchanted Village, so word didn't spread here as it might have, had I not been in Europe."

Ve looked at him. "So I can blame my marriage to Miles on you?"

With a big grin, he said, "Certainly, if it makes you feel better."

She nodded. "It definitely would."

He kissed her temple. "Then I take full responsibility."

As much as I had doubts about Andreus' character, there were times, like now, when I wondered if his "bad" side was just a big ruse to cover a soft heart.

Godfrey spoke around a mouthful of cookie dough. "Let me see that picture."

Ve tossed it at him, then took back her cookie dough. She grabbed her own spoon and stuck it into the bowl.

Mimi scooted over a seat so she could get a view of the picture, too. She squinted. "He looks . . . sad."

Broken.

Godfrey chuckled. "Don't forget, little one, that he'd just married *Ve*. Someday I'll have to tell you of the wedding dress she designed for our big day. A ruffled monstrosity. I still have nightmares about those ruffles."

Ve threw a spoonful of cookie dough at him, but she'd cracked a smile and the tension in the room defused.

Godfrey caught the dough and popped it into his mouth. He then tapped the photo. "Do you have a magnifying glass, Ve?"

She stomped off to what was left of the As You Wish office space. Everything relating to the business was now in its new space at my house. Ve was transforming the room into a home office for herself, but it was a slow process. A moment later she came back with a long magnifying glass with a wooden handle.

"I thought so," Godfrey said after a moment of studying the picture.

"What did you think?" Ve asked, her words clipped.

"I believe Miles himself made this piece. He was fond of this particular design. That disk shape with the geometric edges." He looked at Mimi. "Always reminded me of a gear, which I found highly unappealing. He used it on a lot of his pottery."

"Impossible," Andreus said. "Only someone gifted with creating charms could have made such an amulet. The strength and power it held over these women proves that."

"I wish he was here so I could kill him," Ve said to no one in particular.

It was a wish I was glad I couldn't grant.

"This makes no sense," I said. "Miles was a mortal."

Andreus motioned for the magnifying glass. Godfrey handed it—and the photo—over. Andreus set the picture on the counter and bent over it.

"Aunt Ve," Mimi said, "have you thought about doing the memory spell to remember that weekend? Then you might know what really happened."

Out of the mouths of babes. I'd been meaning to ask Ve that myself.

Ve answered, "Mimi dear, that's exactly why I haven't used the spell. I don't want to remember."

"But why?" Mimi asked. "You don't think you killed him, do you? You wouldn't have. I know you wouldn't have. We all know that."

Ve sighed, then smiled at Mimi. "Your faith in me warms my heart, little one, but I do believe I could have killed him if I knew he'd been controlling me with an amulet. Maybe I found out. . . . Maybe not."

I hated thinking it, but I agreed. Knowing he'd been controlling Ve made *me* want to kill him. Or at the very least, hurt him a lot. "Rightfully so, but you certainly never would have left his body in your garage. You'd have hid him proper in the woods or pushed him into a lake with a cement block."

The others stopped what they were doing and stared at me. "What?" I said. "It's true."

Ve laughed. I loved the sound. "I agree," she said. "I'm much too smart a witch for that. However, it doesn't change my mind. I don't want to know what happened that weekend. It's over and done with. I won't be using the memory spell, and that's that."

That's that.

It was the same phrase Dorothy had used.

There were a lot of stubborn witches in this village.

While the investigator in me wanted Ve to use the spell so I could get more information on Miles and what might have happened to him, the niece in me didn't want her aunt to suffer any more pain. As I couldn't guarantee that the memories she'd recall would be pleasant ones, I let it go. I'd just have to figure out what happened that weekend on my own.

His tone serious, Andreus said, "Darcy, let me see your bird."

"Bird?" I asked. Surely he wasn't asking about my mother in such a roundabout way. He knew who she was—he'd been there when she was sworn in as Elder twenty-four years ago.

"The one from earlier. On the green . . ."

He was being obtuse on purpose, so Ve didn't learn about the altercation with Dorothy. There wasn't enough cookie dough in the world to deal with that right now.

"Oh!" I rushed to my coat in the mudroom and finally found the bird at the bottom of the stash of acorns in the pocket of my now dry and clean-smelling coat.

He hovered the magnifying glass over the bird.

"What are you looking for?" Mimi asked.

He said, "I wasn't sure until I looked at the bird as well, but now I'm fairly positive. . . ."

"What?" Ve looked at the bird oddly.

Godfrey and I both leaned in to get a better look at it ourselves.

Andreus said, "It was Steve Winstead who made this amulet. Not Miles. Steve's clay is unique. It has striations that cannot be covered with glaze. I see the same faint lines in Miles' amulet. Examining it in person would provide even more confirmation." He glanced at me. "Do you think Nick would allow us to see it?"

"I'm not sure he has it," I said. "I think everything that was on the skeleton went to the medical examiner's office."

"Perhaps, then," Andreus said, "Nick could arrange a field trip."

"Oh! Oh! Can I go?" Mimi exclaimed.

No doubt Harper would be champing at the bit to attend as well. I said, "I'll see what I can do."

"Steve?" Ve asked. "That makes no sense, either. He's not a Charmcrafter."

Godfrey was shaking his head. "That piece was made by Miles. Do not question my impeccable eye for detail. The gear shape is his design."

Andreus set his hands on his hips. "The clay does not lie."

I stared at the bird and remembered what Steve had told me earlier about Miles trying to raid his secret clay source. . . . It had probably taken some time for Steve to cast the protection spell on the creek and memory-cleanse Miles, time in which Miles could have returned to the hiding spot.

"Actually," I said to the two men, "you both might be right."

"How?" Mimi asked. "How can they both be right?"

"Magical clay," I told her. "*Stolen* magical clay . . ."

*   *   *

"You're dawdling," Ve said an hour later as we cleaned up the kitchen together. "Go *home*, Darcy. It's where you belong."

I *was* dawdling. I didn't want to leave. "There are still a few boxes left to move. . . ."

I'd been wiping down the counters for the past ten minutes. They were beyond clean. Godfrey had gone back to the boutique half an hour ago, Mimi had headed off to work her shift at the bookshop, and Andreus was upstairs taking a shower.

He'd been very intrigued by the magical clay, and I hoped I hadn't told him something I shouldn't have. Even though Andreus' specialty was rocks and minerals, specifically black opals, I rather hoped Steve still had the protection spell cast over that creek. I made a mental note to ask him.

"Get the boxes tomorrow. Come by anytime. I'll be here." Ve smiled at me, cupped my cheek. "I'll always be here."

Tears welled instantly. "But—"

"No, no!" She shook her head. "Stop that right now. If I start crying today I won't stop. You moving out is . . . bittersweet, but it's still sweet. We're not to be sad about it, do you hear me?"

Sweet . . . and bitter, I wanted to add but held my tongue. I'd had so many great memories in this house. In just over a year it had been more of a home to me than I'd ever had before. And that had been because of Ve. And her love for me.

I threw my arms around her. "I love you, Aunt Ve."

"I love you, too, my darling Darcy." She hugged me back, holding me close for a long minute. Then she pushed back, rubbed her hands together, and said, "Okay. What do we need to send you off right and proper . . . ?" She started rummaging through cabinets. "Salt!"

She set a container of salt on the counter.

"Salt?" I asked.

Ve took a small plastic tumbler and lid from her cup cabinet and filled it from the tap. "Water!"

"Water?" I repeated, watching her make sure no water leaked from the secured lid.

She then rushed across the kitchen and lifted the lid on the bread box. It was empty. "Shoot."

I wasn't sure what she was doing. "Ve?"

She snapped her fingers. "The cookies. They'll work. They're homemade, which is better anyway."

"I'm so confused."

"Salt, water, bread. It's tradition when witches move houses to bring these items with them from the old house to the new one."

"Why?"

"Some say the bread and water are for a life of abundance and the salt is for luck; others say it's to carry good spirits from one home to another. I don't know for certain. It's tradition. We go with it." She packed the items in a paper sack. "And there's one more thing. Come with me."

She bustled off down the hallway toward the front parlor, and I followed along, wondering what she had in mind.

With Ve, one never knew.

In the parlor, she veered off to the fireplace. I stopped short as she reached up for the painting that hung above the mantel.

"Oh no, I can't take that," I said. "Ve . . ."

It was a watercolor painting of a magic wand. With its whimsical swirls and blend of golden colors, it was a visual and visceral reminder of the magic that lived in this home. I'd loved it since the moment I laid eyes on it.

She carried the large painting over to me. "It doesn't

belong to me. It belongs with As You Wish. It belongs with you."

By her tone of voice, I knew it was pointless to argue.

And inwardly, I didn't want to. I loved that painting and knew just where it needed to be hung.

Emotion clogged my throat and I nodded. "Thank you," I managed to say.

She looked pleased with herself as she steepled her fingers beneath her chin. "Now, go *home*, Darcy," she said with a broad smile. "Out, out, shoo!"

I smiled back at her, grabbed the painting and wrapped it in a plastic trash bag, gathered the brown sack, Annie, and Missy . . .

And went home.

Chapter Thirteen

"This wasn't exactly what I expected to be doing to-night in front of the fire." Nick slid me a smile as he opened another manila file folder, gave it a cursory glance, then closed it again.

It was just after nine, and it had been a long, long day.

Laughing, I sipped from my mug of hot chocolate, which had only moments ago been piled high with whipped cream that had now melted into a foamy cloud. "Me neither. But there's still time. And a fireplace in the bedroom . . . We just need to finish these files first."

Nick and Mimi were spending the night here with me, and I couldn't have been happier about that. It was as it should be, since really it was their house, too. I wished they were staying put forever, but we'd decided not to move in together until we were married.

It was a decision I had regretted quickly. While I was

usually quite a patient person, in this matter, I was more than ready to start our lives together.

He grabbed another file. "I approve of your work-place motivation."

"Shh," I teased. "I'll get a reputation."

Flames jumped in the family room fireplace as I sat next to Nick on the shaggy area rug. The mantel begged for knickknacks, for framed photos and artwork. Right now it had only two small items upon it, barely visible against the rich tones of the stacked stone. One was a lovely little white ceramic bird, the other a perfect brown acorn.

I'd kept an acorn in my coat pocket just in case I ran into Dorothy again, then distributed some of the stash I'd harvested this morning around the house in various windowsills and above doorframes. Three of the assort-ment were now residing with a damp mixture of peat mix and sawdust in a plastic bag in the fridge, hibernat-ing. They'd stay there for a couple of months at least. It was the first step in growing my own oak trees, which was a special kind of magic all in itself, one that had nothing to do with the Craft and everything to do with the magic of nature.

Dozens of manila folders tucked into numerous file boxes were stacked in front of Nick and me. They were the As You Wish client files. As scatterbrained as Ve was for most office tasks, she was meticulous about cli-ent records. She said she couldn't locate a file for Miles' visit that day thirty years ago, but I was certain she'd created one. I just hoped it had been misfiled or misla-beled and not destroyed for whatever reason. If it was here, Nick or I would find it eventually.

Atop a fleece blanket on the sectional sofa behind us, Higgins snored sonorously, snuffling every few mo-ments, sucking ever-present drool back into his mouth.

From Annie's spot in front of the fireplace, she shot the Saint Bernard an occasional horrified glance as she stretched languidly, enjoying the heat.

Higgins' drool *was* rather horrifying.

Missy was upstairs with Mimi, who had decided to move a few things into her room to make it feel homier for when she spent nights here, like tonight. Last time I'd checked, her iPod was playing Queen and she was singing "Bohemian Rhapsody" at the top of her lungs. Clothes were strewn about the room, books teetered on the desk, and she'd hung up a *The Princess Bride* movie poster and one of a colorful hipster owl as well. Her beloved pink witch hat sat on the window bench that overlooked the village square. She seemed to be settling in well for someone who didn't quite live here yet.

Nick took a second to check his phone. The preliminary findings from the ME's office were due anytime now, and he was also waiting to hear back about getting a look at Miles' necklace.

Nick had caught a lucky break earlier—Miles had in fact been treated by the local dentist's office, the only one in this area. It took some digging on their part because the records had been in storage, but the office had provided X-rays that proved the skeleton was in fact Miles Babbage.

We just didn't know how—or why—he'd died just yet.

Or why he'd been in Ve's garage.

As with Ve's legal case, Nick was in a limbo of his own until he knew of Miles' cause of death. We presumed that he'd been murdered—but so far there was no evidence that a crime had been committed, and Nick couldn't investigate at full capacity until he knew.

But there was no denying that an abundance of people seemed to want the man dead.

"Are you sure there's a file?" Nick frowned at his phone, then set it on the floor.

"No." We were through the letter *L*. "But I have to look. If we know why Miles hired Ve, then it might open a new door in the investigation."

"You have to consider hiring Ve was a ruse. If Miles was looking for a sugar mama and Penelope was spirited away by her parents to the Cape . . ."

A sugar mama. It did seem that was Miles' type. Like father, like son. "It's possible. Probable, even. And rather despicable. I'm hoping the Chadwicks will have more information on him."

Nick's investigators had discovered some background on Miles. His dad had died years ago, and he had no known living relatives. He'd also had a police record, having been arrested several times during his vagabond life. Shoplifting charges mostly, and one charge of trespassing.

I had called Glinda Hansel earlier this evening, and she'd agreed to accompany me to Wickedly Creative tomorrow morning. Nick was going as well. More fact gathering, as Marcus had said. It was the best we could do right now.

I had told Nick what Dorothy had said about Marcus and he agreed to keep the information under wraps for now. Until we knew if it was true or not. If Marcus was Miles' son, then it was an important factor in the case, but if he wasn't, then any rumors were bound to be hurtful.

Nick opened another file, scanned it, smiled. "Did you know Ve once had to provide an elephant for a bride to ride on to her wedding?"

Laughing, I said, "No, I didn't know. I'm kind of sad for the elephant, though."

Nick leaned over and kissed my temple.

"What was that for?"

"Your big heart. I'm surprised you have room enough in there for Mimi and me."

I closed the file I'd been looking at and glanced at him. "Are you kidding? You and Mimi *are* my heart."

He curved an arm around me, and I set my head into the crook of his neck. I could feel his heartbeat pulse reassuringly against my cheek.

"I want you to stay," I said.

"Stay?"

I leaned back to look at him. "Here."

"I am here," he said, tipping his head to the side in confusion.

"Not just tonight. Always. I don't want to wait until we . . . well, until . . . You know."

Slowly, he nodded.

"It's just, it seems silly," I went on. "Mimi's moving stuff in upstairs. You'll both be here more often than not. So why not? Why wait?"

He took a deep breath. "I've been thinking about this, too, and I agree. I don't want to wait, either. I like it here with you."

"Really?"

"Really. One condition, though."

I groaned. "So close."

"I don't want to wait on the wedding, either. No two-year engagements . . . or anything like that. And yes, I know we should first *get* engaged."

I smiled. "Who's been talking to you?"

He ran a hand through his dark hair, lifting tufts. "Who hasn't been?"

"They love us; that's all."

"I know. It's a good thing. Just a bit . . . much."

It was.

"So, what do you think about a short engagement?" he asked.

"How short?" I asked. Because even though I could

elope tonight and be perfectly happy, Harper would never stand for that. Never mind Mimi, Starla, Evan, Ve, Godfrey . . . There'd be a witch-hunt for sure.

He must have known what I was thinking, because he said, "We can play it by ear."

"Sounds like we have a plan . . . on one condition."

"So close," he echoed. "What's the condition?"

"No elephants."

He laughed. "It's a deal. But maybe it's time we take care of that one technicality in all this. . . ."

"Technicality?"

"The engagement . . ."

"Oh?" I asked coyly, unable to stop a goofy grin from forming.

He took my hands in his. "I've been trying to figure out how to do this right, but I realized there might not be a right w—"

He was cut off by the doorbell.

Higgins lifted his head and blinked his big dark eyes in bewilderment, clearly wondering what had woken him up. Suddenly, his ears perked and he lumbered to his feet. He let out a loud bark, and Annie's fur rose at the sound. She took off for higher ground—which she found atop the fridge.

Missy's sharp bark echoed along the upstairs open hallway that overlooked part of the vaulted kitchen and the family room. That particular stretch of hall separated the master bedroom from the rest of the bedrooms, and while the architect who'd drawn the plans for the renovations had proclaimed it an "interior balcony," we'd taken to calling it the "overlook." As I glanced upward, I could just barely see a ball of fur sprinting toward the staircase. A moment later, she was at the front door. Higgins ran off to join her, his booming woofs joining her staccato barks, creating a bone-jarring harmony.

I fell against Nick, laughing.

The doorbell rang again, sending the dogs into a fresh frenzy.

Nick kissed my head and stood up. "I'll get it."

I glanced at the clock on my phone. It was just after nine, and I was curious who'd be stopping by. If it had been family or a close friend, they most likely would have come to the side door. . . .

Nick said, "Down! Down! *Pzzt!*"

I started laughing all over again. He didn't have Harper's talents as far as *pzzt*ing was concerned. I helped corral the dogs and managed to get them out the rear door and into the fenced backyard with promises of bacon-flavored treats. Neither could resist that particular temptation.

When I returned, I was surprised to see that it was Vince who'd rung the bell. He stood in the entranceway with Nick. I asked, "Is this about Starla?"

"Starla?" Vince repeated. "What about her?"

I took my foot out of my mouth and tried to cover for my slip of the tongue. "Is she okay?"

"She's fine," he said, not looking like it was true. In fact, he appeared a little rough around the edges. Bloodshot, wild eyes. Messy hair. "I didn't come here to talk about her."

Even his voice had a rough, serrated edge to it. His words were said quickly, cutting. I hadn't seen this side of him since I'd first moved to the village.

I didn't like the reminder of the man he'd been back then.

"Why *are* you here?" Nick asked.

He shifted from foot to foot. "I just heard about the skeleton . . . and who it might be. Is it really Miles Babbage?"

Vince sounded like he'd known the man personally, which was impossible.

Nick eyed him curiously, then nodded. "Dental records confirmed it a couple of hours ago. Why do you ask?"

Vince bent at the waist and drew in a deep breath. Then he stood upright and looked between Nick and me. "I've been looking for him for years. Miles Babbage is . . . was . . . my father. And now that I know of their marriage, I suspect Ve might be my mother."

Chapter Fourteen

Nick handed me a glass of water and sat next to me on the sectional. I wished desperately the tumbler was full of wine instead. I needed something to calm my nerves. My mouth was Sahara dry, and any words I might have had were stuck in my parched throat. A fidgety Vince sat in an armchair. His legs jiggled. His fingers thrummed the tops of his thighs. He'd declined anything to drink.

Nick finally broke the silence. "Honestly, I don't know where to start."

I heard a creak and looked upward in time to see a long shadow dart into the reading nook that was notched into the back wall of the overlook. Mimi was listening in. I was surprised she wasn't sitting front and center on the balcony, her nose pressed between the turned-iron spindles, her legs dangling.

"I hate the secrets in this village." Vince's lips curled

in anger. "If I'd known about Ve's marriage to Miles,
I'd have put this together sooner, that Ve is my mother."

His *mother*. That was quite the leap he'd made.

"Do you know where she is?" he asked. "Ve? I went
to her house, but she's not there. And her cell is going
straight to voice mail. I really need to talk to her."

"I don't know," I said. "But Andreus is in town, so
they're probably on a date. Probably a movie, which is
why her cell is off."

He glanced at his watch, frowned.

I took a sip of water. "Ve's not your mother. And I
thought you had a mother? I met her at the Midsummer
Ball. . . ." Brenda Paxton seemed like a lovely woman.

Vince stood and paced. I noticed the dogs pressing their faces to the French doors, and I debated letting
them back in. Probably not a good idea. "She's my adoptive mother," he said. "I didn't find out I was adopted
until my senior year in college. I had a ruptured ap-
pendix and had complications. I needed a blood trans-
fusion. Neither of my parents' blood types matched
mine. They confessed at that point I'd been adopted a
day after my birth."

What a way to find out. I felt for him, but why did he
think Miles was his father and Ve his mother?

"If I'm being honest, I wasn't completely shocked.
I'd always felt a little . . . different. I started asking about
my birth parents. That was about seven years ago, right
after I graduated college. I was curious. My parents
clammed up, refusing to tell me anything." He glared
at me. "How do you know Ve's *not* my mother? If she
and Miles were married . . ."

If he *was* Ve's son, he'd have inherited Wishcrafter
traits and wouldn't appear as anything but a bright light
in photos. I'd seen pictures of him, so I knew it wasn't
possible. I couldn't very well tell him that, though. I

struggled with how to explain when Nick saved me the trouble.

"The timing is off," Nick said. "If you were a product of that marriage, you'd be a year younger than you are now. Ve didn't know Miles until the weekend they eloped. The marriage was a . . . spontaneous decision."

Spontaneous. Felonious. Both fit.

Vince shoved his hands into his hair and started pacing again. It was then, as he turned, that I noticed he shared the same jawline as Miles.

Was it really possible . . . ?

Suddenly uncomfortable, I asked, "How do you know Miles is your father?"

Vince sat. His leg resumed its jiggle. "I first heard Miles' name shortly after I asked my parents about my birth family. I heard them arguing about it one night. I eavesdropped, desperate for any information, since they wouldn't give me any. Apparently, my father wanted to tell me everything, because he thought it was right I should know, despite some deal made to never tell. My mother was adamant in her refusal. She said no good whatsoever could come of me knowing that my father was that 'loser' Miles Babbage and that my mother was some *witch* from the Enchanted Village. That I'd never be able to accept the truth. It was the last I'd ever heard out of them on the situation. They agreed I should never know and vowed never to talk of it again. It was then I was determined to figure out the truth on my own."

Some witch. Had she meant "witch" as in Crafter? Or as a euphemism, as Sylar had used earlier referring to me?

Vince went on. "I went to file a petition to have my adoption records unsealed, only to find I had no adoption records. None. My birth certificate lists only my adoptive parents' names. They both refused to admit that I had been placed with them via black-market adoption, but it's the only logical conclusion. I searched and searched for Miles Babbage and found nothing I could follow up on. So I did the only thing I could. I moved here. I ask from time to time about anyone knowing someone named Miles Babbage, but no one seems to know much other than he was some sort of homeless gigolo or something."

He obviously hadn't asked anyone with the Roving Stones, or he'd know about Miles' artistry as well.

"I was forced to stop looking for him. Instead, I studied witchcraft and sought out witches to try to find my mother."

I knew he'd once been connected with Alexandra Shively, who'd also been a Seeker who believed she was a witch . . . and she had been. Unfortunately, she'd been killed before knowing exactly what kind of Craft ability she possessed.

"With witchcraft," Vince said, "I found my calling. It resonates in me. It feels . . . normal."

Normal.

A chill swept down my spine. Growing up, I also had felt different and as though I didn't fit in. It wasn't until I learned of my abilities and moved here that I truly felt like I belonged for the first time.

"It's because *I'm* a warlock," he said. "I'm sure of it."

Well, this certainly explained why *he* was a Seeker. But was he *really* one of us?

I had no way of knowing if he was a Crafter. For now I tried to downplay any possible Craft involvement. "Perhaps your mother meant 'witch' as a euphemism," I said. "I was called one today myself."

Nick scowled. "By who?"

"Sylar," I said. "Long story."

Vince narrowed his eyes. "It could be a euphemism,

but I don't think so. I think there are witches in this village. And that I'm one of them."

My heart started to race. I recalled what Starla had said this morning, about his sorcery research. "Do you have any magical powers?"

"It's not the point, Darcy. The point is, I need to know for sure who my birth parents are." He turned eager eyes to Nick. "I was hoping Nick could help me get Miles Babbage's DNA sample from the medical examiner's office."

"You'll need a court order for a paternity test," Nick said. "A good lawyer can help."

A lawyer like Marcus Debrowski.

My throat went dry again. If what Dorothy had said about Marcus was true . . . and what Vince suspected was true—at least about Miles being his father . . .

Vince and Marcus would be half brothers.

I searched for similarities. Both men were tall and thin. Both had brown hair, though Vince's was curly like Miles' had been and Marcus' was straight, like Penelope's. Both men wore glasses.

It was where the resemblances ended. The shapes of their faces were different. Marcus had green eyes; Vince's were blue. Different noses. Different jawlines.

Still, it was . . . possible.

Nick squeezed my hand, and I looked at him. I had the feeling he'd followed my train of thought.

It was confirmed when he asked Vince, "Have you thought about contacting Marcus Debrowski?"

"I have. He turned down the case. I suspect his father told him to."

"Oliver?" I asked. "Why?"

"Once when I searched my parents' house for any information about my birth, I found Oliver's business card in a box with a stuffed bear and a blue baby sweater. I contacted him and he knew immediately who

I was, but he refused to confirm or deny that he handled my adoption. But I know he did. I know it."

As far as circumstantial evidence went, it was pretty damning. I wondered if lawyer-client confidentiality included lawyers and clients involved in black-market adoptions.

Secrets. Yes, the village was rife with them.

Vince clasped his hands together. "I hired Glinda Hansel to help find my parents. She's the one that told me Miles was likely the skeleton in Ve's garage and that he had been married to her."

Because *I'd* told Glinda. No wonder she'd been acting oddly. If she'd been searching for Miles to fill in those empty family tree branches, she was probably shocked to know he'd been in Ve's garage.

I couldn't blame her for not telling me—when we spoke earlier we hadn't known for certain the skeleton belonged to Miles. It would have been premature— and unethical—on her part to share Vince's adoption with me.

Still, I wished she would have.

"In addition to trying to trace my family tree, I've asked her to collect DNA samples from villagers for comparison to mine. I'm related to someone in this village, and I'm determined to find out who. My mother lived here. Or lives here. I want to find her."

"DNA samples? That can't be legal," I said, horrified by the thought of it.

Anger flashed in Vince's eyes. "It requires participant signatures, which Glinda said might be hard to get. She said she wouldn't do anything illegal, but she'd try to get people to agree. If she can't, I'll collect the DNA on my own and forge the signatures if I have to. What are the people going to do if they find out? Throw me in jail? I'm already living in a prison created by the people who didn't want me."

The bitterness in his voice hurt my heart, but I couldn't help replaying his words in my head. About his collecting DNA samples from the villagers.

"Starla," I suddenly said. "You tried to get her to do the ancestor testing with you."

Apparently if Glinda was tasked with comparing samples, he'd had his DNA sample done already. He'd lied to Starla.

She had believed he wanted her tested because he was trying to find out if she was a witch, but in reality he was trying to find out if they were related.

Or maybe he was seeking answers to both.

The thought turned my stomach.

Vince didn't even try to deny it. "One more person to rule out."

"Why now?" Nick asked. "Why the big push at this point?"

"I just had another birthday. I want to know who I am. What if I want to start a family of my own one day? There's too many questions. I need answers."

A family of his own . . . Was he planning that potential family with Starla? "Does Starla know about all this? Your adoption?"

"No," he said. "Other than Oliver and Glinda, you two are the only ones in the village who know my truth."

It was something else he'd kept from Starla. One more nail in the coffin of their relationship. I suddenly realized that she probably knew Miles' name from seeing it on Vince's computer. If she'd seen his sorcery searches, she'd probably seen his paternity searches as well but hadn't known what she was looking at.

With a sigh, I said, "You need to tell her."

Slowly, he nodded. "I will. Tonight."

Nick asked, "Why the secrecy? It might have been easier to find out information on Miles or your mother if you'd been more open."

"Maybe so," he admitted, "but I wanted to find out what I could on my own first. This village is known for keeping secrets, and I believed that if I came straight out with my search that whoever was keeping the secret would go out of their way to make sure I never found out."

It was a real possibility. Villagers, especially Crafters, were used to nurturing their secrets, tending to them as one would a prized garden.

Vince's leg finally stopped wiggling. "Now I don't care who knows. Miles is dead. My mother is all I have left."

I wondered how his adoptive parents felt about that.

He added, "I need to find her. She holds the key to my magic."

Studying him, I wondered if the magic was the root of his mission. He didn't sound like he cared to know the woman who gave birth to him but wanted only the knowledge she could share with him. If he was a Crafter, it was an unsettling notion. Rogue, power-hungry witches were dangerous.

I opened my mouth, then closed it. I didn't know what to say to him.

"I'll get a lawyer and request a DNA sample from the medical examiner's office, just to make things official with Miles," Vince stated. "I need to get Ve's DNA to check to see if she's my mother. Will you help me, Darcy? Talk to her? Smooth the waters, so to speak?"

"She's not your mother," I said once again.

"You don't know that," he insisted.

"I do so. Look, Vince. If I thought there was even a chance Ve was your mother, I'd help you in a heartbeat. I don't think it's right that you don't know who your parents are, but she's not your mother. She's just not." I would call her as soon as possible to let her know of Vince's suspicions, even if I had to leave the news on a voice mail. As Glinda had said, forewarned was fore-armed.

Vince looked on the verge of tears. "Then who, Darcy? Who is?"

"I don't know," I said as gently as I could.

I thought about Dorothy's affair with Miles and wondered if it was possible she was Vince's mother, but the timing wasn't quite right. She would have been out of the country on her second honeymoon when Vince was born. If he was adopted the day after he was born, it seemed likely his mother had been right here in the village, not halfway around the world.

Then I thought about what Dorothy had mentioned to me this afternoon, about Marcus. And then of another tidbit I'd heard today. About how Penelope had dated Miles once before they'd nearly run off together. Right around the time Vince would have been conceived . . .

Had that tryst produced a possible son as well?

The more I thought about it, and how Oliver had handled Vince's adoption, the more I believed in the likelihood that Marcus and Vince weren't just half brothers.

But *full* brothers.

Chapter Fifteen

Saturday dawned bright and sunny.

I'd slept well. Remarkably well considering it was a new house and a new bed and my mind was full of troubling thoughts.

Having Nick next to me all night helped. We'd agreed that he and Mimi would move in immediately, and Mimi had been over the moon with excitement. During the coming week, Nick would put his house on the market, and we'd officially move all their belongings here next Sunday, since the housewarming was already scheduled for Saturday.

From the doorway, a patient Higgins watched my every move as I made the bed. I'd had to remove Annie from beneath the blankets three times before accomplishing the task.

Mimi was still asleep, Nick had already headed off to work, and I'd already gone for my morning jog. Usually Starla joined me, but she'd texted that she had a headache and would catch up with me later today at the playhouse.

I wondered what had happened between her and Vince last night. The headache wasn't a good sign. She'd been planning to break up with him, and before he'd left last night, he'd promised to tell her all about his adoption. I wanted to text her and beg for details but decided it was a conversation best to have in person.

The bedroom was one of my favorite places in the house. As part of the addition, it was all brand-new and held none of the memories of the murder that had taken place in the old master bedroom when the house was for sale. Where that room had once stood was now open air, part of the vaulted family room.

At the far end of the master, at the back of the house, were the bathroom and walk-in closet, which had built-in shelves and drawers. At the front of the room was an upholstered bench below a set of double windows that overlooked the village. It matched exactly the one in Mimi's room. In the middle of the long space was an area rug, atop which was the king-sized bed, flanked by wooden nightstands. On Nick's nightstand were a lamp, his phone charger, a woodworking magazine, and a framed sketch I'd done of Mimi. On mine were a lamp, a clock, and a small vase full of fresh daisies. Most of my knickknacks were still at Ve's. I'd swing by her house later, as she had suggested I pick up the rest of my boxes then.

Higgins' and Missy's dog beds were at the foot of the bed, though last night Higgins had ended up in bed with Nick, Annie, and me while Missy had slept with Mimi. I was thinking that soon enough Missy's bed would reside in the room down the hall. The two had a strong bond.

My cell phone rang, a loud hound-dog *arr-ooo* that had Higgins' ears perking up in confusion.

Higgins often seemed confused.

I patted his head and answered before the phone rang again, knowing immediately who was calling: The ringtone was one I had assigned to Harper.

"Did you know that Miles is *Vince's* father?" she said in a high-pitched voice as soon as I answered. "And that Vince thinks he's a warlock? A warlock of all things?"

The news had made the rounds quickly. "He mentioned it to me last night. Where'd you hear the news?"

"Angela just called me. She heard it at the Witch's Brew this morning from Vince himself. And he also thinks Ve is his mother? Has he gone crazy? He's lost his mind," she added, answering her own question.

When I'd spoken to Ve last night, she'd been stunned silent by the news, which was quite the feat. By the time I hung up, she'd been grabbing her cape to pay a midnight visit to my mother. She wasn't so concerned that Vince thought she was his mother, but rather that he was talking about witchcraft so openly. A plan for damage control was desperately needed.

"The part about Miles being his father might be true. . . ." I explained last night's visit, including Vince's insistence that he was a witch.

She said, "I guess, I mean, at least his Seeking makes sense now. No wonder he was obsessive about it. Did you check with Mom yet to see if he really is a Crafter?"

"On my to-do list."

Light flooded the room from the many windows, two of which flanked the fireplace opposite the bed. Tall and arched, the windows overlooked the backyard. I drew back one of the thin curtains and peeked out. Behind the back fence loomed a stand of trees. Beyond them, I glimpsed part of the Enchanted Trail, the paved path that looped around the village. It acted as a divider between the village and the Enchanted Woods.

Deep in that forest was the Elder's meadow, where my mother lived. I planned to go see her, to see if she knew if Vince was a Crafter. As the Elder, she would know. It was just a matter of whether she'd share the knowledge with me.

"Does Starla know all this about Vince?" Harper asked.

"He said he'd tell her. I don't know if he did. She canceled our morning run."

I wondered if the news had changed her mind about breaking up with him. At least the timing of it. Somehow, I doubted it. She'd made up her mind before knowing he'd been keeping lots more secrets.

Harper said, "Well, that's not the only big news today."

"Oh?"

"Marcus is going to drop Ve's case."

My heart sank. "He is?"

"Well, he admitted he's thinking about it. That's as good as dropping it."

I breathed a sigh of relief. Marcus was the best lawyer around, hands down. I wanted him on Vc's side if she needed legal help. "No, it's not. He just needs time to process his mother's involvement."

I debated whether to say anything to her about Miles potentially being Marcus' father as well as Vince's. Harper was already freaked-out, so I let it be. For now.

"That's not the problem," she said. "The problem is that Marcus' parents have a strong hold over him. He's influenced by their opinions."

Ah. I suddenly realized that this was perhaps the heart of why Harper didn't care for the pair and why they had rattled her so. She was scared of their opinion of her and whether they would use it to suggest Marcus break up with her.

I had to admit, I'd be scared, too. "Marcus loves you. That is a powerful influencer in itself. . . ."

Background noises suggested Harper was making breakfast. I heard the buzzing of her coffeemaker, the telltale sound of cereal being poured into a bowl. I could easily picture her moving about her kitchen, a tiny tornado.

"But is it enough?" she asked. "Will it be enough when it comes down to making a choice between me and them? Because it will come down to it. Eventually."

"You don't know that."

"We'll see, won't we?"

I didn't like how confident she sounded on the matter. It made me worry on her behalf.

She added, "The only good thing that's come out of this new development is that dinner tonight has been canceled. That's a silver lining if I ever saw one."

"I for one am glad you didn't have to go the scurvy route to get out of it."

She laughed and the microwave dinged in the background. "Me, too. I have to go. Call me if you hear anything else about the case. Or Vince."

I promised I would, then hung up, wondering if Penelope would also cancel on Evan and not show up this afternoon at the playhouse. I'd planned to ask her a few questions after we wrapped up. . . .

Higgins followed behind me as I tiptoed along the overlook hallway, past the reading nook, the staircase, and the back bedroom I was using as my art studio, to peek on Mimi before heading downstairs. Her door was ajar. She was sound asleep, one of her legs stuck out from beneath the covers and her head buried under her pillow. Missy immediately hopped off the bed to greet me and wagged her tail when I asked if she needed to go out, then wagged harder when I asked if she was hungry. Higgins greeted her with droplets of drool, and she looked up at me with dismay.

"Sorry," I whispered to her as I grabbed a towel from the linen closet to wipe her off.

Downstairs, I let the dogs out. They raced from one side of the yard to the other, making me smile at their size difference. Annie watched me patiently as I filled food bowls, then pounced on hers. I made coffee, then walked into the As You Wish office and immediately grinned. On the mantel above the office's fireplace—which was original to the house—sat the framed magic wand painting. Ve was right. It did belong here.

In front of the fireplace was a seating area with a couch and two chairs with a low table in between. It was where I'd meet with clients.

My desk area was a good three feet behind the couch. I picked up the phone and checked voice mails, making notes to return calls as soon as I reopened for business. Behind my desk were wall-to-wall custom cabinets and shelving. Several of the cabinets had been doctored to hold files until I could get the existing files computerized. Nick and I hadn't finished sorting through the boxes last night, as Vince's visit had thrown us for a loop.

Vince.

I let out a breath and looked at the clock.

Although I was due to meet Glinda soon at Wickedly Creative, if I hurried, I could make a quick trip into the woods. . . .

I let the dogs back inside and left a note for Mimi telling her where I was off to and asked her to text when she woke up. I left it on the kitchen island, where she'd find it easily. She was thirteen and more than capable of staying home alone, but I was glad for the extra security measures of Higgins' drool, Missy's barking, and the alarm system Nick had had installed. Plus, there were the acorns. Truly, no one in the village was safer than Mimi Sawyer this morning.

I grabbed my cape, set the alarm, locked the doors behind me, and headed out to see if my mother would tell me what was going on with Vince . . . and whether he was a witch or not.

Chapter Sixteen

As soon as I was through the back gate, I followed the Enchanted Trail path for a bit before veering off into the woods.

Under the thick canopy of red oaks, hemlocks, and sugar maples, I slipped my cape over my shoulders and drew the hood over my head. By doing so, I was now invisible to all mortals. It was a precautionary measure to keep the location of the Elder's meadow a secret.

Breathing in the rich forest scents, I followed a path I'd come to know well. Pine was the predominant smell, followed by the earthy aroma of the dirt, moss, and decaying leaves that littered the ground.

Mindful of the time, I walked quickly, almost jogging. I hoped my mother was home and that this trip hadn't been a waste of my time. When I reached a rock in the shape of a piece of cake, I turned right, and the Elder's meadow soon came into sight.

I drew my cape tight around me as I stepped cautiously into the grassy open and glanced around. Surrounded by forest, the meadow seemed out of place; an oasis. In the middle of the area stood a single tree, its weeping branches hanging low, its silvery green leaves glistening in the early-morning sunshine.

I smiled broadly as those branches suddenly lifted. In a blink the grassy meadow turned into a field of vibrant wildflowers. The cool wind turned warm, inviting. A bird flew out from the top of the tree, swooping my way.

My mother *was* home.

A beautiful mourning dove with bright blue rims around its eyes landed before me. A moment later, it disappeared into a glittery cloud, from which my mother floated, dressed all in white and barefoot as usual.

I smiled as I always did when I saw her. I didn't know if I'd ever get used to the idea that she was back in my life. All I knew was I'd never take it for granted. "I was hoping you'd be here."

She smiled, then kissed my cheek. "I usually am. Are you here about Vince?"

Nodding, I followed her as she motioned me toward the tree.

Normally when I visited with her, a tree stump seat typically arose from the ground for me to sit on, but not today. With a wave of her hand, a swinging bench that matched one that hung at my house appeared on a branch of her tree.

The magic in this village never ceased to amaze me.

"Coffee?" she asked. "I know I could use a cup. It's been some kind of morning already. I've been inundated with messages about Vince telling everyone he comes across in the village that he's a warlock."

"I'd love some," I said, letting down my hood. I was

safe here in her presence. "Harper's already called me about Vince. Angela Curtis called her after she ran into Vince at the Witch's Brew. I'm sure Ve explained everything to you last night, about how he's . . . on a mission to figure out his parentage and prove he's a witch."

"She did." With another wave, two mugs filled with coffee appeared in her hands.

She handed one to me, and I sipped. It was perfect, with just a bit of cream and sugar. Hers, I saw, was as black as night. Just the way she liked it.

I marveled at how spirits and familiars still could enjoy earthly pleasures, such as coffee. One of Pepe's favorites was cheesecake from Evan's bakery. And Archie delighted in anything consisting of carbs.

I sat next to her on the bench swing. "Is Vince really a Crafter?"

Drawing in a deep breath, she gazed into her mug as though looking to it for advice. So much of the Craft was secretive, and the only one privy to all was the Elder. Until I knew the Elder was my mother, I never realized the burden of her power.

Her gaze came up and curiosity filled her golden brown eyes. "What do you think?"

She was always challenging me this way. Making me dig deep, looking for answers that I didn't know I possessed. Was there really a way for me to tell if Vince was a Crafter?

Silvery leaves rustled around me as I thought about it, and the sweet scent of the wildflowers filled the air.

"Don't think too hard, Darcy," Mom said as she sipped her coffee. "Do you think Vince is a Crafter?"

"Yes," I said, surprising myself.

She smiled over the rim of her mug. "Why?"

Why? Why? I didn't know *why*. I searched for an explanation. "I'm not sure. It's just . . . a feeling. Last night Vince talked about how witchcraft made him finally feel normal. It was something I related to. Growing up, I always felt different. Out of place. I thought it was because you were gone and Dad was lost in his grief, but it wasn't until I moved here . . . and started practicing my Craft that I, too, felt normal. Whole." I wrinkled my nose. "Does that make sense?"

Her long fingers had wrapped around the mug, her fingertips touching on the opposite side. "Perfect sense. Magic dwells within every Crafter. Some feel it more acutely than others. It is common for a Crafter who doesn't know of their powers to feel peculiar. Or as an outsider."

I let what she said sink in.

Crafters who didn't know of their powers.

Like me. Like Harper.

Like Vince.

Like *Seekers*.

"Are all Seekers simply Crafters who feel the magic but don't know they're witches?"

Warmth filled her eyes, which in turn filled me with warmth. With it came a contentment I never knew I'd been missing until she came back into my life. There was something about a mother's love that was irreplaceable.

"Not many are so insightful to make that connection. Yes, it's true that most Seekers are Crafters who do not know of their heritage for one reason or another. It is why we don't run all the Seekers straight out of the village."

"Why don't we just tell the Seekers who are witches that they *are* witches?" It seemed to me that it would solve a lot of problems that Seekers caused.

"As Elder, it's not my place to interfere in what's been decided for that particular Crafter," she said, tucking one leg beneath her as we swayed. "I must abide by what the fates have set in motion. I must respect the choices others have made. I can only offer guidance from afar."

"Why not interfere? It seems to me that of anyone, it is *our* place. If Ve hadn't told Harper and me about our magic, we'd probably still be floundering in Ohio."

"That's just it, Darcy. Your fate had already been set in motion. Your daddy and I had a deal, a deal that was seen through when he"—she swallowed hard—"passed on."

The grief in her voice nearly tore me open. I hadn't thought about what it had been like for her to see the man she'd loved live his life without her. And die without her as well.

I blinked back tears, wondering what life would have been like had that accident not taken my mother away so long ago. . . .

Fate. Sometimes I hated it.

"Vince's fate," she said, "is already in motion. It is my job to guide him, whether or not he uncovers the truth of his heritage. Even though he knows nothing of me, I know of him, and I'll look after him the best I can."

Vince was a Crafter. I could hardly believe it. All his rantings and ravings had been valid. Justified. "But what about him going around talking about witchcraft? Isn't he violating our laws?"

"No, but only because he doesn't know he's a Crafter."

That was a pretty big loophole, in my opinion.

"Now that I know he's a witch, I could tell him, right?"

Her eyes darkened. "You could, but you should not. You know only because I have confirmed it. You would be interfering with his journey, altering his destiny."

I was beginning to dislike the word "interfere." "It doesn't seem fair he doesn't know."

"No," she agreed. "It doesn't. But it is the way it is."

Taking a sip from my mug, I said softly, "Maybe we need to change those ways."

She smiled. "I'll take that suggestion under advisement and bring it up at the next Coven gathering."

I'd only recently learned of the Coven of Seven's existence. They were my mother's form of a village council and she needed their unanimous approval to make any big changes to the Craft. Their identities were a mystery to me, and I figured they always would be.

I asked, "What about his dabbling in sorcery? What do we do about that?"

Over her shoulder, I spotted the hollow in the tree where Crafters could leave her notes if they wanted to trek into the woods. The much quicker route was using Archie as a messenger. By now, my mother had undoubtedly received Starla's message from the loquacious bird.

"It's troublesome and something to keep an eye on. He doesn't realize the power that comes with the dark arts."

I thought perhaps he did. And that's why he'd been looking into it.

"We will intervene if we have to. Hopefully it will not come to that, as it will put our identities at risk."

By the haggard tone of her voice, it sounded as though intervening was the last thing she wanted to do. To me, it seemed we had a better shot at getting him to listen to reason if we had his family on our side.

As casually as I could, I asked, "Who is Vince's mother?"

She gave me *that* look. The one that told me she couldn't tell me. I was beginning to dislike *it* as well.

"Would you tell me if I guessed?"

"No."

I pressed. "Not even if it was a factor in Miles' death?"

"What are you thinking, Darcy?"

I told her my theory about Penelope, Miles, Marcus, and Vince. "It seems coincidental, doesn't it, that Vince's birthday is right around the time Miles returned to the village? What if he returned for his son's first birthday?"

"Do you have any proof Vince's paternity is a factor in Miles' death?"

"Not yet, but it would be easier if I knew for sure that Penelope was his mother."

"I cannot tell you who his mother is." She pressed her lips together and made a zipping motion across them.

"Does his mother know who *he* is? That he's her child?" After all, he'd been given up for adoption as an infant. Had his mother kept tabs on him?

"Not for me to say."

Really dislike it.

I let out a breath and tapped my fingertips on the arm of the swing. "Is Marcus Debrowski's birthday really in August?"

"What a curious question."

I explained about Dorothy.

One of her eyebrows rose, and a corner of her mouth twitched as she nodded. "His birthday *is* in August. He is not Miles' son."

Which meant that he and Vince were not full brothers, after all.

And that Dorothy had purposely misled me.

I was beginning to hate her, too.

It was still entirely possible that Marcus and Vince were *half* brothers. Penelope did have a relationship with Miles around the time Vince would have been conceived. I just didn't know how to confirm—or rule out—the possibility. I had the feeling Penelope would not consent to a DNA test.

And I still didn't know whether any of this paternity information factored into *why* Miles was dead.

It was something I was going to have to keep pursuing. I did, however, wonder why Dorothy had lied to me about something that was so easily refutable; she had to have known I'd ask my mother.

"Should I be worried about Dorothy?" I asked, honestly curious. Her firebug tendencies had always bothered me, but especially more now that I owned a house.

"Darcy, we should always be worried about Dorothy."

"Why does Dorothy hate us? Is it like Penelope? That she's jealous?"

"Penelope is not jealous of us. She's envious. There is a difference, as subtle as it may be. She's envious because she had little freedom to make her own choices and longed to have the freedoms Ve and I, and now Harper and you, enjoy."

Evan had said something similar, and it was easy to see that it was true. Penelope had been forced to practice law. Her husband had been handpicked by her parents. "How about Dorothy? What's her issue with us?"

"Dorothy is . . ." Her voice trailed off as she searched for a word. "Misguided."

I used my toe to keep us swinging. "How so?"

"She believes our family has something that belongs to her family. It's why she's . . . not very nice, I'm sorry to say."

I couldn't imagine what we possessed that would cause Dorothy to despise us so much. Our wishing abilities, perhaps? "What do we have?"

"The Eldership."

My mouth fell open. "Why in the world does she think it belongs to her family?" Wait. I realized I didn't know how the Elder was even chosen. "How is it you even became the Elder?"

"It's a complicated situation," she said on a heavy sigh. "Needless to say, Dorothy is displeased and holds a mean grudge."

That was putting it mildly. "She can't do anything to harm you, though. Right?"

Mom cupped my cheek. "Leave Dorothy to me. I know just how to deal with her."

"But—"

"Nope. No buts."

I had the feeling I would get nothing else out of her about Dorothy or the Eldership. I had to trust that those kinds of secrets would be divulged in time. I just needed to be patient. I let it go. For now.

Mom said, "You need to keep your focus on what happened to Miles."

I asked, "Did you know Miles had been using a seduction amulet?"

"Not until yesterday, thanks to what you uncovered. It is possible the Elder before me knew, but it was never mentioned to me when I took over. It was reprehensible on Miles' part to have used magic that way, but it's important to know something about charmed amulets such as his."

"What's that?"

"If, as we suspect, enchanted clay was used to create his amulet, its magic falls under Craft laws. And in such, our rules of Do No Harm apply. Miles could not have attracted any woman who did not wish to be seduced."

Wait. What?

She went on. "Without the power of that amulet the women might not have chosen him as a potential mate, necessarily, but while he was with them, wearing that amulet, no harm was done to them. None at all. And that's not all."

"There's more?" It was hard to believe there could be.

"Because Miles infused that clay with its power, its magic died when he did. That amulet will lure women no more."

"I don't understand. I thought amulets retained their charm, even after their creators passed on."

"Not when the amulet is made of enchanted clay."

I didn't think I'd ever learn all the ins and outs of the Craft.

"That's good news, I suppose."

"Very good."

"But I'm still struggling with the do-no-harm part. The fact that the women wouldn't have chosen him on their own . . . doesn't that factor as harmful? It feels like, I don't know, as though he took them hostage or something."

"The amulet would have only lured the women to him. It would not have kept them there if they wanted to leave. They retained free will. I can only presume that once the women spent time with him, they chose to stay."

"You mean on some level, they *wanted* to be with him?"

"That's exactly what I mean. It's not to say that Miles didn't have his motives for the women he chose, rich women, for example. But those women freely gave him what he wanted."

"I'm having trouble grasping that these women stayed with him willingly. Penelope, for example. She was in love with Steve Winstead when Miles came back to the village. Surely she wasn't looking for someone else to seduce her. . . ."

"Was she in love with Steve?" my mother asked. "Has she said so?"

She hadn't. It had been Steve who'd told me. Had he been lying? Or had he been misled?

I stammered, "But Ve . . . The elopement . . ."

My mother raised her eyebrows, sipped her coffee, and said nothing.

I nearly fell off the swing. "You mean Ve *willingly* eloped with Miles?"

"In light of the revelation about the amulet, I'd say yes. Yes, she did. She's always been rather impulsive, especially when it comes to marriage. And she'd just broken up with another man. Miles showed up at the perfect time for a rebound relationship."

"Did you tell her all this?"

"Last night."

"How'd she take it?" I asked.

"Better than I expected. She's now willing to do the memory spell to recall that weekend. She'd like you to be there, so she's waiting until you stop by later."

I gripped my mug. "For decades Ve believed she hated the man. What do you think she'll do when she realizes she actually *liked* Miles?"

"I don't know," my mother said. "But we'll soon find out."

Chapter Seventeen

I was on my way to Wickedly Creative to meet Glinda when I spotted Oliver Debrowski coming out of the Witch's Brew with a cup of coffee in hand.

Ever so slightly, I altered my course and headed his way.

As I stepped up next to him, he didn't slow to a stop or change his stride. He walked with purpose, and I noticed he had an unusual gait, a slight hitch like speed-walkers used. A lot of hip swing and small steps. I almost smiled, thinking of him speed-walking around the village in his power suits.

"Hi. Beautiful morning, isn't it?" I asked.

A dark eyebrow rose as he glanced at me out of the corner of his eye. He adjusted his glasses, kept steady on his course, and said, "Yes, it is."

I was grateful that we were headed in the direction

of Wickedly Creative, so I wouldn't have to backtrack. I was running a bit late as it was.

He walked like a man on a mission to get away from me, so I knew I didn't have time to beat around the bush. "I heard Marcus is thinking about dropping Ve's case. Do you know if that's true? Because it would be a shame. If this case progresses, Ve will need his help. As he's practically family, there's no one she trusts more."

"Family?" he scoffed. "Let's not get carried away."

A knot grew in my stomach, twisting hard. Harper's concern that Marcus' parents were out to break them up suddenly seemed very valid.

"Marcus is family to *us*," I said.

Oliver glanced at me with what looked like pity, but he said nothing.

It was clear by his expression that he believed Harper and Marcus weren't going to last. Well, I didn't want his pity. He clearly didn't know Harper if he thought she'd give up Marcus without a fight. Truly, it was the Debrowskis who deserved any pity.

There wasn't even a hitch in Oliver's step as he said, "Technically, there is no case involving Ve. There's been no retainer. There's been no crime committed. It is a waste of Marcus' valuable time to continue to engage in the matter."

"Actually, we don't know yet that there's been no crime committed. Nick should be getting the preliminary report from the ME's office today."

"I reiterate: Until it is known whether Mr. Babbage was a victim of a homicide, there is no case. Marcus' talents are in high demand. He should not be wasting his time fighting imaginary battles."

Mr. Babbage. So formal. "Did you know Miles?"

His stride faltered then, but only for a moment. "I knew of him, yes."

"Did you ever meet him face-to-face? Have a conversation?" *Did you handle the adoption of his illegitimate child? A child born to the woman who was to eventually become your wife?* "A fight? That kind of thing?"

"I struggle to see why this is relevant, but no, I did not. I knew him only from sight and reputation. I've never had a fight in my life."

There was a hidden "yet" in his voice as he looked my way.

It hinted that I was pressing my luck.

I was. As he said, I really had no business questioning him. So I bluffed. "It's relevant because I'm investigating the case for the Elder, which you know."

"As I keep saying," he said, as though I was too dense to understand his previous meaning of "reiterate," "there is no evidence of a crime. Therefore, there is no 'case' and nothing to investigate."

"There was a dead man in my aunt's garage. That's certainly something to investigate—don't you think?"

"Not necessarily."

"How's that?"

"Any number of reasons. He could have been drunk and went to sleep it off in the corner of the garage, only to die of natural causes. Heart failure. Hypothermia. A stroke. He could have fallen while trying to reach something from a top shelf. There are any number of reasons he could have died in that space, and none of them need investigating."

I was getting nowhere fast with him. I changed tacks, thinking it was better to be up front with him in my questioning than roundabout. He seemed like the kind of man who abhorred the long way around anything. "Did you broker Vincent Paxton's adoption?"

At that, he came to a sudden stop. Momentum pro-

pelled me forward, and I actually had to double back
to him.

His eyes were hard as he glowered at me. "I do not
think I need to remind you of attorney-client privilege."

"I was wondering about that," I said. "Because Vince
can't find any adoption records. None. Nothing sealed.
They don't exist. Even private adoptions have proper
protocols. Which hints that it was an illegal adoption?
Or maybe even a magical one. If that's the case, then is
privilege a factor?"

"I think we're done here," he said as he started walking away once again.

Faster this time. It was amazing how fast he could
move taking such tiny strides.

He looked back at me. "I have nothing more to say
to you, Darcy. If the Elder wants to speak with me, she
can contact me directly."

I had to jog to keep up. "Vince is looking for his
parents. He suspects Miles is his father, which will soon
be proven or disproven by a DNA test. But he has no
idea who his mother is, except that she's from the village. He thinks she might be a witch as well, which has
fostered his Seeking."

Oliver suddenly darted right, crossing in front of me,
his hips working hard. He clicked a key fob. A car
parked nearby beeped as it unlocked its doors.

I had no other choice than to ask, "Is it true that
Penelope had a relationship with Miles around the time
Vince would have been conceived?"

His jaw came up, clenched. He pulled open the driv-
er's door. "Leave Penelope's name out of your mouth.
She went through enough with that man when he was
alive. She should not have to deal with him when he's
dead as well. Leave her out of it."

He ducked into the car, slammed the door, and

backed out of the parking spot. I'd been expecting him to zoom off, but instead he kept his hands at ten and two as the car crept down the road.

My gaze turned toward the Trimmed Wick's storefront.

Why did it seem that the men in Penelope's life were intent on protecting her?

Why, exactly, did she need protection at all?

Wickedly Creative was a beautiful studio located about half a mile from the village square on old farmland that belonged to George and Cora Chadwick. The property held the couple's rambling farmhouse, a stable, outbuildings, a large garage with an upstairs apartment, and the art studio. I once thought the land felt more like a secluded compound, and I still felt that way.

The recently renovated two-story dairy barn was in itself a work of art, a mix of old and new. Gone were any traditional wooden barn doors, replaced with tall double doors made of steel and glass, with transom windows above and sidelights to the left and right.

In front of those doors stood Glinda. She headed my way when she spotted me. I glanced around for any sign of Nick but didn't see him or his police cruiser, which would have been easy enough to spot. I called it the Bumblebeemobile. It was a black-and-yellow MINI Cooper. There were other colors in use on the village police force, all chosen by Sylar Dewitt when he'd been village council chairman. He believed the cars would be less threatening to tourists.

He'd been right about that.

"George is waiting for us inside," Glinda said as she met me on the wide walkway. Today her hair was pulled back in a low ponytail. She wore jeans, boots, and a belted sweater. "Is Nick joining you?"

"I thought he'd be here by now." After all, I was

running late after having chased down Oliver Debrowski.

I pulled my cell phone from my coat pocket and checked for messages. Sure enough, there was one from Nick waiting for me. I'd most likely been pestering Oliver when it had come in.

"Here's a message from Nick from ten minutes ago," I said. "He's on hold with the ME's office and says not to wait for him. He'll catch up with us when he can."

As we headed for the doors, Glinda said, "Has he heard anything about Miles Babbage's preliminary cause of death?"

"Not yet. It's probably what he's waiting on hold to hear." I glanced at her. "So, you knew exactly who Miles Babbage was yesterday, didn't you? Not from your mother but from Vince."

"Sorry. Vince swore me to silence, but now it seems as though he's telling anyone and everyone. I heard he paid you a visit last night."

"He came to my house after he couldn't get ahold of Ve. He thinks she is his mother."

"We both know she's not," she said. "He didn't steal a hair from your head when he left, did he?"

"Not that I know of." The thought alone made me uncomfortable. "You're not really going to try to get DNA samples from villagers, are you?"

Groaning, she said, "It's ridiculous. But I'm afraid if I don't string him along a bit, then he's going to go off and start stealing toothbrushes or something."

He'd pretty much admitted to that last night. "He tried to get Starla to take a test. She thought it was because he was trying to see if she was a witch. Little did we know."

Glinda pulled open one of the glass doors. "Darcy, I wouldn't rule out the witch notion, either. He probably figured two birds with one stone. . . . He's obsessed with witchcraft, and I don't say that lightly."

I was grateful we'd gone inside and had to nix the witch conversation. I felt guilty I couldn't tell her Vince *was* a witch. It wasn't my place, though it certainly seemed like it was.

The studio was buzzing. Weekends were often their busiest hours, filled with classes in just about every art imaginable. People filled dozens of tables on the main level. Some worked with beads, others with fiber. The painting studios were toward the back of the space, walled off with glass. I could see Will Chadwick teaching a class, his students engrossed with their canvases.

The barn's second story was open to the main floor. The lofted space held additional classrooms, including the basket-weaving area, where Glinda worked part-time, and also the metal workshop, where Liam was often in charge.

Mimi was the reason I'd first come to this place, last January. She'd been working on a special gift for my birthday. A charm bracelet. It was still at Ve's, tucked away in the box that held all my favorite things. I wanted to wear it more often, but I feared losing a charm or, worse, the whole bracelet. Instead, I kept it by my bedside, where I saw it every night before going to sleep.

Octagonal skylights let in natural light that filled the space with warmth and energy. I followed Glinda as she weaved through the room. Cora was standing at a far table, watching over students as they repeatedly jabbed a blob of fiber with long-handled needles. She smiled and offered a wave.

I waved back.

I had nothing against George and Cora, but the whole ordeal with their son and Starla had been nothing short of heartbreaking. But seeing Cora's smile relieved some of the tension I'd been feeling.

And I realized it wasn't as uncomfortable to be around them as I'd feared.

Time was working its magic, after all.

"What are they doing?" I asked Glinda, pointing to the table where Cora stood.

"Needle felting. Today they're making a mouse, I believe."

"One with a red vest that has gold buttons?"

She looked over her shoulder and smiled. "That's a little advanced for the beginner class, though I'd love to see it happen."

Me, too.

We found George in the classroom adjacent to the painting class. It was a pottery studio, and it looked like a class had just ended. Freshly made lumpy pots and shallow dishes sat on a long table, and he was transferring them to a rolling cart.

"Darcy," George said, greeting me with a grin. "It's good to see you again. It's been a while."

A little more of my anxiety evaporated when I saw the kindness in his eyes.

I wanted to joke about always meeting under lousy circumstances, but I couldn't bring myself to do it. "It has," I said. "Thanks for agreeing to talk to me about Miles."

"No problem. I hope you don't mind that I talk while I work. Another class is due in here in fifteen minutes."

"Not at all," Glinda said. "Do you need help?"

He gave Glinda a kiss on her cheek and I noted the happiness shining in her eyes. The Chadwicks were essentially the normal family she hadn't had. Happy. Stable. Secure. "If you could move these pots to the cart, I'd appreciate it."

She gave a nod and set about carefully making the transfers, handling each creation as though it was a piece of Tiffany crystal.

"Horrible situation with Miles," he said to me as he walked over to a long stainless steel counter and started separating chunks of clay.

I trailed behind him and asked, "I know it was a long time ago, but do you remember much about him?"

Pale blue eyes blinked, and he took his time in answering. Finally, he smiled. "I might have lost my trim figure over the years, but my mind is still sharp. I remember those days well."

He was a big-boned man, and even heavier now than the last time I'd seen him. There was a teddy-bear quality about him with his benevolent eyes, salt-and-pepper beard, and round cheeks that was comforting. Despite the lingering awkwardness of what had happened this past winter, I liked him.

George said, "Miles wasn't naturally outgoing, so he often came off as a loner, and people didn't like that about him. They thought him odd. But others found him charming once they got to know him."

"And you?"

He set a flat slab of clay next to a potter's wheel. "I liked him well enough. He was creative, funny. But he was also a wounded soul. Those wounds made it impossible for him to stay in one place for very long or to have any kind of meaningful relationship." George went on. "He'd had a rough childhood, moving around a lot. Never had much schooling. He was a self-taught artist, and a damn good one."

I said, "Steve said Miles' dad was a con man?"

"Only when it came to women. Natural charm, Miles once told me. Women fell at his feet. When Miles turned sixteen, his dad made it known that he'd become more of a hindrance than a help where his con was concerned. Miles left home and never looked back."

"Harsh," Glinda said, shaking her head.

"It was probably best for Miles." George grabbed

another slab of clay. "He suffered at his father's hand for many years."

Her eyes widened. "His dad was abusive?"

George said, "Let's just say he was a firm believer in corporal punishment."

Glinda frowned, and I once again felt a rush of sympathy for what Miles had endured as a young boy.

I stepped back as George passed by me, headed to the next potter's wheel. I asked, "Did you know Miles was using a charmed amulet to lure women to him?"

Glinda glanced my way, her eyes wide. "He was?"

"He was," George confirmed. "As I said, he wasn't naturally outgoing. Wooing took too much energy, and he was awkward at it. What came naturally for his father was a real struggle for himself—until the women got to know him. Then he was as charming as all get-out. He found a way around his awkwardness using the amulet."

"Was he a con man, too?" Glinda asked.

From what I'd heard, he was. But George shook his head.

"I know some in the village think so, but he never took anything that wasn't offered. That wasn't insisted upon, really. A little money to get to the next town, a hot meal. Nothing over-the-top."

"But what about his Casanova reputation?" I asked. "Seems like he tended to use women. Love 'em and leave 'em."

"Maybe so, but like I said, he didn't know how to have a meaningful relationship. I'm not sure he even knew what real love was, but I think he was trying to learn. He broke a lot of hearts, but none were as broken as his own."

A wounded soul. It seemed an apt description of Miles Babbage.

George continued. "When he came back to the village after being gone for a year, I was a little surprised when he mentioned that he was ready to settle down and get married. He started looking for the right woman."

In his world, with that amulet, it was as easily said as done.

"He said he was looking for love, that he wanted to stop living in his father's shadow and start making his own."

So Miles had gone looking for a wife to love. He'd found Penelope. And when that didn't work out, he'd found Ve.

If he'd been so easily able to jump from one woman to another, I figured he hadn't learned anything about true love in the time he'd spent away from the village. But the fact that he was ready to put down roots told me a lot. He'd been serious about staying here . . . and trying to learn how to truly love someone.

"Do you know if he had any kids?" I asked.

"Kids?" George's bushy eyebrows shot up. "Not that he ever said."

It was no surprise to hear. If Vince was Miles' son, there was a chance he hadn't even known of Vince's existence. And also a chance he had. Maybe he'd agreed to the adoption. "Any living relatives that you know of?"

He shook his head, then snapped his fingers. "You know, his stuff is still out back if you want to look at it. There's not much to speak of, but you're welcome to see what's there."

"You kept it all this time?" I asked.

"Miles was a little funny about people touching his things, and we weren't needing the space. We always thought he'd be back. So we left it all there. We did clean up some. Stripped the bed. Put away his supplies. Protected his canvases from dust. That kind of thing, and we still go in from time to time to keep up with the maintenance. But it's all there, including an address

book with some phone numbers. I tried calling a few of
them when he hadn't come back after a month or two,
but they were mostly old flames. There might be one in
there that will help you find a next of kin."

I thought I might kiss George right then and there.
"I'd love to see his things."

"Glinda, can you take Darcy out?" George asked.
"I have a metal sculpture class in ten minutes. It's bunkhouse ten. You can get the key from the office. Just lock
up when you're done."

"Sure." She crossed to a deep sink to wash her hands.

"Thanks, George," I said. "And one more question . . .
Do you know where Miles got that charmed amulet?
Did it look familiar at all?"

"Familiar? Not especially. I don't recall ever getting
a good up-close look at it. I assumed Miles got it from
one of Charmcrafters at the Roving Stones. That kind
of power isn't easy to come by. Why?"

"I don't think it came from one of the Roving Stones.
I believe Miles stole some of Steve's creek clay to make
that amulet, but I don't understand how he charmed it,
necessarily. Do you know "

I was cut off by an angry voice coming from behind
me. "What did you just say?"

Spinning around, I saw Steve Winstead standing in
the doorway, fury etched into every line on his face.

Chapter Eighteen

"It is possible Miles was able to sneak back to the creek site before I cast the protection spell over it," Steve said as he walked alongside Glinda and me as we headed to bunkhouse number ten.

It turned out that *he* was the instructor for the pottery class George had been prepping. When Steve found out why Glinda and I were there, he volunteered to accompany us to the bunkhouse. I suspected it had nothing to do with escorting us and everything to do with wanting to get a peek at Miles' belongings, as though he was hoping to find a stash of contraband clay that he could reclaim.

Steve went on. "If he did steal it, he's lucky I didn't catch him. I'd have—"

His unfinished sentence hung in the air between us, and Glinda and I left it right where it was. The theft of his magical clay was just one more reason for Steve to despise Miles. He'd already hated him for stealing Penelope away.

The wind kicked up as we crossed an expanse of wet grass. Glinda seemed to know where she was going, which was good, because to me it didn't seem as though any of these buildings were marked. It appeared as if there were fifteen or so outbuildings and bunkhouses spread out behind Wickedly Creative, nestled into manmade hollows in the woods behind the property. Only the kiln house had a well-worn path that led from the rear door of the studio to its entrance.

Steve said, "I can't know for sure if the amulet was created by the enchanted clay unless I see the amulet, hold it."

It was going to be *quite* the field trip to the medical examiner's office. "Andreus said the same thing. We're waiting to hear from the ME's office to see if we'll be allowed to get a closer look at that amulet. It'll have to stay with them as evidence, unless a next of kin comes forward to claim Miles' body and belongings."

"Is there a next of kin?" Steve asked, his eyes desperate.

I slid a look to Glinda. Her forehead had wrinkled and her lips pulled down into a deep frown as she said, "Not that we know of."

Officially, that was true. It would take weeks, maybe months, for Vince to get paternity test results.

"If it is made of my clay, I want it back. It should be destroyed and returned to its source."

"Destroy it how?" Glinda asked.

Steve said, "A piece of that size? A sledgehammer will do the job. I'd smash it to dust, then return it to the creek."

Absently I thought of the broken candle. I shouldn't have thrown away the pieces. They didn't belong in the trash.

I was glad I'd worn a pair of boots today as we sloshed across the damp meadow. "I don't understand how Miles made a seduction charm from your clay. Your pottery infuses its owners with warmth and serenity. Vastly different emotions."

"The clay emits what it's imbued with. I choose serenity, peace, comfort—those kinds of qualities—for my ceramics. Miles obviously chose desire, allure, appeal. The clay would have the same propensities as my candles. Heat would release the sentiment."

"But how did he know to do that?" Glinda asked. "He's not a Crafter; it wouldn't be instinctual for him."

It was a good question.

"I told him," Steve said. "Not in a Crafter kind of way, but more peer to peer. Potters often infuse their works with emotions and tenderness. Miles must have caught on that my emotions came out in my candles."

It seemed like a Craft violation to me, but that would have been decided by the Elder back then, and she obviously had deemed it harmless.

"Since Miles wore the amulet around his neck, his body heat might have been enough, but most likely when he was ready to attract a specific woman, he gripped the amulet, warming it quickly in his hand." Steve glanced at Glinda and me. "No wonder Penelope found him irresistible. She didn't stand a chance against that kind of magic." His hands curled into fists.

Yet it was Miles' inherent charm that had kept her at his side.

It was a good lesson on not necessarily judging books by their covers.

At this point, I decided not to share this knowledge with Steve. He was already vibrating with anxious energy, and knowing Penelope had freely chosen to stay with Miles might push the man over the edge.

Glinda led the way into the hollow. Once off the

grass, we stepped onto a narrow fieldstone walkway nearly covered in forest detritus. It led to the front door of a tiny slate-shingled house that sat in the clearing, its steeply pitched metallic roof covered in leaves, pine needles, and a layer of moss. Other than the moss, it seemed well tended. In the space between an arched wooden door and a small paned window hung a piece of smooth gray slate from a weathered cord. The stone had the number ten stenciled upon it in crackled white paint.

Glinda unlocked the door and slowly pulled it open. She stuck her hand inside the house and flipped a light switch next to the door.

It was unusual to see a front door swing out rather than in, but as soon as I stepped inside, I saw why. There was no room for it to swing inward.

I wasn't sure what I'd expected when I'd heard "bunkhouse," but it wasn't this. The only thing bunkish about this space was the lofted bedroom. Otherwise, it could be labeled a small cottage. A teeny-tiny cottage, but one nonetheless.

Natural wood paneling covered the walls. Oak floors creaked beneath our feet. Sheets had been thrown over a sofa that took up most of the living space. A wood-burning stove, a wooden easel, and a maple blanket chest acting as a coffee table took up the rest of that area. A hot plate, a mini fridge, and a two-foot expanse of countertop created what could be called a kitchen at the far corner of the cozy room. A bathroom slightly bigger than what you'd find on an airplane took up the other corner. In a narrow closet, paint supplies and sculpting tools filled the shelf space.

I climbed up a ladder rung to peek into the loft. It held only a bare mattress, not even encased in plastic. No bed frame. No accessories.

It was evident that George and Cora had been keeping up with the cleaning and maintenance. There were no visible cobwebs or other signs that the bunkhouse had been invaded by nature. Only the stale air, a light coating of dust, and the absence of personal effects and bedding hinted that the place hadn't had a resident in quite some time.

Steve poked around the closet. I assumed he was looking for any leftover clay. "Is this everything?" he asked.

I was wondering if the place had been robbed of Miles' belongings when Glinda pulled back the sheet on the sofa, which was upholstered in an ugly plaid that was better left covered. There was nothing on the dirty cushions, but several canvases peeked out from behind the heavy piece of furniture.

While Glinda tried to wrestle the canvases out from behind the couch, I opened the blanket chest, fully expecting to find the bedding for the bare mattress. Instead, I found a large duffel bag and an overwhelming scent of mothballs.

I pulled out the bag and started digging through it. Miles traveled light. There was a pair of jeans, a pair of shorts, two shirts, and two pairs of nasty-looking socks. No underwear. I wasn't sure if I was grateful or grossed out by the knowledge that he probably didn't wear any.

Grateful, I decided.

The fabrics were stiff with age, and I wished I'd had gloves with me as I made a growing pile on the floor next to me.

I cast my spell and everything, ever hopeful.

No gloves appeared.

Cringing, I continued to look through the bag while Steve helped Glinda move the couch.

George had been right. There was an address book in the duffel bag. I pulled it out as Steve finally freed the canvases.

There appeared to be three of them wrapped together in plastic. Steve used one of the sculpting tools from the closet to slice through the plastic, and he and Glinda laid out the paintings.

Steve went as white as a ghost.

It didn't take long to see why.

On one of the canvases was a half-finished painting of a nude woman. It was very obviously Penelope. She was sprawled out on a plush rug in front of a wood-burning stove, and if I wasn't mistaken, it was the very stove in this room. The rug, however, was long gone.

It was more of Penelope than I ever needed to see.

Still pale, Steve backed away from the canvas as though it were alive, a snake rearing to strike.

Still holding the address book, I stood up to get a better look at the paintings.

They were stunning. One was of a resplendent rainbow-hued sparrow in an elaborately gilded golden cage. The bird's sorrowful gaze contrasted so dramatically with the painting's bright colors that it suddenly filled me with sadness.

The other was a lovely landscape painting of the road that led into the village. With meticulous brushstrokes, it expertly portrayed the enchantment of the village's entrance. Of the yew trees and branches that lined both sides of the road, twining above the road to create a natural tunnel, the lush flowers and bushes, and the glittery lights and shops in the far distance. It captured the village's whimsy. Its fantasy. Its beauty. Its heart. Its magic.

Glinda said, "Did Miles paint? I thought he was a ceramics artist."

"Miles didn't paint those," Steve said, his voice hard.

"Who did?" she asked, eyeing the nude.

I studied the canvases. I felt the one of the village entrance had to have been created by a Crafter. Only a witch could reflect the heart and soul of this village so

beautifully. Then I looked at the bird, at the dichotomy
of the painting. The vibrancy. The melancholy. It reflected
someone who was torn in half. My gaze slid to the nude,
and I took a closer look at the background, at the lightly
penciled grid marks, and the answer came to me.

"Penelope did," I answered. The nude had been a
self-portrait. The grid marks told me she'd been painting the portrait from another source, most likely a photograph. They were probably her painting supplies in
the closet.

Steve said, "She'd been working on finishing the bird
painting the week Miles came back to town that last
time."

Glinda quickly stacked the paintings again, trying
to replace the plastic as best she could. I didn't think
I'd ever seen her move so fast.

Steve slowly slid down the wall to sit on the floor. He
dragged a hand down his face, and his voice was ragged.
"How could he have done this to her? I should have
known. I should have been able to stop him. This is my
fault. It was my clay."

I turned to offer him some sort of comfort, and the
address book slipped out of my hand. It hit the floor
and a piece of paper slid out from its pages and disappeared under the couch.

I got down on my knees, put my head close to the
floor, and tried to see where the paper had ended up. I
couldn't see a thing, and I didn't want to stick my hand
into the unknown.

"What was it?" Glinda asked, her tone clearly wondering whether we could just leave it be.

I sat up. "I don't know."

Glinda looked at Steve, then at me. "We should go."

He had his forehead resting on top of his bent knees
and his arms wrapped around his legs.

I nodded. "I can come back with Nick later."

I set my hands on the floor to push off as I stood up. It was then that I noticed the stain on the foot of the blanket chest. Leaning in, I took a closer look. My gaze rose up the side of the chest, to the corner. I cocked my head, looking beneath the edge.

"Do you have a flashlight?" I asked Glinda.

"Not on me," she said. "What do you see?"

"I think it's a bloodstain." I felt a little woozy just saying the words. I didn't like the sight of blood, even dried.

Steve's head snapped up. "Blood?"

Glinda dropped down next to me, edging close to the table. "It looks like it."

Steve knee-walked over to us. "I don't know. Could be paint."

"Could be," Glinda said, sounding like she didn't believe it at all. She pushed my leg, and I moved aside. "There's a stain on the floor, too. It's hard to see unless you're looking for it."

I jumped backward, away from it, as though I'd just been told I was sitting on a fire-ant hill.

"Help me move this couch," she said to Steve.

Together, they lifted the couch, moving it at a ninety-degree angle from where it had been. Dust balls scattered, and I reached over to grab the folded paper that had fallen from the address book.

Glinda knelt down and traced the stain on the floor with her finger. As she had said, it was easy to see once one was looking for it. Whatever it was, blood or paint, at some point in time it had flowed from the table and pooled beneath the sofa.

"We need to get this area tested to see if this is blood," Glinda said.

Steve had his hands on his hips. "Someone probably knocked over some paint. No big deal."

We both looked up at him with narrowed gazes. No

big deal? A possible bloodstain of this size? Had the dust gone to his head?

In mock surrender, he held up his hands. "You can do what you want, but this is an artist's retreat. Makes sense that stain is paint."

Normally, I'd agree with him. It did make sense, especially with the easel right next to the couch. Except Miles was dead. And this had been *his* retreat.

Glinda slid me a what's-going-on-with-him glance as she stood.

It was reassuring that she also noticed how hard Steve was pushing the paint theory, as though he didn't want to know the truth of the matter.

Or perhaps . . . it was *because* he already knew the truth.

Was he protecting himself?

Or someone else?

Someone like Penelope?

Again.

"What is that? A love note?" Glinda asked, nodding to the paper in my hand.

I'd been so entranced by the floor stains that I hadn't looked. It didn't feel like notepaper, which would have been heavier in weight and bigger in size and different in texture. I unfolded the paper and read what was printed on it three times before I fully understood what I was looking at.

Glinda sidled up to me to read over my shoulder. She whistled low. "It looks like Oliver Debrowski has some explaining to do."

It did. Because in my hand, I held a copy of a cashier's check. It had been made out to Miles Babbage for one hundred thousand dollars. It had Oliver's business card stapled to it.

On the surface, it reeked of a bribe, which would

have been ingenious of Oliver. An easy way to get Miles to leave town without Penelope.

But when I looked more closely at the check, the date that had been printed on it caught my eye.

It was dated just thirty-one years ago . . . on October second, the day after Vincent Paxton had been born.

Chapter Nineteen

" 'They barely speak anymore. They're like strangers.' "
Archie's deep voice greeted me as I strode through the side gate at Ve's house. Between the rain yesterday and the wind today, the climbing roses were nearly bare of their petals. The color of the leaves on the trees beyond the back fence had deepened overnight, promising that autumn had well and truly arrived.

As I approached his cage, Archie gave me a woeful look and blinked pitifully.

I said, "*The Sixth Sense.*"

"Drat!" he cried, throwing his wings in the air.

The bright colors of his feathers, the brilliant red, blue, and yellow, reminded me of Penelope's painting in the bunkhouse, which then reminded me of the stain on the floor.

I hoped it was paint.

"And," I added, "I moved only yesterday. It hasn't even been twenty-four hours. Hardly stranger status just yet, so I'm not sure why you chose that particular quote."

"'Tis just a matter of time until we drift apart. Your house is so far away. I barely see you anymore."

"I'm literally on the other side of this yard."

Dramatically, he lifted a wing to cover his face as though he couldn't bear to look at me. "If only we could spend more time together. If only there were an upcoming event in which we could both participate . . ." He peeked out at me, a glimmer in his dark eye.

Ah. I saw where he was going with this. On an ordinary day, I would have seen right through his acting straight off the bat. Today, however, my mind was occupied with thoughts of Miles and Steve and Penelope.

And bloodstains.

I'd called Nick about those stains, and he'd told us to leave everything where it was including the cashier's check receipt and the address book—to not touch anything else, and to lock up. He was waiting on yet another infernal call back from the ME's office. After that, he'd then have to go speak with George and Cora to get their official permission to send a team into the bunkhouse. Without probable cause, he wouldn't have been able to get a warrant to go in on his own, so going through the Chadwicks was the path of least resistance.

For a while I'd waited for him to arrive at Wickedly Creative, but after an hour I decided I couldn't take Steve Winstead's anxiety any longer and left Glinda to deal with him. She was practically family, with his being Liam's uncle, so I didn't feel too badly about my defection.

I was sure she'd forgive me.

I'd send her some cookies.

"Not to worry, Archie," I said to him. "I talked to Evan. He's giving you one of the best roles there is."

He practically bounced on his perch. "Do tell! Is it Max? I have a soft spot for him."

"Well, nothing quite so . . . visible. You would be rather difficult to costume—don't you think?"

"Darcy Merriweather, are you gaslighting me?" He cleared his throat. "'I knew from the first moment I saw you that you were dangerous to me.'"

I didn't bother to identify the quote from the movie *Gaslight*. It hadn't been a trivia challenge on his part. Just more dramatics. "Not in the least. Like I said, you're going to have one of the best roles. One of the most *important*."

He hopped closer, stuck his face through the iron bars of his cage. "What, pray tell, is that? As the theater custodian? Am I to pick up wayward popcorn after theatergoers have departed? Will you have me cleaning chimneys, mopping floors, mending dresses, and talking to mice, too?" He tapped his chin with a wing tip. "Hmm. Perhaps the latter was not the best reference. . . ."

I smiled. He and Pepe were the best of friends. "You do enjoy popcorn."

"Inconsequential!" he squawked.

Laughing, I said, "Don't worry, Cinderella. You've been assigned the role of assistant casting director."

The wind ruffled his feathers as he cocked his head. "I'm listening."

"You're going to help Evan conduct auditions, which will make good use of your excellent critiquing skills."

"Go on."

"You'll get," I said in a stage whisper, "the chance to see Dorothy Hansel Dewitt audition for the role of Maria."

Slowly, he nodded. "I'm intrigued. Why, might I in-quire, is my title as an *assistant* only? No one judges others more spectacularly than I. I should be the lead casting director."

"I think a role as a casting *assistant* is pretty darn good. Especially after you conveniently forgot to mention to me yesterday that following Dorothy's affair with Miles she reconciled with her husband, Joel, renewed her vows with him, and had come back to the village after their lengthy second honeymoon pregnant with Glinda. . . ."

"Yes." He coughed. "I see your point. I suppose the role will do. For now."

Ve's back door opened and she popped her head out. "Darcy! I thought I heard your voice. We've been waiting for you."

I told Archie that Evan would pick him up at three thirty, said my good-byes, and headed for the house.

Ve waited for me at the back door. "I was just wondering when you'd stop by."

"I called but it went straight to voice mail."

"I had to turn off my phones for a while. People keep calling, wondering if the news that I have a son is true! It's driving me crazy. Well, craz*ier*."

Archie called out. "If you're handing out cigars, I'd be more than happy to take one off your hands."

She laughed and waved him off.

I tried to picture him with a cigar sticking out of his beak, and I knew I had to sketch the image. Which reminded me that I needed to retrieve the box that held my sketchbook and other favorite things from upstairs before I left. It was, after all, one of the reasons why I was here.

The other reason was to see what Ve remembered about her marriage to Miles with use of the memory spell. With its help, hopefully Ve would be able to fully accept what had happened that weekend and then put it behind her.

Ve gave me a kiss on my cheek and a tight hug, as though I was a long-lost relative she hadn't seen in years. I couldn't help smiling and holding her back just as tightly.

I'd missed her just as much as she apparently had me in the less than twenty-four hours that I'd been gone.

Maybe the length of time didn't warrant stranger status, as I'd mentioned to Archie, but it *was* long enough to feel a loved one's absence.

Pulling away, she patted my cheek. Today she was dressed in a batik tunic top in deep reds and browns that picked up the bronze tones in her hair. She'd paired it with jeans that were cuffed at the ankle and flats.

As I stepped into the kitchen, I was surprised to see Marcus sitting at the peninsula. He had a plate of shortbread cookies in front of him.

Ve had been baking again.

Tilda sat on his lap, looking like she'd just won the lottery as he ran a hand over her fur.

His way with cats never ceased to amaze me.

Andreus sat there, too, puzzling over the crossword in today's *Toil and Trouble*. He glanced up at me. "Five letters, the word 'storm' is the clue."

Squinting, I searched my brain as I slid onto the empty stool between the two men. Ve handed me a plate with shortbread cookies and a cup of coffee. "Rains? Rages? Winds? Chaos?" I offered.

"None fit." He shook his head, then sighed and waved his hand over the paper, his fingers spreading out as though he'd just sprinkled invisible water onto the page.

It was the same motion Godfrey had used yesterday on my coat.

My eyes widened as letters slowly filled the tiny squares.

Andreus *tsk*ed. "Ah, *furor*."

My jaw dropped. "How'd you do that?"

He patted my hand. "You've much to learn still, Darcy."

I looked at Marcus. "Can you do that?"

He waved his hand over his plate of cookies, did the finger thing, and suddenly his cookies appeared on *my* plate.

Stunned, I said, "Is that some form of the Special Delivery Spell?"

I'd learned of the spell and its ability to transfer objects this past winter, except that spell came with a flash. Literally.

"It's not a spell at all," Marcus replied. "It's a manifestation of the magic inside us. You'll eventually learn how to handle your own. It takes time."

I stared at Ve. "You've been holding out on me!"

She laughed. "As Marcus said, it takes time. You've already tapped into some of your inner talents, hiding Melina's journal the way you do."

I realized she was right. I did. I hadn't truly thought there was more I could do. There was still so much to learn about this Craft. And its people.

I grabbed a cookie and ate it.

"Hey!" Marcus said. "That was mine."

"Finder's keepers." I chewed, swallowed, then looked at Ve. "Has Vince stopped by here?"

"He came by earlier," she said, "with some sort of DNA test kit."

I thought my mother would be here, but Marcus' presence had probably squashed that plan. He didn't yet know that she was the Elder. And I wasn't sure he would ever be told, which suddenly struck me as odd. After all, my mother had allowed me to tell Nick and Mimi, so why hadn't Harper been allowed to tell Marcus?

It was something to ask her the next time I saw her.

Though . . . I supposed it was possible she was still

here somewhere. As Elder, she could use any form she pleased. From gnat to bee, lion to rhinoceros.

A rhino in the village would certainly be something to see.

I glanced around for any sign of her presence. There wasn't so much as a fly to be seen, though for some reason I felt like she was here. I'd come to learn I could sense her presence and wondered if it had something to do with what she'd told me this morning. How Crafters had magic within them. Perhaps we could use it to fill in crossword puzzles . . . and feel it within one another as well. It might explain why Vince had been drawn first to Alex Shively, then to Starla.

Kindred spirits.

No, kindred *witches*.

"Did you take the test?" Marcus asked Ve.

"Yes," Ve said. "The Elder assured me that the best way to handle Vince is to give him what he wanted. She also said that no trace of the Craft would show on the test. I do feel badly for the boy. He seemed crushed that I didn't claim him."

As far as mothers went, Ve would have been a good one. I could understand why Vince had been deflated. I reached over to scratch Tilda's head, and her tiny pink tongue darted out and licked my hand. I wasn't sure I'd ever received a kitty kiss from the cranky cat.

She must have missed me as well. Either that, or Marcus' petting had sent her into a state of euphoria.

I chose to believe she missed me.

"Any news from Nick this morning?" Andreus asked me.

"Not that I know of. But Glinda and I found something interesting at Wickedly Creative."

I debated whether to tell them everything, mostly because Marcus was here. But I finally relented. If I were in his position, I'd want to know all the details.

As Glinda had warned me yesterday, forewarned was forearmed. If Marcus was going to stay on this case, he needed to know everything, even if his parents were involved.

Especially because his parents were involved.

I told them about the bloodstains, the receipt for the cashier's check, and Penelope's paintings, though I did leave out the mention of the nude specifically.

"What was the check for, do you think?" Ve asked. "Did Oliver bribe Miles to leave town to get him away from Penelope? If so, smart man."

Marcus winced a bit.

"I don't think so," I said. "It was dated the day after Vince was born. I think Oliver handled Vince's adoption. The money was probably a payout to Miles for severing his parental rights."

It was a lot of money. Someone had deep pockets. Someone like Penelope's parents?

"Then Oliver most likely knows who Vince's mother is," Andreus said.

"If he knows"—Marcus reached for a cookie from my plate—"he would never tell. Even if the adoption wasn't legal by mortal standards, he's still bound by privilege."

By mortal standards. He obviously knew the Craft was involved somehow, but did he know Vince was a witch? I wasn't sure. Instead, I asked him, "So you knew about the adoption? And that it was illegal?"

He took off his glasses, rubbed his eyes. "Vince mentioned the adoption to me a long time ago, trying to convince me to get my father to talk about it. As a courtesy, I asked my father. He declined to speak to Vince about it, but mentioned to me that it had been an extremely private adoption. Strings were pulled since a friend was involved."

"Oliver didn't say who the friend was?" Ve asked.

I was dying to know if the friend had been Penelope. It made sense. Perfect sense.

Marcus checked his watch and said, "He said nothing more at all. That was the end of it. I need to go soon. I have things I need to do."

"Yes, yes," Ve said after a moment. "I think we're all more than ready to get the memory spell over and done with, yes?"

I had high hopes the spell would shed a lot of light on that weekend and what had happened with Miles.

"I've asked Marcus here just in case I see anything that might implicate me. This moment is covered under attorney-client privilege, and you two"—she pointed at Andreus and me—"are simply sworn to secrecy."

Andreus crossed his heart and then poked me with his elbow until I did, too.

"All right," she said, rubbing her hands together. *"Mind blank; conscious spark; lost memories; return to me."*

She repeated the spell two more times to cast it properly. Her eyes were squeezed shut, and Marcus, Andreus, and I all leaned toward her, waiting on the edges of our seats.

Ve frowned deeply, her eyebrows pulled low, her lips tight.

"Well?" Andreus asked.

She held out a finger and cast the spell again. After a moment, she shook her head and her eyes opened. "I recall opening the door to find Miles on the front porch, and then nothing else until the next night. There's nothing there."

"How is that possible?" I asked.

"You should have *some* recollection," Marcus added. "As far as I know the amulet doesn't have the power to erase your memory. There's only one kind of magic. . . ." He trailed off.

I picked up where he'd been going. "A memory cleanse. It's the only explanation. But Miles was a mortal. He couldn't have been the one to give it to you."

Andreus said darkly, "Correct. It had to have been a Crafter."

Ve massaged her temples. "But who? And why?"

Marcus stood up. "You obviously know something someone wanted you to forget."

"But what?" Ve said, her voice cracking as she looked among us.

My heart hurt for her. I didn't know the answer to her question.

But I was determined to find out.

Chapter Twenty

My box of favorite keepsakes was heavier than I'd thought. I struggled with its weight and the wind as I walked home, glad I lived so close.

Archie wasn't in his cage. Smiling, I thought about him getting ready for the auditions later on, taking a bath, combing his feathers.

It reminded me of the sketch I wanted to do of him with a cigar. I hoped I'd have some time to work on it before I was due at the scene shop this afternoon. I should still be out investigating what had happened to Miles, but there was time enough for that later, when I saw Penelope at the playhouse. I couldn't help feeling that she was the key to this case, and now that I knew about the magic inside me, I didn't discount the notion.

I'd grill her later.

And as much as I just wanted to curl up in front of the fire with my sketchbook, the very first thing I wanted to do when I got home was to check to make sure Mimi was still alive. Because it was nearing noon, and she still hadn't texted me that she was awake. So when I glanced up at her bedroom window and saw her smiling face, I was a bit surprised.

I smiled back as she opened her window.

"Do you need help?" she called down.

"I've got it." I headed for the front walk. "How long have you been up? You didn't text."

"Text?"

"I left you a note."

She laughed. "So that's what that confetti in the kitchen was. Annie must have found it. I called Dad to see where you two were. Are you sure you don't need help?"

I used my knee to keep the box from slipping. "I'm almost there. . . . I'll be right in."

She laughed again and closed the window.

I was halfway up the walkway when the Bumblebee-mobile pulled into the driveway. I set the box on the stone path and waited for Nick to get out of the car.

He smiled as he walked over to me. "Is it me, or does it feel like it should be eight, nine o'clock at night?" He leaned in and gave me a kiss that would have had Archie catcalling—or gagging—if he'd seen it.

It *had* been a long day already, and it was barely noon. "It's not just you. Did you ever make it over to Wickedly Creative?"

"I was just there. Everything's set. A forensics team is on its way to process the bunkhouse."

I rocked on my heels. "Did it look like paint or blood to you?"

"With the Chadwicks' permission, I tested a small sample of the stain on the table. It was positive for blood."

Instantly, I felt queasy. "Miles'?"

"No way to tell yet. More tests need to be done."

"Well, I guess this at least suggests what Miles might have died from. Wait," I said, bending to lift the box. "Did you hear from the ME's office? Do you *know* what he died from?"

Nick took the box from my hands. "I was on hold forever to be told that the office is understaffed and overworked. I've been promised a preliminary report by tomorrow."

"Tomorrow? You waited all that time just to hear that?"

"Pretty much. Not all was lost," he said. "Marcus came by and worked some magic and found out that Dorothy's first husband, Joel Hansel, was in fact out of the country the weekend Miles went missing. And I was able to check into Vince's adoptive parents. Brenda Paxton worked as a secretary for Oliver Debrowski. She retired about fifteen years ago. She and her husband live in Salem, near the college."

His secretary? Was she the "friend" Marcus had referenced earlier? Had she paid one hundred thousand dollars to adopt Vince? "What does her husband do for a living?"

"He's a college librarian. Why?"

I explained what Marcus had said at Ve's about the adoption. "A secretary and a college librarian wouldn't earn very much money, would they?"

Nick shrugged. "You wouldn't think so, but they could have family money. There's no way I can check into their finances without a warrant, and right now . . ."

"Limbo," I said.

He nodded, and then took a step and said, "I don't like all the question marks with this case. There are plenty of leads, but we don't know what we're investigating just yet."

"Speaking of leads, another one just opened up at

Ve's. . . ." I told him about the memory cleanse. "I don't know what it means, or if it relates to Miles' death, but it's another fact to keep in mind."

"This case just keeps getting odder and odder."

It did. We headed for the front steps. "If a memory cleanse was used, there's absolutely no way to recover those memor— Oh no!"

Nick had just taken a step when the bottom of the box gave out, and its contents crashed to the ground. He dropped the now-empty box and dashed after a drawing that had come loose from my sketchbook and was now blowing down the driveway.

I fell to my knees, trying to keep my sketchbooks from soaking in the moisture from the puddles on the walkway, especially my favorite sketchbook, which was leather bound. I quickly picked it up, but the wind caught the cover just right, flipping it out of my hand. It fell facedown on the grass behind me, splayed open. I grabbed it, immediately checking to see if the tiny dried four-leaf clover that had been nestled between the cover and the first page was still there.

It wasn't.

"Oh no," I murmured, glancing around. "Oh no, oh no."

"Got it!" Nick returned with the sketch. He stuck it into my leather sketchbook, then turned the box over. He bent the flaps this way and that, folding the box so tape wasn't necessary to keep the bottom secure.

I put my face close to the grass, searching for that clover. It had to be here somewhere. *Please be here somewhere.*

"What're you looking for?" Nick asked as he started packing the box up again.

A gust of wind sent hair flying into my eyes, and I said loudly, "I wish the wind would stop!"

It didn't. It had been worth the try, though. I ran my

hand over blades of grass. Moisture soaked through the knees of my pants and dampened my palms as I crawled around.

"Darcy?" Nick knelt next to me. "What is it? An earring? A contact lens?"

"A clover," I said, hearing the panic in my own voice. "Do you see it?"

"A clover? There is lots of clover in the yard."

There was. Weed control had been low on my to-do list as the house neared the end of its renovation. I'd planned to tackle the bulk of the landscaping next spring. "It's an old four-leaf clover. Dried. I kept it in one of my sketchbooks. . . . It blew away."

"With this wind, it could be anywhere."

Tears came unbidden to my eyes. "I need to find it."

He took one look at me and started crawling low to the ground, searching. "We'll find it."

We looked for a good ten minutes, but it was nowhere to be found. I sat back on my haunches and wiped my eyes. "This is pointless. It's gone."

"I'm sure we'll find it if we just keep looking." The knees of his khakis were soaked through and ringed with grass stains. Blades of grass stuck to his palms.

He went back to looking.

"I just need to let it go," I said. "It . . . I mean, my wish came true, so I guess I really don't need it anymore. It did its job."

"Wish?" he asked, crawling back toward me.

"Do you remember the day Mimi gave me a four-leaf clover on the green?"

It had been almost directly across the street from this house, near Mrs. P's bench under the birch tree.

"I do. It was what? Two weeks or so after you moved to the village. Mrs. P was there. You had cupcakes. Devil's food, if I remember correctly. Mimi and I were waiting for you so we could return Missy after we found her at our house, running loose. Mimi found you a four-leaf clover and told you to make a wish . . . ," he said, his voice growing softer the more he spoke. "You kept it? The clover?"

That day was forever etched in my memory. It was so easy to recall how I'd felt standing next to him. The heat of his body. His stare. I felt it now as he searched my face with those dark eyes of his. I shrugged, trying to play it off as no big deal. "Of course I kept it."

He moved closer. "Why?"

It felt to me as though the world around us stopped. The birds quieted. The leaves settled. The wind didn't blow. It was just us, sitting here on the wet grass, in our own little bubble. Him and me. I swallowed hard. "I'm a sap. Everyone knows that."

Our knees touched. Sunlight glinted in his eyes. "Is that so? No other reason?"

I gestured with my hands as though they were the scales of justice. To tell the truth? Or gloss over it? I glossed. Surely he didn't want to know *everything*. "Okay, I admit it. I had a lot riding on that wish. Plus, Mimi gave it to me. It's sentimental."

"What did you wish for?"

Apparently he *did* want to know everything. Heat rose into my cheeks. I could feel them starting to burn and imagined them to be bright red. "I can't tell you. . . ."

"But you said your wish came true. So you *can* tell me. There's no risk of negating it."

"It's embarrassing."

His forehead crinkled in puzzlement. "I doubt that."

I couldn't even face him. "Oh, it is. I'd just met you. . . ."

"Me?" He nudged my chin upward. "What did you wish for, Darcy?"

I wanted to bluff and bluster, to brush off the question. But when I looked into his eyes, I couldn't bring myself to do it. Not when I saw the emotion shining there. Taking a deep breath, I said, "I wished to love again. To love you. And for you and me and Mimi to be a family. It's so silly. I mean, I'd just met you. . . . But I knew. I knew I wanted to be with you."

"It's not silly. I knew, too. And I still know."

I tipped my head. "You did? You do?"

He took hold of my hands. "I knew from the moment I—"

A shadow fell across us and someone cleared his throat. "I hope I'm not interrupting."

Nick hung his head. "So close," he murmured.

"Terry? Is everything okay?" I asked as I stood up to greet my neighbor. "Is Archie all right?"

"He's fine," Terry said. "But if hear 'So Long, Farewell' one more time, I'll be saying the same. I can only tolerate so much. A vacation with Cherise will be in order."

"A vacation with Cherise should be in order, whether Archie stops singing or not."

He narrowed his eyes. "She's been talking to you, hasn't she?"

I laughed. "No, but I'll be sure to bring it up next time I see her."

Nick rose to his feet, shook Terry's hand. "Good to see you out and about."

It was a rare occasion for Terry to leave his house, especially during daylight hours. For someone who didn't like to call attention to himself, he'd certainly dressed to impress for this excursion. He wore a slim-fitting blue suit that looked like it could be vintage from the beatnik era. He'd topped it with a Red Sox hat.

The outfit, if meant to distract from his Elvis-like looks, had failed in its job.

He looked like an older version of Elvis in his *Viva*

Las Vegas days who happened to be wearing a Red Sox hat. He'd fool absolutely no one.

"I have information I wanted to share with the both of you, so I came straight out when I saw you crawling about so intently, like you were looking for your hopes and dreams or perhaps the engagement ring Darcy has yet to receive. . . ."

Nick groaned. "Subtle."

Terry jutted his big jaw, curled his lip. "I don't do subtle."

"Good to know," Nick said with a smile.

"What kind of information?" I asked.

Terry turned his attention squarely on me. "When I witnessed your altercation with Dorothy yesterday afternoon, I was reminded of another altercation of hers."

I didn't doubt that there had been many.

"It was thirty years ago," he said, "and I recall it only because it occurred the weekend Ve married that low-life scum bucket Miles Babbage."

Low-life scum bucket.

Nope. There was nothing subtle about that at all. I wanted to hear what he had to say, so I didn't tell him that Miles wasn't nearly as bad as he had seemed. There would be time enough for that later.

"Was Dorothy fighting with Ve?" I asked.

"No, I didn't see Ve at all, though the fight happened on her side porch."

"Who was Dorothy fighting with, then?" Nick asked.

Terry took off his hat, ran his hand over his pompadour. How he didn't have hat head was a mystery to me, and I figured some sort of magic had to be involved.

"It was a full-fledged shouting match between Dorothy," he said, "and Miles."

"Miles?" I repeated. "Dorothy told me she hadn't seen Miles that weekend at all."

Terry looked at me with sympathetic eyes. "Is it truly any surprise at all that Dorothy lied?"

Knowing what I knew of Dorothy, it shouldn't have been a shock at all.

But it was.

Now I was more determined than ever to uncover what she was hiding and was left wondering if she'd had something to do with Miles' death after all.

Chapter Twenty-one

An hour into the set build and it felt more like we were on the set of a soap opera. Animosity hummed in tandem with the power saw. Uneasiness punctuated the air with each *pop* of the nail gun.

The Sound of Music movie soundtrack played in the background. Evan believed it would provide inspiration as we worked, but I thought it might be adding to the disharmony.

Mimi kept sending me worried glances as she painted a faux stained-glass window onto muslin for the convent scenes. I'd already sketched the piece and labeled it. All she had to do was paint by number. I sent her reassuring smiles as I worked next to her, painting an exact replica of her window on my own sheet of muslin.

I wished Nick was here. He was supposed to be, but

he'd been sidetracked by a call from the medical examiner's office, whose preliminary report was finally complete. It was being faxed to Nick's office, so he had
headed off to the police station instead of coming here
with me.

I hoped he'd walk through the door at any moment,
not because I wanted to know what he'd learned from
the report, but because I wanted him here if a fight
broke out.

At the moment, it was unclear who the fight would
be between.

It could be Vince and Oliver. The two were giving
each other a wide berth and the evil eye.

Or Oliver and Steve Winstead. Oliver had looked
like a vein was about to pop in his forehead when Steve
walked into the scene shop, declaring he was there to
help with the sets.

Despite the fact that no one had asked for his as-
sistance.

So far he hadn't done much other than try to get time
alone with Penelope, but Oliver kept heading off the
advances.

Then there was Starla and Vince. She had, in fact,
broken up with Vince last night. She said she had taken
it harder than he had, especially when she learned
he'd been keeping his search for his biological parents
from her.

She insisted he'd taken it well, but his glowering said
otherwise. He'd probably just been trying to act brave
in front of her. I wished he'd backed out of coming today, but I'd never known him not to honor his word.

He looked like he hadn't slept a wink, and I couldn't
imagine what he was feeling today. Between Miles'
death and the breakup . . . it was a lot to bear.

I sighed, wishing it had turned out differently for

him and Starla. I had to keep telling myself some things weren't meant to be.

It turned out that I hadn't needed to worry about any lingering uneasiness between Glinda and Starla this afternoon, because Glinda had been a no-show. It was so unusual for her to be late that I'd called to check on her. The call had gone straight to voice mail.

Mimi said, "Maybe you should take the nail gun away from Vince. Give him a paintbrush instead."

Vince was glaring at Hank Leduc, who seemed to be the only one in the room who hadn't picked up on any tension.

Probably because he was too busy staring at Starla.

I could tell she was at war with herself, wanting to enjoy Hank's attention but feeling horrible about Vince. She was doing her best to keep busy.

It probably hadn't been wise to allow Vince use of the nail gun, but he was whipping out framing for the canvas stretchers faster than Steve could transport them from one side of the scene shop to the other, where Starla then stapled canvas to the pine strapping.

Pop, pop, pop.

Vince tended to discharge the nail gun in threes.

"Very nice," Steve said to Mimi on one of those trips across the space. Then he bent down to me and whispered, "You might want to give Penelope some guidance." More loudly, he said, "I would do it, but I can't get past her *guard dog*."

Oliver looked over at him like he wished he'd been holding that nail gun instead of Vince. I'd assigned Oliver to be Hank's assistant. Currently, he was connecting a spindle to a railing. I was mighty glad he had only a screwdriver in hand.

I glanced over at Penelope and frowned. After seeing her paintings at the bunkhouse this morning, I'd given her the job of creating the mountain scene. It was a challenging piece, and though she'd tried to resist taking on such a big responsibility, I'd insisted.

Now I wished I hadn't.

Her mountains looked like lumpy clouds. I set down my paintbrush and told Mimi I'd be right back.

Pop, pop, pop.

My shoulders stiffened at the noise. It was getting on my last nerve.

Penelope saw me coming and said, "I'm having trouble with the canvas."

An understatement if I'd ever heard one. "It can be tricky," I reassured her, though I was lying though my teeth. Any advanced painter should have had no trouble with the material.

She certainly looked the role of an artist. Her hair was pulled up in a loose bun; paint flecks dotted her cheeks. She wore an old pair of paint-splattered jeans and a loose sweatshirt, its collar cut out. I liked this version of her much better than the one I had met in the bookshop yesterday.

I asked, "Do you want me to create some guidelines?"

She nodded and handed over a paintbrush. "Thank you. It was probably a mistake to come here today. My mind is preoccupied. I can't focus on my work."

I set about outlining mountain shapes in the background and a hilly expanse in the forefront, taking extra care to get the perspective of the scene just right. It was a good time to speak to her, to see what she would tell me about Miles Babbage. "I saw some of your paintings this morning. They're lovely."

"My paintings?" She tipped her head. "Where did you see them?"

"At Wickedly Creative. They were in one of the bunkhouses. The one Miles used when he stayed in the village."

She glanced over her shoulder, searching the room. She was looking for Oliver, I realized, but he wasn't to be seen. He'd probably stepped out to use the restroom.

"One was of the village entrance, the other of a bird in a cage. The third wasn't completed."

I hadn't needed to tell her it was the nude. Her fast blush told me she knew well enough.

"When was the last time you saw Miles?" I asked. "Do you remember?"

Again, she looked around. "This isn't a good time to be talking about this."

"Penelope, it's never going to be a good time."

"You should let it be."

"You know I can't do that." I dipped the paintbrush. "Did you see him after he and Steve had that fight in front of Third Eye?"

Resigned, she sighed. "No. The last I saw him was the night before that. We had plans to run off to elope the next day. Then Miles and Steve had that fight, my parents found out, and I was sent off to stay with an aunt down the Cape." Her eyes moistened, but no tears formed. She glanced away. "I never saw Miles again."

Steve must have noticed Oliver's absence as well, because he bustled over. "Penelope," he began.

She rubbed her temples. "Not now, Steve."

"We need to talk," he said, reaching for her hands.

She folded them across her chest. "I'm busy." She picked up a spare paintbrush, dipped it in green paint, and attempted to create a line of pine trees dividing the mountains from the grassy area of the picture.

The strokes were wrong. Too broad. And she'd used too much paint. They weren't Bob Ross happy little trees but rather gelatinous green blobs with no discernible definition.

Oliver's voice came from behind us. He said, "You heard her plain and clear, Steve. She's busy. Back off."

Steve pulled his shoulders back. "Stay out of this, Oliver. It's between me and Penelope."

Oliver stepped closer. "I don't think so."

"She needs to know the truth."

I looked around. Everyone else had stopped working. It was definitely a soap opera in here.

"What truth is that?" Oliver asked. "She chose me over you. The end."

"No," Steve said, his tone cold and hard. "She chose Miles over me. Then her parents made her marry you. And she wouldn't have chosen Miles except he'd been controlling her with an amulet."

"What amulet?" Vince asked.

Oh jeez. We were going to have to memory-cleanse him before this day was through.

"Stay out of this," Oliver said to him.

"You can't tell me what to do," Vince said. "You're not my *father*."

Pop, pop, pop.

I said loudly, "Maybe we ought to take a break."

Everyone ignored me.

Steve kept trying to reason with Penelope. There was a plea in his voice as he said, "Don't you see, Penelope? It all would have been different if not for that amulet. You would still be with *me*."

She closed her eyes, sighed. "I knew about the amulet, Steve."

"You did?" I asked.

"What amulet?" Vince asked again.

No one answered him.

"Miles told me after I agreed to leave town with him," Penelope said. "It didn't matter. I still wanted to be with him. It turned out, however, that he hadn't wanted to wait for me." She faced Steve. "Now, please . . . It's been thirty years. Please let it go."

She turned her back on him and started attacking the canvas with green blobs again.

The whole thing was going to need to be repainted.

"I can't let it go," Steve said. "I love you."

Gasps rippled through the room. Mimi's eyes were as wide as saucers.

Tears filled Penelope's eyes. "I love Oliver. Please, please, Steve, let it go."

"Fine," he said stubbornly. "I'll let it go for now."

"Let it go forever," she said. "It's over. It's been over for a long time. I never wanted to hurt you. . . . *Please*," she begged. "Just go."

He glanced around, saw the sympathetic glances everyone was giving him, then turned and left.

Penelope watched him leave with tears in her eyes.

"We should go, too," Oliver said to Penelope. His color was high, and he looked about to come undone. "It's ridiculous that we came in the first place."

"It is not," she said, sighing. "You know how I feel about the arts."

It sounded like an argument they'd had a time or two.

He dragged a hand down his beard. "Be that as it may, we have no business being here. You can't even p—" He broke off as her face drained of all color. "I'm sorry," he said quickly.

Tears spilled from her eyes as she set down her paintbrush, pivoted, and said, "I need some air." She walked out.

I glanced at Oliver, at the painting, then back at Oliver. . . .

"You can't even p—"

Paint.

He'd been about to say "paint."

As realization hit, I lowered my voice. "She's lost her abilities, hasn't she?"

He didn't answer as he turned to follow his wife out of the room.

Fortunately for me, he'd said all I'd needed to hear.

There were several ways to lose your abilities, but the most common was to tell a mortal of your gift. Suddenly and instinctively I knew she'd told Miles.

I watched Oliver go, and as he flew out of the doorway, he nearly knocked over Glinda as she came inside.

"Sorry I'm late," she said to the room, then hotfooted it over to me. "What'd I just miss?"

I closed the paints Penelope had been using. "Long story."

She eyed the canvas. "Are those green sheep?"

I cracked a smile. They did look like green sheep. "Also a long story. Are you all right? I tried calling. . . ."

She didn't look all right. Her eyes were rimmed in red as though she'd been crying.

"Family emergency," she said, her voice sounding funny. "I had to talk to my mother."

I put my hand on her arm. "You're worrying me."

"Glinda!" Mimi rushed over to us. "We were worried about you."

Glinda smiled and said to me, "She's becoming your mini-me."

It might have been the best compliment I'd ever received.

She put her arm around Mimi. "I'm okay."

"Really?" Mimi asked, concern etching her gaze. "Because you don't look okay. You look like you've been crying. Did you have a fight with Liam? Oh no! Did you break up with him like Starla broke up with Vince? You were so happy with him."

"Mimi," Glinda said, smiling. "Take a breath!"

Mimi sucked in some air.

"Liam and I are fine. I *am* happy with him. It wasn't that. Starla and Vince broke up?" Glinda looked to me for explanation.

Yet again I said, "Long story."

Mimi said, "Then what happened? Is it Clarence? Did he run away again?"

Only Mimi could get away with peppering her with these kinds of questions. But I was glad she was asking, because I was curious as well.

Pop, pop, pop.

Glinda's gaze whipped to Vince and that nail gun. She swallowed hard. "Clarence is fine. Everything's fine. I just got some surprising news in the mail."

Vince picked up a length of pine, eyed it, made a cut with a jigsaw, then set it in place on the frame he was working on.

Pop, pop, pop.

"Who knew Vince was so good at building things?" Mimi said. "I'm glad you're here now." She gave Glinda another hug and went back to her painting.

She was right about Vince. Who knew? I'd never known him to build a single thing. He'd especially taken right to that nail gun. Men and power tools. It was like it was natural instinct.

Some women had natural instincts for it, too. I was reminded of Glinda and what she'd told me yesterday, of how she was *"really handy with power tools."*

Of course the Broomcrafting helped.

The Broomcrafting . . .

My head snapped up. Wait.

I looked between her and Vince, Vince and her.

"I need to talk to you," Glinda said, grabbing my arm. "It's important."

My jaw practically hit the floor. They had the same eyes! That same brilliant blue. Oh. My. God.

"H-how?" was all I could stammer as she tugged me

along. Dorothy had been out of the country when Vince was born. . . . This didn't make sense.

"Long story," she said drolly.

Penelope and Oliver came back inside, cutting us off.

"I'm sorry, Darcy," Penelope said, "but I think it's best we left. I just need to get my things; then I'll get out of your hair."

"I understand," I said, mentally shooing them out the door. I wanted to hear what Glinda had to say.

"A family emergency," she'd said.

It was putting it lightly.

I glanced over at Vince. He'd abandoned the nail gun.

Thank God.

Unfortunately, he was headed this way.

He sauntered over and stared at Penelope. "You said earlier you were going to run off with Miles Babbage. You had a relationship with him?"

Her eyes narrowed in confusion. "I'm not sure how that's any concern of yours."

Oliver stepped in close to his wife. "Leave her alone, Vince."

"No," Vince returned as he folded his arms across his chest. "If she had a relationship with Miles, then I have a right to know." He faced her head-on. "Are you my mother?"

Her eyes flew open wide. "What? Your *mother*?"

Oliver sighed.

"Is Miles your *father*?" She gasped. "Oh my God. You have his chin."

"Are *you* my mother?" Vince asked Penelope again.

She kept staring at him as though seeing him in an all-new light. Tears brimmed in her eyes, pooling along the lashes. "How didn't I see it before?"

"She's not your mother," Oliver said to Vince in a firm voice.

Vince jabbed Oliver in the chest. "You expect me to believe you? I want a DNA test."

Oliver jabbed back. "Keep your hands to yourself, son."

"Don't call me 'son,'" Vince said, taking a swing at him. It connected with Oliver's jaw and sent him reeling backward.

Penelope screamed.

Oliver rubbed his jaw, then lurched forward. The two men fell into each other, punching and grunting and shoving as they yelled nonsense at each other.

I recalled how Oliver had said he'd never had a fight in his life and felt sorry for the man as I backed up to protect Mimi. Hank hurdled a sawhorse to break up the pair as Evan came sprinting into the room, Archie on his shoulder.

"What's going on?" Evan cried.

"They're going to kill each other," Mimi said, poking her head out from behind me.

Glinda joined in the fray, trying to get a grip on Vince, while Hank tugged on Oliver. I glanced at Starla across the room. Tears streamed down her face. She shook her head, turned, and ran out of the room.

I'd grabbed Mimi's arm to follow Starla out when Archie let out an earsplitting whistle and Evan bellowed, "Enough!"

It was enough to startle Oliver and Vince so they could be separated. Glinda pushed Vince behind her, and Hank held his arms wide, corralling Oliver.

"I'm pressing charges!" Oliver huffed. Blood seeped from a cut above his eye, and I went instantly woozy.

I had to look away.

"Do it!" Vince prodded, and after he adjusted his

glasses, he pushed against Glinda as though he wanted to continue the fight with Oliver. "I'll be glad to tell them all about my *adoption*."

I continued to edge my way out of the room with Mimi.

"What is he talking about, Oliver?" Penelope asked.

"Stay out of this," he told his wife.

"Let me at him." Vince tried to bob and weave around Glinda, but her police training had prepared her well.

"Settle down," she told him, keeping him contained.

"Enough!" Evan said again, coming to stand in between the warring parties. "What is going on?"

If anyone thought it odd that Archie was perched on his shoulder, they didn't say.

Archie was practically rubbing his wings together, delighting in this drama. For him, seeing this might be even better than helping with the auditions.

"I'm just trying to find out who my mother is." Vince's left eye was quickly blooming black and blue. "No one will tell me. I have a right to know!"

"Well, it's certainly not me!" Penelope cried.

"No," a voice said from the doorway. "It's not."

Mimi and I froze as Dorothy *click-clacked* into the room.

"Then who is it?" Vince demanded of her.

Dorothy walked past me with nary a sideways glance. She stepped up to Vince, looked him straight in the eye, and said, "It's me."

Chapter Twenty-two

" 'Nobody knows the trouble I've seen; nobody knows my sorrow.'"

It was a line from a song in *The Lion King*. Archie had perfected the despondence of the lyric in his mournful delivery. His imitation of Zazu, the red-billed hornbill in the movie, was spot-on. No wonder. They were very much birds of a feather.

I patted his head. "The auditions will be rescheduled."

Evan had postponed tonight's auditions in light of the fight and the revelation that Dorothy was Vince's mother. Everyone had been in such a tizzy that it wouldn't have been fair to the actors trying out for the play. No one would have been paying much attention.

"If I'd known building sets would be so exciting, I would have signed up," Harper said glumly.

We were sitting at my kitchen island, pints of ice cream dispersed among us. Archie sat on the edge of the counter, his long tail hanging down. Higgins and his drool were patiently waiting for his share of dessert.

"It wasn't exciting. It was dreadful," Starla moaned from the sofa. Her headache had turned into a migraine. She was lying on the couch with a wet cloth on her head. Annie was curled on her chest. "Vince was . . . out of his mind. Now that I know he's Dorothy's son, it kind of makes sense. Like mother, like son? She's always been loony tunes. No offense, Glinda."

Glinda jammed a spoon into a pint of rocky road. "None taken."

Mimi sat with Missy on her lap. The little dog kept trying to lick her spoon. She said, "Starla, do you think you'll get back together with Vince now? I mean, he's a witch, right? You wouldn't have to keep any more secrets. Wait. Is Dorothy going to tell him he's a witch?"

Glinda sighed. "That's her plan."

"You don't think he should know?" I asked.

"It's not that," she said. "It's . . . complicated. And it's going to be weird."

"Totally weird," Mimi agreed. "Especially when he finds out you were a witch all along, Starla."

Starla sat up and groaned. "Don't remind me." The washcloth fell into her lap. Annie wiggled out from beneath the damp rag and hopped onto the floor. "And I don't know what I'm going to do about Vince. I just don't know. It's a lot to think about and my head hurts."

"Should I call Cherise?" I asked.

"Maybe," she said, closing her eyes and putting her head back down. She replaced the cloth on her head and said, "Why didn't he tell me he was adopted?"

I didn't think she was looking for an actual answer. She was talking out loud, trying to make sense out of something that didn't.

Mimi spooned a helping of cherry vanilla ice cream

and looked at Glinda. "You really didn't know Vince was your brother?"

"I really didn't," Glinda said. "I only took the DNA test as a lark, wanting to see how it worked and what it would show in terms of the Craft. I'd planned to show it to Vince as a way to stretch out the case until I could convince him to drop the warlock nonsense. Which I guess wasn't nonsense after all. When the results came in today's mail, I couldn't believe what I was seeing."

At that point, she'd gone straight to her mother, who'd explained everything.

Dorothy had been pregnant with Vince during her vow renewal and second honeymoon. She and Joel had stayed away long enough for her to give birth and get pregnant again so no one suspected. There had been no trip around the world. They'd been staying up the coast in Marblehead. Only Oliver, the family attorney, had known the truth.

"Apparently," Glinda said, "my father insisted she give the baby up for adoption. He didn't want a constant reminder of her infidelity. She wanted Dad back, so she agreed. When the time came, Oliver promised her the baby would have a good home. She knew only that she had a son. Not who his new family was, or where he lived. She said she wondered just about every day what had become of him. . . ."

I wondered if somehow what she had gone through with Vince spurred her decision to adopt a baby with her second husband. To give a home to a child who needed one, as her child had once been the one in need.

If so, Dorothy might have a heart under all that cleavage after all.

"What of the weasel?" Harper asked. "Did he know your mom was pregnant?"

Glinda pushed the pint of rocky road away from her.

She set her elbows on the counter. "He did. They were dating when she found out. As soon as she told him, he told her to get rid of the baby, that he wasn't cut out to be a father. She refused. He quickly left town. Almost as soon as she reconciled with my father, Miles came back. Apparently he was having second thoughts about fatherhood. My father decided the best way to get rid of Miles was to pay him off. A hundred thousand once the baby was born to sign over his parental rights, leave town, and never come back. Mom said it took some convincing, but Miles eventually took the deal."

"But return he did," Archie said. Higgins tried to lick his tail, and Archie flicked him in the face with it. *"Pzzt!"*

Glinda said, "He came back to town on what would have been the baby's first birthday. He wanted to know what happened to the baby and wanted to see him. Kept going on and on about having made a mistake with the adoption."

Roots. Miles had been trying to plant them. Too little, too late, it seemed.

Glinda put the top back on the pint of ice cream. "My mother says they fought about it."

I'd bet that was the fight Terry had witnessed.

"Miles threatened to track down the whereabouts of the baby and challenge the adoption. He said he'd use Ve and As You Wish to look into the adoption. Mom still refused to tell him anything. Later that week, he eloped with Ve. Mom tried to contact Miles to work out a solution to their problem but was never able to reach him. He'd disappeared." She dropped her head into her hands. "I thought my mother was going to be sick today when I told her about Miles' amulet."

It had to have been startling, but I knew that Dorothy had stayed with Miles of her own free will.

In light of all that had happened, it was probably best if she never knew that.

I kept thinking about what Glinda had said about Miles threating to use Ve to find the baby. . . . I'd been wondering why he'd chosen her to marry, and I suspected he'd taken advantage of opportunity. He'd gone to see her about the baby . . . and probably liked what he'd seen. The next thing Ve knew, she'd woken up a married woman.

"Weasel!" I said suddenly, hopping off my stool.

Starla leaned up. "Are you okay?"

I dropped in front of the file boxes that were still on the living room floor. "Ve called Miles a weasel."

"Fittingly," Archie intoned.

I found the box that held the *W* files and thumbed through the tabs. "Weasel!" I said as I pulled out the file. I flipped it open. "This is it. He wanted Ve to find Baby Boy Babbage. A child he'd had with . . . Dorothy. There's a dozen exclamation points after that last part."

"Whoa," Mimi said.

Harper set her spoon on the counter. "If Dorothy knew that Ve knew . . ."

Archie said, "Then she would've gone to great lengths to make sure Ve unlearned that information."

"The memory cleanse." It made perfect sense. Dorothy had to erase the knowledge of the baby from Ve's memory . . . and in doing so she'd also taken away all Ve's memories of Miles.

Dorothy, I realized, had also given herself away yesterday, but I'd been too preoccupied to catch it.

Pepe had told me how Ve had told only a trusted few that she hadn't been able to recall the wedding. Yet Dorothy had taunted me during our altercation that Ve might not remember that she'd killed Miles.

Dorothy wasn't one of Ve's trusted few; she shouldn't

have known that Ve had no memories of that time. Unless she'd been the one to erase them in the first place.

The things people did to protect themselves. It baffled me.

As I stood up, the front doorbell rang. Higgins looked conflicted. Stay and hope someone shared ice cream? Or greet the visitor?

When the doorbell rang a second time, he couldn't resist the lure of its magical tone. He let out sonic woofs and ran for the door.

Starla moaned at the sound.

Glinda said, "I'm calling Cherise."

Missy yapped and wiggled in Mimi's lap, but she kept a firm hold on the dog.

It was utter chaos.

It was *home*.

I peeked out the sidelight and saw Steve Winstead on the porch. Instead of inviting him into the bedlam, I slipped past Higgins and wiggled out the door, closing it firmly behind me.

It wasn't late, not even five yet, but there was a chill in the air, and I was instantly cold. "Steve?"

He paced. "I didn't tell you everything yesterday."

"About?" As he paced my way, I caught the scent of alcohol. He'd been drinking.

"I was so stupid, thinking she loved me, too, all this time."

"Steve," I said softly. "Maybe you should come back tomorrow."

"No." He stopped, shook his head. "No. I've been keeping this secret all these years, trying to protect her." His voice cracked. "To protect the woman I loved, because I thought she loved me, too. . . . So *stupid*."

He might have been drinking, but he was too lucid to be drunk. He knew what he was saying and why.

"What secret?" I asked, rubbing chill bumps on my arms.

"Penelope might have been whisked away to the Cape by her family after that fight I had with Miles, but she found a way back. I saw her two nights later, at Wickedly Creative. She'd just come running out of Miles' bunkhouse. She was crying." His shattered gaze lifted to meet my eyes. "I went to see what was wrong. She had blood on her hands."

I leaned against a porch column. "Blood?"

"She told me . . . she told me she cut herself on a sculpting blade. I brought her inside the studio, helped her clean up, and made sure she got home safely." He held my gaze. "I knew the whole time she'd been lying to me about the blood."

"How did you know for sure?"

"Darcy, there wasn't a scratch on her. The blood wasn't hers."

"Did you check on Miles?"

"Not right away. I drove Penelope home first. By the time I went back to the bunkhouse, the door was ajar. I went in. There was no sign of any blood. And no sign of Miles, either. He was gone."

Gone? Where? "What did you do?"

A tear leaked from the corner of his eye. "I closed the door and went home to wait for Penelope to come back to me. I've been waiting for thirty years. Today . . . today I realized she was never coming back. And that I needed to finally tell the truth."

Half an hour later, the side door opened, and Nick's voice came from the mudroom. "Darcy?"

"In here," I said in a stage whisper from the living room.

Starla and I were on the sectional, watching *Toy Story*.

We'd needed something light after the day we'd had.

Well, I was watching. Starla was sound asleep, thanks to a little magic from Cherise Goodwin. Starla's headache was history. For now. I had the feeling that as she sorted through her feelings for Vince it would return.

As soon as Harper heard what Steve had told me, she had set off to find Marcus, and Glinda had gone home. Once Starla had drifted off, and I kept shushing Archie and Mimi, they headed out to fill Ve in on what had happened today.

It had been a lot.

But despite all I'd learned, I still had no clue what had happened to Miles.

If Penelope had killed him, what had happened to his body in the time Steve had driven her home? Had she used the Special Delivery Spell to move Miles to Ve's garage?

"I went to the playhouse, but it was"—Nick stepped into the kitchen, took note of Starla and me huddled on the couch—"dark. What's happened?"

Higgins and Missy went to greet him as he set a briefcase on the island.

Trying not to disturb Starla, I dislodged Annie, who'd been snoozing on my lap, and carefully stood up and motioned for him to follow me.

Higgins took my warm spot on the couch, and Missy trotted behind Nick and me. In my office, I slid the doors closed behind us.

"What *didn't* happen?" I asked, holding up a hand. I began to tick off fingers. "Penelope has no powers. Vince and Oliver got into a fistfight. Dorothy is Vince's mother. Steve saw Penelope with blood on her hands. Thirty years ago," I amended. "Not today."

Nick held up both hands, palms out. "Hold up. Dorothy?"

"Long story," I said, dropping onto the sofa and drawing up my legs to tuck beneath me. "And I'll tell you, but first tell me what you learned from the ME's office."

He sat next to me and pushed his palms into his eyes. It had been a long day for us all. "The death has been ruled a homicide. The postmortem exam revealed that a small bone in Miles' neck was broken. The hyoid. It usually only breaks when someone is strangled to death."

"What about the blood in the bunkhouse?" And on Penelope's hands . . .

"No way to know," he said. "Could be related somehow. Maybe not. Now tell me what happened today."

I spent the next half hour filling him in. He just kept shaking his head as though he couldn't believe what he was hearing.

I said, "Are you going to go talk to Penelope?"

"I'll call, but any questioning will likely have to be tomorrow. There's no way she or Oliver would agree to meet with me without counsel present."

Counsel *would* be hard to come by this late. Unless they turned to Marcus, which was always a possibility. Especially if he dropped Ve as a client.

"It's amazing, isn't it? That one little amulet caused so much grief. Though, really, it wasn't the amulet's fault, was it?" I couldn't stop thinking about Miles. His life. His choices. And all the choices that had been made for him by his father.

"It seems to me that there are a lot of factors at play where Miles is concerned. And about that amulet . . ."

I didn't like the warning in his tone. "Oh no. What? Is the ME's office refusing to let us see it? Surely they understand that we won't—"

"Darcy," he cut me off. "They can't let us look at it because they don't have it. The amulet isn't part of Miles' belongings. There's no record of it."

I processed what he was saying. "So he wasn't wearing it when he died?"

Nick shook his head. "Again, I'm feeling as though this case is full of question marks," he said. "The more we dig, the more questions come up."

"We can't rule out Dorothy. If she was trying to keep Miles from learning about their baby's new family, she definitely had motive to kill him."

"We can't rule out *anyone* at this point," Nick said. "And if we don't get a big break soon, this cold case might stay cold forever."

Chapter Twenty-three

I awoke Sunday morning to bright sunshine streaming in the windows and Annie sleeping in Nick's spot on the bed. Sleepily, she looked at me, and I patted her head until her eyes closed again.

Leaning up on my elbow, I glanced at the clock on my nightstand. It was after eight in the morning. Way past my usual wake-up time. I yawned, stretched, grabbed my glasses from where they sat on a stack of three sketchbooks on my nightstand, and eyed the one made of leather, wishing I'd been able to find that four-leaf clover. In the grand scheme of life, it was such a silly thing to want back, but to me it represented so much more than a gift from Mimi.

It represented family.

My family.

I sighed and told myself to let it go. I had the family, and that was all that mattered. I lifted the charm bracelet Mimi and Nick had given me for my last birthday. Three charms dangled from the sterling silver band. Two of which Mimi had made at Wickedly Creative: a paintbrush to represent my art and a book to remind me that I'd first met Nick in front of Spellbound. Nick had bought a sun charm to add to the collection. He'd said it represented the light I brought into their lives.

Just remembering the moment filled me with such love that I sat there staring at the charms for a long moment, thanking my lucky stars.

And that clover.

Wherever it might be.

Annie stayed in bed as I brushed my teeth, pulled my hair into a high knot, put on my robe and slippers, and went in search of Nick. And for Higgins, too, since he hadn't greeted me with his usual slobbery morning kisses. I knelt on the window bench that looked out over the village square to see if Nick was walking the dogs on the green. And though the paths were busy, I didn't see them.

Down the hall, I peeked in on Mimi. She was sound asleep, her pillow over the top half of her face. Missy's tail wiggled when she spotted me, and she leaped off the bed and ran to the door.

I picked her up and let her give me slobbery morning kisses. In all honesty, I'd missed them. I couldn't fault her for loving Mimi the way she did, however. I knew the feeling. "I don't suppose you know where Nick and Higgins are?"

Her tail stopped wagging.

I took that as a no.

In the kitchen, I checked for a note from Nick, found none. No confetti, either, which told me that Annie hadn't stolen it before I had the chance to read it. The coffee carafe was full, and Nick had set a mug out for me. It was from the Witch's Brew and was in the shape of a cauldron. I checked the pets' food dishes. Annie's and Missy's were full—because Nick had left them on top of the washing machine. Higgins' bowl was on the floor and licked clean. I set Missy and her bowl on the floor, and she happily dug in.

I took my cup of coffee and opened the French doors leading out to the back patio. It was a beautiful, balmy morning. I breathed deeply, hoping to catch a whiff of the magical scent that I loved so much, but it wasn't in the air.

The bad juju was lingering, and I wished it would just go away already.

A moment later, a mourning dove landed before me, then disappeared into a glittery white cloud that dissipated, revealing my mother floating there. She was dressed in white jeans and a white cashmere sweater. Her hair flowed over shoulders, and I wanted to know her secret to keeping stray strands from sticking to her clothes. My hair tended to shed like crazy, which was why I shied away from white outfits.

"Good morning," Mom said as she kissed my cheek.

I gave her a hug and wondered if seeing her every morning was going to become a routine. I rather hoped so. "Coffee?"

She shook her head. "I can't stay. I have a meeting with Dorothy."

"How's Vince?" I asked as I walked over to the porch swing that hung from a trellis that ran along the back of the house. "I assume he's been told by now that he's a witch?"

She sat next to me, lifting her feet up to tuck beneath her. "He has. He's processing. It's a lot to take in."

He'd wanted so badly to know who his mother was, and also to be a witch. He'd gotten those wishes, but at what cost? "Has he met you?"

Missy toddled out, saw my mother, and picked up

her pace. With a not so graceful leap, she joined us on the swing. I patted her head, and she settled in between us.

"Not yet. Dorothy will take him under her wing for now. I'll be keeping in close touch with her."

"Lucky you."

She laughed and the sound filled my soul. "The luckiest."

The sun lit the dazzling leaves on the trees beyond the fence. The reds, oranges, and golds appeared to be glowing. We swayed. "Did Dorothy really not know that Vince was her son?"

"She hadn't a clue."

Birds chattered from the woods, and a squirrel ran along the fence pickets. "But you knew. . . ."

"Yes," she admitted.

"Did you know Dorothy had memory-cleansed Ve?"

"No. I wish I did. It would have saved me a lot of worry over the years about what had taken place that weekend."

"Seems dangerous, Crafters being able to cleanse anyone they please without consequence, yet I have to admit, it is handy at times." I'd had to use it myself more than once.

She smiled. "Whether to limit the usage of the memory cleanse is one of those things that has been brought up time and again at Coven of Seven gatherings. No one can ever agree on limitations, however, so it remains ungoverned for the most part."

I gave us a push with my slippered toe. "Who, exactly, is in the Coven of Seven?"

She patted my cheek. "Good try."

It had been.

We swung in silence for a few moments. I could have sat with her, like this, all day long.

I said, "Do you know if Miles' death involved Crafting at all?"

"Other than the Crafters themselves who are involved?"

"Other than."

"I'm not sure what you mean . . ."

"I've been thinking about what Steve Winstead told me last night. About Penelope and the blood on her hands. If she killed him, there's only one way she could have transferred his body to Ve's garage. The Special Delivery Spell. The Elder would know if she'd used it, wouldn't she? Since Penelope had used magic in a criminal manner?"

"A record of that would have been kept, yes. However, I've searched the archives for any infractions relating to Miles Babbage and there was only one, and it didn't relate to that particular spell."

One? Then I remembered. "Penelope's powers."

My mother nodded.

"She told Miles, didn't she?"

"Yes. From what I've discovered, she felt the need to be honest before they eloped."

"Was he memory-cleansed?"

"He was, shortly after Penelope was whisked away to Cape Cod."

We swayed for a moment before I said, "If Penelope killed Miles, his body should have been in the bunkhouse. But it was gone by the time Steve returned to check on him. . . . So what happened to the body?"

"Do you know for certain she killed him?"

"No, but she had a lot of blood on her hands, so something tragic happened."

"But according to the medical examiner Miles was strangled, wasn't he?"

I rubbed my temples. "Yes."

"Then how does the blood factor in?"

"I don't know . . . yet." I needed to speak with Penelope. The sooner the better. Right now all I had was Steve's word of what had happened that night, and suddenly I wondered if he'd been telling me the whole truth.

Glancing up at the sun as if judging its placement in the sky, Mom gave a little sigh. "I must be going. You'll figure out what happened to Miles, Darcy. I have faith in you."

At least one of us did. "Thanks."

"You know where to find me if you need me."

I did.

I waved and Missy barked as my mother disappeared into a glittery cloud. A mourning dove flew off, headed in the direction of the magical meadow where she lived.

As I watched her go, I wished I'd thought to ask her if she knew where Miles' amulet was. Even though it no longer held any power, it was still made of enchanted clay, so there was a chance she would be able to find its location. I'd trek into the woods later to ask her.

I sat on the bench a little while longer before heading back into the house to refill my coffee. Afterward, as I headed for my office to check voice mail, I happened to glance at the front door.

Looking in, Higgins had his nose pressed to the sidelight, and drool dripped down the glass. "What in the world?"

It sounded like someone knocking as his tail thumped the front porch. I peeked outside. Nick was in the grass on his hands and knees with a magnifying glass.

I pulled open the door and Higgins gave me a bath in kisses. I gave him lots of love and he soon turned his attention to Missy, who didn't tolerate his kisses nearly as well as I did.

I sat on the bottom step of the porch stairs, set my coffee next to me, and tightened the sash on my robe. Higgins and Missy darted about the yard, sniffing far corners. I stretched out my legs, felt my heart swell. Softly, I said, "How long have you been out here?"

"Not long," Nick said.

"Why are you doing this?"

He looked over at me. "I'm going to find it."

"Nick . . ."

"No, Darcy." He stood, stretched, and rolled his shoulders back as though he'd developed some serious kinks. He left the magnifying glass on the ground as he walked over to me and sat down. "It's too important to let go. I'll spend every morning for the rest of my life out here if I have to. I'll find it."

"You don't have to do that."

He thumbed a teardrop from the corner of my eye. "I want to do that. Just like I want to spend every day of the rest of my life here with you." He took hold of my hands, drew in a long deep breath, and said, "Darcy, will you—"

"Is this a private party?" Harper asked as she strolled up the walkway, carrying a paper sack from Spellbound. "If so, you need to work on your party clothes, Darcy. Godfrey would be appalled."

Nick stared at me, smiled. "So close."

I couldn't help smiling back. I leaned my forehead against his. "I love you."

"I love you, too." He gave me a kiss and went back to his search.

Harper's face scrunched in disgust. "You two . . ."

"Hush," I said. "You and Marcus are just as bad."

Something flashed in her eyes as she took Nick's spot next to me. Something bleak.

"What's wrong?" I asked. It was clear something was. "Is it Marcus?"

The bleakness turned to despair and Harper looked away, suddenly fascinated with the paint on the newel-post.

I bumped her with my shoulder. "Harper?"

When she finally looked back at me, I could tell she was trying hard to keep her emotions in check. "He, um, he . . ."

"What?"

Nick, I noticed, had stopped looking for that clover.

"He's just kind of torn up about what's going on with his parents. He's taking it hard. What Steve Winstead said about Penelope . . ." She swallowed. "He went to talk to her about it last night. He didn't come home."

Home. To Harper.

"Did he call?" Nick asked.

She nodded. "Eventually. After I left eight thousand messages on his phone. He gave me some excuse about needing to stay at his parents' house last night. I knew this would happen."

"What?" I asked.

Her eyes were clear and bright with moisture as she said, "That they would tear us apart. It's starting. I can feel it."

As much as I wanted to discount what she said, I couldn't. Harper's feelings weren't to be taken lightly. She knew things. I didn't know how. Maybe it was part of the magic that lived within *her*. And I couldn't help but recall the look of pity Oliver had given me yesterday as well. I said, "You won't let that happen."

She gave me a wan smile. "I know I'm stubborn, and I'm up for the fight, but I don't know if I can compete against them. They're his parents. . . ."

I took hold of her hand. "He loves you."

"I know he does. I just don't know if it's enough."

"It is," I insisted.

Holding my gaze, she nodded. But I could tell she didn't believe it.

She gave my hand a squeeze, then released it. "Enough about me. I brought you something. A housewarming gift." She handed me the bag.

"But the housewarming is next weekend," I said, trying to hand it back.

"I was going to save it, but as I watched Nick crawl around out here on his hands and knees for the past three hours, I thought he needed a break."

"Three hours?" I said to him. "You said 'not long.'"

He gave me an impish smile. "When you compare three hours to the rest of my life . . . it's not that long."

"Nick."

"Open the present," Harper said. "I'm getting a headache. I think Starla's migraine was contagious."

Yeah, they'd caught it from the men in their lives. I looked at my sister and immediately wanted to go find Marcus to shake some sense into him.

"Open it," she said, dragging the words out. "I have a store to open in two hours."

I laughed. "All right."

From the bag, I pulled out a heavy square-shaped package. It was badly gift wrapped in red paper, the corners bunched, the edges uneven. Harper never had the patience for wrapping, and I'd come to love the way she presented gifts. If I ever received one that looked professionally done, I'd have to question her wellness.

I slowly peeled back an edge.

"For the love," Harper wailed. "Today is not the day to torture me, Darcy."

Nick laughed and motioned to the present. "What is it?"

I quickly ripped off the rest of the paper, squeezing it into a ball. I tossed it at Harper.

I'd managed to tease a smile out of her.

It was a start.

The gift, which felt like a frame, had been double-wrapped. I was more careful as I undid the tissue paper protecting the glass. When I saw what Harper had framed, my mouth dropped. "How did you—"

"What is it?" Nick asked, standing up.

The frame had wooden trim, but its center was made up of two panes of glass. Sandwiched between them was a slightly frayed four-leaf clover.

Nick stared. "Is that what I think it is?"

Harper said, "Terry told Ve about seeing you and Nick out here, crawling around, and Ve told Mimi, and Mimi told me. I'd just read about this spell in one of my books, about finding lost objects, so I decided your little clover was a good way to test the spell." She nodded toward the iron fence that divided our yard from Terry's driveway. "It was snagged in the bushes in Terry's yard."

I hugged the frame, telling myself not to cry. If *I* started, *Harper* would start. I was afraid that she wouldn't be able to stop, thanks to the emotional roller coaster Marcus had her on. I might have been able to manage to keep my tears in check, but my voice cracked as I said, "I love it so much. And I can't thank you enough."

"Thank you, Harper," Nick added.

She stood up. "You're both welcome. That kind of keepsake should be treasured."

It should be. It *would* be.

Nick set his hands on his hips. "So three hours you let me crawl around?"

She smiled. A real smile. "It was kind of entertaining." She kissed our cheeks noisily, then strode off across the green.

I watched her go, a smile on my face as I wondered if she knew she'd given me *two* gifts this morning. The clover, of course . . .

But she'd cast a spell to find that clover.

She'd finally used her witchcraft, and knowing so was almost better than the gift of the clover.

But the more I thought about it, the more I realized that casting that spell wasn't so much a gift for me . . . as for herself.

Chapter Twenty-four

No sooner had Harper left than a new visitor appeared.

I was shocked down to my toes to see Penelope Debrowski lingering at the gate and could only wonder what would have happened if she and Harper had crossed paths.

Immediately I was glad it hadn't happened.

Penelope cleared her throat. "Is now a bad time?"

She wore wide-leg trousers, a floral blouse, and a cropped cardigan. Her hair had been pulled back into a tight bun at the nape of her neck. I rather missed her paint-splattered clothes.

"Not at all," Nick said as she came up the walkway.

"Hello, Darcy." She eyed my robe and slippers and lifted a judgmental eyebrow. Her attitude seemed to shift depending on which of her personalities was present.

Yesterday, it had been the Colorcrafter. She'd been friendly, relaxed.

Today she was in Lawcrafter mode. Stiff and starched.

It was interesting to watch, especially considering she had lost her powers. I supposed you could take the Craft out of the witch, but not the witch out of the Craft.

"Hi, Penelope." I picked up my coffee and sipped.

Nick leaned on the stair railing. "Should we go inside?"

Penelope shook her head. "If it's all right with you, I'd rather stay out here. It's such a beautiful day." She sat next to me on the steps. "Since I'll be locked up soon, I'd like to enjoy it as much as possible."

Nick said, "What do you mean? Locked up soon?"

"I have a few legal matters to wrap up this afternoon, but I wanted to let you know that I'll be turning myself in by evening."

"Turning yourself in for what?" I asked, though I had a good idea.

"I know Steve Winstead paid you a visit last night. Marcus told me." Her voice cracked when she added, "It's long past time the truth comes out. I'm tired of living in fear. I'm just . . . tired. It's my fault Miles Babbage is dead."

"Does Oliver know you're here?" Nick asked, his voice gentle.

"No." She watched a leaf fall from the tree in the front yard. "He's against my decision to turn myself in, but I'm done living a lie. I see what these last couple of days have done to Marcus and it makes me sick to my stomach. It should have never gotten to this point."

Nick said, "Why don't you start at the beginning?"

She picked at her manicure as she said, "Miles and I dated briefly before he dumped me for Dorothy, breaking my heart the first time. It took a little while to get over him, but soon enough I started dating Oliver and Steve. Oliver because my parents insisted and Steve because he was fun and fed my creative side. But I never forgot about Miles. He was . . ." She shook her head. "I loved him. It's that simple. And that complicated."

I thought about Miles not knowing how to love and realized the same was true. It was that simple. And that complicated.

Penelope shifted so the sun wasn't in her face and said, "I was at Wickedly Creative the next time I ran into Miles. I remember it so well; it was a Tuesday night that had been so very ordinary until he waltzed in like he hadn't been gone for a year. All it took was one look, and I fell for him all over again." She glanced between us. "And yes, I know some of that was the amulet, but some of it was just that I found him alluring. He was funny and kind and talented, and he had a wicked sense of humor. We picked up where we left off. The next day, he asked if I wanted to get married. I said yes. We planned to do it that weekend. . . . That's when he confessed about the amulet. And I told him I was a witch. We wanted to start the relationship on a clean slate."

Missy trotted up the steps and lay down on the porch, her head on her paws. Higgins, I noticed, was rolling in the grass . . . and over the daisies, flattening them.

"How'd he take the news that you were a witch?" I asked.

"Like it was no big deal," she said. "He said he'd always suspected there was more going on in this village than met the eye."

I imagined that using enchanted clay had heightened that awareness.

Penelope's voice hitched again as she said, "Then Steve and Miles got into that fight and all hell broke loose. My parents sent me off to Cape Cod."

"But you came back . . . ," Nick said.

"Two days later. I snuck out and called Oliver from a pay phone. He came down to the Cape and picked me up. I think the only reason he did was because he wanted to warn me that Miles and Ve had eloped the day before. He was trying to prepare me."

My coffee had gone cold. I set the mug aside. "How'd he know?"

Seemed I'd heard over and over again the past few days that only a few people had known about the elopement at the time it happened.

"On the day of the elopement, Ve had called him to see if he could work some magic on a Massachusetts marriage license. He refused and tried to talk her out of marrying Miles. She didn't listen and told him that they'd just go up to New Hampshire. I couldn't believe what I was hearing. I cried; I wailed. I was in hell. Absolute hell. I ranted and raved about Miles, that amulet, and about how I told Miles I was a witch."

I could only imagine the shock she had been in.

"When I got back to the village that Saturday afternoon, I called Miles at Ve's house. He agreed to meet me at the bunkhouse that night. When I finally saw him face-to-face, I wanted to know *why*. How could he plan to elope with me one minute, then run off with Ve the next? It had been only a *day* since my parents sent me away that they eloped. A single day."

My heart hurt for her. She'd honestly loved the man, and he'd just married another woman.

She clasped her hands together. "He tried to tell me that he didn't know what I was talking about. That we hadn't had any plans to marry and that he was sorry I was upset but he'd married Ve, and he wasn't going to break that vow, even though he did have feelings for me. I was so angry I couldn't even see straight," Penelope said, her cheeks flushing at the memory. "His ceramics tools were on the table, and I grabbed his sculpting knife and went after him. I slashed him a few times. When he jumped back from me, he lost his balance and fell, hitting his head on the coffee table. There was blood everywhere."

The mental image I conjured made me queasy. Queasier, I should say, because my stomach had already started to churn. All I could think about was what my mother had told me this morning. . . . About how Miles Babbage had been memory-cleansed after Penelope was sent away.

He'd been telling Penelope the truth that night—he had no memory of asking her to marry him.

It had been wiped out by magic.

I wasn't sure whether that knowledge would help her or hurt her more at this point, so I kept quiet for now. I'd seek the counsel of my mother on the matter.

Penelope went on, her voice dropping to a whisper. "He was alive when I left, still pleading his innocence." She blinked away tears. "With the way he was bleeding, I should have called for help."

Nick ran a hand through his hair, and then said, "I don't quite understand. If Miles was alive when you left, why do you think you were responsible for his death?"

I glanced at Nick, and his gaze met mine. We knew that Miles had died from strangulation, but did Penelope?

She glanced upward at the clear sky, then back down. "I didn't think so, not for many years. Not until I learned his skeleton had been found in Ve's garage. Until then, I simply believed that he had left town like he always did. That maybe he felt some remorse for what he did to me and had decided never to come back to the village ever again. Looking back, I believed it because I wanted to believe it. It was easier than believing he'd used me."

"But now?" I asked. "What do you think happened?"

She started wringing her hands, and then stopped and clasped them tightly. "I can only surmise that he'd bled to death the night I attacked him."

This still wasn't making sense to me. "But you never saw him again after you ran out of the bunkhouse, right?"

She nodded. "That's correct."

Nick said, "That doesn't explain how Miles ended up in Ve's garage."

Her eyes brimmed with tears. "No, it doesn't."

I fought the urge to put my arm around her. "How do you think Miles ended up in Ve's garage?"

She swiped tears from the corners of her eyes. "Steve."

"How so?" I asked.

"He was so worried that night when he saw the blood on my hands, and he pretended to believe what I told him about cutting myself."

"You knew he was pretending?" I asked.

"Oh, Darcy. It was so obvious I was lying. I took full advantage of how he felt for me." Her lower lip trembled until she pressed her lips firmly together. "He had to have gone back to the bunkhouse that night to clean up the mess . . . and"—she blinked away tears—"took care of Miles' body."

"You think Steve found Miles dead in the bunkhouse?" Nick asked. "And hid the body to cover for you?"

"I do," she said. "It's the only explanation I could come up with over the past couple of days that makes sense. Steve knew my dislike for Ve, and that's probably why he put the . . . body . . . where he did." She looked at me. "I'm sorry."

It wasn't me to whom she owed the apology, but Ve. And I suddenly wondered at Penelope's motives for coming here this morning. Was she here only to drag Steve down with her, since he'd ratted her out? Would she be here at all if he'd kept the secret about her blood-stained hands?

I doubted it.

Birds chirped as I asked, "Did you ever love him? Steve?"

"It's not as easy a question as you think. I hate that I hurt him. I hate it more than I can ever say. He's a good guy. We had fun. At one point I thought we could end up together."

"But?" I asked, hearing in her voice that there was one.

"But with Steve, it never felt quite right. I always felt as though he loved only the artsy side of me. And though I couldn't Lawcraft very well, it was still inside of me. I liked reading court cases. He didn't understand that. Then Miles happened. He turned my world upside down and inside out. I would have done anything for him. Left my family, walked away from this village."

Roots, Steve had said.

"How did you end up with Oliver?" I asked.

Torment filled her eyes. "I was so lost after what happened with Miles. Sick. Ashamed. Brokenhearted. I didn't want to live without him. The next day, I took a bunch of pills. Oliver was the one who found me, got me medical help. When I was better, I told him what happened and that I didn't know if I could go on. He visited me every day. And each day, I looked forward to his visits more and more. Oliver was the only one I could talk to, who knew everything. I realized that any-time I ever needed something, I went to Oliver. If I was sick, it was Oliver bringing me soup. If I had a fight with my parents, he was the one who brokered peace." She looked at me. "He knew I didn't love him when he asked me to marry him, but he thought it was best to get me out from under my parents' thumbs. I agreed. I felt like I owed it to him, after all he'd done for me."

As much as I couldn't imagine marrying someone under those circumstances, I could see why she had agreed to it.

There was still moisture in her eyes when she glanced at me. "About six months after we married, a funny thing happened. I looked at Oliver one day. I mean, truly looked at him, and it hit me like a ton of bricks that he loved me. Truly loved me. Both sides of me. He'd seen it all. I fell hard after that."

I believed it. I'd seen the way they looked at each other.

"I wish . . . ," she began.

My nerves danced as I readied to cast a spell.

Then she shook her head. "If only Miles had never come into my life . . ."

A warm breeze blew, loosening more leaves from their branches. They floated peacefully to the ground, and I wondered what would have happened if she'd actually made that wish. How so many lives would have been different.

"I'm sorry to do this, Penelope," Nick said, "but I just have a couple more questions about what happened with Miles."

A shudder went through her. "Go ahead."

"If I have this right, you said you slashed Miles, he fell and hit his head, and that you ran out."

Her chin lifted. "That's right."

He nodded. "What did you do with the sculpting knife?"

"I left it on the table with all the other sculpting tools."

"You used no other weapons?" he asked, fishing. "Another ceramics tool? Your hands, even?"

"No. Just the knife. And those wounds were only

superficial. It had to be the fall that killed him." She winced. "He probably cracked his skull. The blood . . ."

My stomach ached. Head wounds were notorious for bleeding copiously.

"What about the amulet?" he asked.

"The amulet?" she repeated. "What about it?"

He shoved his hands in his pockets. "Was Miles wearing it?"

"He was always wearing it. Why?"

"Are you certain he was wearing it that night?" he asked.

"Positive," she said. "I remember asking him if Ve knew about it. Why does the amulet matter at all?"

I said, "The amulet is missing. It wasn't found with Miles' body."

She didn't move a muscle, but something shifted in her eyes, and I figured she believed Steve had taken the amulet.

Had he been lying to Glinda and me about not knowing of its existence?

If so, he was an excellent liar.

"I don't know where it is," she said, then glanced at her watch. "I should get going. I have a lot to do before this afternoon. Will you be at the police station?"

"I'll be there," he said. "But, Penelope, I'm not sure anything much will happen other than taking your statement."

"Why?" she asked. "I need to take responsibility for what happened."

"The thing is," Nick said, "I don't think you had anything to do with Miles' death, not physically anyway."

The breeze ruffled her bangs as her forehead furrowed. "I don't understand. It's my fault he fell and hit his head. . . ."

"That might be true, but his official cause of death

is strangulation." He explained the medical examiner's findings and what it all meant.

"I don't understand," she finally said, shaking her head.

"You said he was alive when you left the bunk-house . . . ," Nick began.

"He was, but . . ." She stared at Nick for a long moment, then suddenly stood up. "I need to go."

Although she didn't run, she moved at a fast clip across the village green. We watched as she knocked on the door of the Trimmed Wick. The shop wasn't due to open for another couple of hours, so it was no surprise no one answered the knock. After a moment, she turned away and rushed off in the direction of her house.

I said, "She was looking for Steve, but he's probably at Wickedly Creative. He teaches a morning class there on the weekends."

Nick nodded. "I want to talk to him, too, and also check the bunkhouse for that knife. Do you want to come with me?"

I jumped up. "Did you even have to ask?"

He laughed. "Well, go get changed. If we hurry, we'll be back before Mimi gets up."

Chapter Twenty-five

Fifteen minutes later, we walked behind Wickedly Creative, traipsing through the grass on the way to the bunkhouse.

We'd had no luck tracking down Steve Winstead; George and Cora weren't expecting him at the studio for another fifteen minutes. We decided to bide our time by looking at the bunkhouse.

Nick had changed into his uniform, but he wanted to question Steve informally before bringing him to the police station.

I kept thinking about that wish Penelope almost made about Miles never coming into her life.

If he hadn't, there was a chance Steve would have had his happily ever after, after all.

And it was likely she wouldn't have married Oliver. There would be no Marcus.

Destiny.

My mother had spoken of it, referring to Vince. But it was applicable here, too.

This had been Penelope's journey, and altering it with a wish would have drastically changed the lives of so many.

Including Harper's.

I shuddered at the thought of her not having Marcus in her life and wondered if the wish would have even been allowed by the Elder.

She said we weren't to interfere with destiny. . . .

"You okay?" Nick asked, stopping to look at me.

"I'm all right." I looked down. "This case is getting to me a little bit."

"Me, too."

We started walking again, and as we strode through a clump of clover, I stopped again. The clover . . .

"What is it?" Nick asked.

"I think I know how we can find that amulet." I pointed downward.

"You want to look for a four-leaf clover?"

I laughed. "Not the clover specifically. Harper's spell. It's how she found our clover. She said it could be used to find lost objects, right? We use that spell, Bibbidi-Bobbidi-Boo, we know who has the amulet."

He said dryly, "Bibbidi-Bobbidi-Boo?"

"Sorry. *Cinderella*'s been on my mind since Archie complained about cleaning up popcorn."

He ran a hand through his hair. "I'm not sure I want to know that story."

"Oh, but it's a good one. Lots of theatrics."

Grinning, he said, "With Archie, I wouldn't expect it any other way. You can tell me later. We'll stop by Spellbound on the way home to see Harper about that spell."

Home.

I liked the sound of that very much.

Nick took down the yellow police tape crisscrossing the door of the bunkhouse, handed me a pair of gloves, and pulled open the door.

The bunkhouse didn't look all that different from the day before except it was a lot dustier. Fingerprint powder. I imagined after thirty years it had been quite the task to collect all of them.

Penelope's paintings had been unwrapped once again, and I was grateful it was the bird painting facing out from the stack.

I poked around a bit but didn't see anything I hadn't yesterday. I watched Nick over his shoulder as he sorted through ceramics tools. He held up the only one that looked as though it could do damage to someone. It was spotless. If it ever had blood on it, it had been thoroughly cleaned.

I heard a soft tap at the front door and turned to see Marcus stick his head in the doorway.

"Marcus, hi," I said, instantly worried about his pasty appearance. He didn't look well at all.

"Sorry to bother you," he said solemnly.

Nick leaned out of the bathroom. "Something wrong?"

Marcus' voice sounded as though it was being dragged over hot coals. "I just left my mom at my office. She said she thought I'd be able to find you here since she told you about the knife she used . . . that night."

Anguish shone in his eyes, and I knew that if Harper could see him right here, right now, she would have understood why he'd stayed the night with his parents.

"She's still planning on going to the police station this afternoon," he told Nick. "She wants the truth out, no matter what that truth turns out to be. She said she owed that much to Vince, since it looks like Miles was his father. Do you think she'll face any charges?"

Nick said, "I'm not sure. The case isn't close to being closed yet."

Marcus nodded. "I'll be representing her, so I'll be with her as well."

Nick nodded, and I wondered if this meant Ve was off the hook altogether. I hoped so.

Marcus cleared his throat and looked around. "My mother wanted to see if I could take her paintings home . . . before they're stowed away in an evidence locker."

Nick looked like he was battling his inner policeman. Finally he said, "Go ahead. If I need them again, I know where to find them."

"Thanks, Nick."

As he crouched to gather them up, I nearly jumped out of my skin when the front door suddenly slammed closed.

Had the wind slammed it? I didn't think so. There was no wind today.

That slamming was quickly followed by another sound, a loud clunking. Very unnatural clunking.

Marcus rushed to the door. Pushed. "It's stuck."

Nick gave it a shove as well, but it remained shut. He then ran at the door, kicked it. It didn't budge.

"Maybe if we all try at once?" I said, trying not to panic because suddenly the bad juju in the air was suffocating.

I jumped again when something hurtled through the kitchen window. A rock. It was quickly followed by a bottle that smashed when it hit the closet door. The scent of paint thinner filled the air.

Another rocked hurtled through the window, this one wrapped in a cloth that was on fire.

The kitchen ignited instantly.

Now I panicked.

All three of us rammed the door. Using shoulders, kicking. Anything we could think of. It wouldn't budge.

Smoke plumed, easily filling the small room.

The kitchen window was the only possible way out.

"Stay here and keep low," Nick said, edging that way. "I'm going to jump out the window and get this door open."

Coughing, I pulled him back. "No, don't go."

"Darcy, I have to."

Tears gathered in my eyes. I knew it was the only way, but I didn't want to let go of him. I tried not to think of Mimi. Or Harper. Or anyone. I finally nodded. "Be careful."

"Wait, wait!" Marcus called.

"What is it?" Nick asked.

In the growing darkness, I saw Marcus flash a smile. "I wish we were outside."

I could have kissed him then and there. *"Wish I might, wish I may, grant this wish without delay."* I cast the spell by blinking twice, and suddenly we were outside, huddled together behind the bunkhouse.

"My mother's paintings!" Marcus surged to his feet and ran for the front door.

Nick went after him. "Marcus! Stop!"

I followed them, wishing he'd just *wished* for the paintings. As I rounded the front of the bunkhouse, I noticed people had started running out of the studio, rushing toward the fire. George was leading the pack.

Neither Nick nor Marcus was at the front of the small cottage. The front door was open wide and a couple of thick branches were on the ground. I realized they'd been used to brace the door, locking us inside.

"Nick!" I yelled into the building.

A moment later, he stumbled out, half carrying Marcus. Marcus had a tight grip on the soot-covered paintings. Two of them, at least. The nude had been left behind.

Covered in soot himself, Nick pulled me into a hug. It was then, as I looked over his shoulder, that I saw a figure step out from behind a tree in the woods. A chill went down my spine.

Dressed all in black, the man had some sort of towel draped over his head like a monk's hood. He knew immediately that he'd been spotted.

I grabbed Nick's hand and pulled. "There's someone in the woods."

Nick squinted and then sprinted into action. I followed him. "Who was it?" Nick yelled over his shoulder. "Could you see?"

I hurdled a log. "No. Just that it was a man. He's hiding his face with a towel."

The man ran ahead of us, getting away even though it didn't appear as though he was even moving that fast. I could hear the sound of water and realized we were near a creek. Swollen with rainwater, it appeared suddenly as we crested a hill. It had flooded the area, cutting off any effective means of escape.

The darkly dressed man doubled back, tried to forge deeper into the brush. He tripped and fell.

Nick surged after him. He, too, fell hard. He let out a gut-wrenching moan. I caught up to him and bent down. Breathing hard, I said, "Are you okay?"

Pain filled his eyes. "My ankle . . ."

I took a look at his left ankle and felt woozy. It had already ballooned, looking like he had a baseball under his skin. I tried to give him a reassuring smile. "It's nothing Cherise can't fix."

"I wish she was here."

"Me, too," I said. My gaze went to the man, who was not even ten feet away. It felt like a mile. The forest was thick with undergrowth. He stumbled again before gaining his feet. When he spotted a path not covered in water, he darted to the right. I stood up to go after him.

Nick tugged me back down. "Let him go."

"I can't. He tried to kill you in that fire."

"He tried to kill *you*, too, and I'm not going to let him have a second chance to do it again."

Anger built in me, that this person was going to get away with trying to kill us. My fury grew and grew until my skin practically sizzled with it. The man looked back as though wondering why he was no longer being followed, and I pounced on his hesitation.

I shot my arm out, made a circular motion with my hand. Three circles, counterclockwise. Just like Marcus and Andreus had done in Aunt Ve's kitchen. Then I made a fist and shot my fingers straight out.

A log lifted off the ground, tripping the man.

He fell with a jarring grunt, followed by a long moan.

I did the finger thing again, and a branch came down on his head for good measure.

Nick's eyes had gone wide. "Uh, Darcy?"

I kept an eye on the fallen man. "Yeah?"

"How'd you do that?" he asked, doing his own version of the finger move.

I kissed him quickly and stood up. "Old witches *can* learn new tricks. Andreus and Marcus taught me yesterday. Do you have your handcuffs on you?"

Wordlessly he handed them over. I rushed over to the form writhing on the forest floor and quickly pulled the man's hands behind his back and snapped the cuffs on him. I then tugged him into a sitting position.

The towel had fallen from the man's head, but I'd already known his identity.

I'd known the moment he'd darted to his right, as I'd seen him do the same maneuver just yesterday, cutting me off in order to get to his car.

Oliver Debrowski stared at me, his eyes filled with remorse beneath a cut over his left eyebrow. "I'm sorry," he said. "I didn't know what else to do."

I sat on the log I'd used to trip him, trying to catch my breath. When I heard a noise behind me, I turned to find Nick hobbling this way, using a branch as a makeshift crutch.

Quickly, he patted Oliver down, and when he got to his sock, he hesitated. A moment later, he pulled forth Miles' amulet. With a heavy sigh, Nick handed it to me.

I felt ashamed of Oliver and sorry for him at the same time.

He knew of the amulet's power because Penelope had told him during the ride home from Cape Cod, and he'd undoubtedly believed that for the past thirty years, that amulet was the only thing keeping his wife by his side.

He'd been wrong. So wrong.

"You tried to kill your own son?" Nick said, his disbelief loud and clear in his outraged tone. "Why would you do that?"

"Marcus?" Oliver blustered. "What are you talking about? I'd never hurt a hair on his head!"

"He was in the bunkhouse with us," I said as calmly as I could. "He came to pick up Penelope's paintings."

The color drained from Oliver's face, and he swayed. For a moment there, I thought he was going to pass out, but he soon steadied.

"Is he okay?" he whispered.

"He'll be fine," I said. At least he would be physically. Mentally, I wasn't so sure. Not after he found out what his father had done.

"No thanks to you," Nick snapped.

Oliver hung his head. "I didn't see him go in. I didn't know he was in there," he repeated.

As though that excused the behavior.

"It was you who strangled Miles, wasn't it?" I asked, having put two and two together after seeing that amulet.

His head snapped up. "How'd you . . ." He trailed off; then his eyes widened. "Does Penelope know Miles was strangled?"

"You haven't spoken to her since she paid us a visit this morning?" I asked.

His face drained of all remaining color. "No, I only saw her speaking with you in front of your house. Then I followed you both here. She knows . . . the truth?"

Nick said, "She thinks Steve killed Miles."

I had thought so, too. I sent silent apologies to him. "How'd you even come across Miles that night?"

It had to have been that night, sometime between when Penelope fled the bunkhouse and when Steve went back to it. According to Steve's account, the place had been spotless when he'd returned, no sign of any blood at all.

"I followed Penelope there. I didn't trust Miles and wanted to make sure she would be okay. I was watching and listening at the kitchen window and heard everything that happened inside. His denial of being engaged to her, her anger. Everything. After Penelope ran out, I went inside. . . . Miles was holding a washcloth to his head and cursing up a storm. He didn't even question why I was there. He just kept cursing and telling me Penelope was crazy."

Miles had most likely known who Oliver was because of Penelope. The memory-cleanse wouldn't have erased that knowledge. Not questioning *why* Oliver was there had been a mistake for which Miles had paid dearly.

"The more Miles told me Penelope was crazy, the angrier I became." Oliver's head dropped as he added, "I was blinded by fury and lunged at him to get him to shut up. I didn't even realize what I'd done until Miles was on the floor, not breathing."

He might not have intended to kill Miles, but getting rid of him had eliminated a lot of Oliver's problems, especially where Penelope was concerned.

"I panicked. I quickly wrapped him in a rug, used a little magic to clean up the mess, and carried him through the woods to my car."

My stomach rolled as I asked, "Why did you put Miles' body in Ve's garage? Is it because Penelope never liked Ve? Why not just bury Miles in the woods?"

He shook his head. "How Penelope felt about Ve had nothing to do with it. It was simply because Ve was the most obvious person to use as a scapegoat, since she'd just married a man she barely knew. I never dreamed it would take this long to find the remains, but I knew eventually they'd be found."

"You *wanted* them to be found?" I asked.

"As much as I hated Miles, I didn't want a question mark to continually hang over the heads of the people who would wonder what happened to him or fear his return."

People like Ve or Dorothy. George. Steve. Maybe even Vince.

That plan, however, had backfired.

Tears built in his eyes. "Penelope came to me this morning and told me that she was going to turn herself in for her perceived role in Miles' death. I thought I'd talked her out of it, so I panicked when I saw her speaking to both of you earlier, when I was on my way to the Witch's Brew. All I could think was if I could silence the two of you, then get Penelope out of town . . . I followed you here and when I saw you go into the bunkhouse, I saw my chance. I broke in to the empty bunkhouse next door and grabbed supplies. . . ."

Silence.

He meant *murder.*

I shivered.

Voices rose from behind us. "Darcy!" George Chadwick called out. "Nick!"

"Over here!" Nick yelled back.

"She's going to hate me now," Oliver said quietly.

"Doubtful. Penelope loves you," I said unable to hide the revulsion I suddenly felt for him. "That's not going to change."

Oliver's voice rose in despair. He motioned to the amulet in my hand. "She only loves me because of that."

I shook my head. "The charm on this amulet died with Miles, Oliver. Penelope was with you because she wanted to be with you."

He studied my face, looking for the truth. He must have found it, because he suddenly dropped his chin to his chest and started sobbing.

George and Marcus thundered through the dense brush. Several police officers jogged behind. Nick stood and hopped over to talk with them.

"Dad!" Marcus yelled when he spotted his father. His gaze shot to me. "Why is he handcuffed?"

I held up the amulet by way of explanation. He was smart; he'd know what it represented.

His eyes flared with anguish; then he sank to his knees in front of his father. "Don't say anything else, okay, Dad?" His voice broke. "Nothing else, do you hear me?"

I couldn't help but think of Harper and how this was going to affect her and her relationship with Marcus. The more I thought about it, the more my stomach hurt.

George put his arm around me. "Come on, Darcy; let's get you back to the studio."

Nick joined us. We left Marcus and Oliver in the care of the police officers. It was a quiet walk back, George helping Nick navigate the woods and me lost in my thoughts.

When we emerged from the woods, Wickedly Creative was swarming with emergency personnel, including firefighters, who were still working to put out the flames on the bunkhouse. All that remained at this point was its slate shell.

In the distance, I spotted Steve Winstead, covered in dark gray soot. He was carrying a charred painting into the art studio. I realized it was Penelope's nude. He glanced back and saw me watching him. He gave me a nod, then turned and went inside. I didn't try to stop him.

Nick waved off treatment from the paramedics and put his arm around me. "If we hurry, we might be able to make it home and clean ourselves up before Mimi wakes up and hears what's happened from someone else."

There was that word again. *Home.*

I gave him a hug, so grateful to be able to wrap my arms around him. So grateful for the man that he was, full of love and honor and integrity. I glanced at his swollen foot, then whispered in his ear. "I'll race ya."

Chapter Twenty-six

The housewarming was in full swing Saturday afternoon when I sat next to Starla in the courtyard. Flames crackled in the stone fire pit, and she held a twig with an impaled marshmallow over the heat.

I loved seeing all my friends here, celebrating what this house meant to me, Nick, and Mimi.

The living room and kitchen were full of people I'd come to know and love, including Cherise, Colleen and Angela Curtis, Godfrey, and Ve, and even Andreus. Like pros, Pepe and Mrs. P were dodging the mortals, who didn't even bat an eyelash that Archie was singing karaoke along with Mimi, Hank, Terry, and Evan on the other side of the patio. And be still my heart, those Elvis look-alikes could even *sing* like the King of Rock and Roll.

"They're impressive," I said, motioning toward them as I rammed a marshmallow onto a stick.

"Seriously. They could go on the road. I'd buy tickets."

"Me, too."

Starla pulled off her marshmallow and stuck it in her mouth while looking over my shoulder, into the house.

"He's not here yet," I said, knowing she was looking for Vince.

Her gaze met mine. "Did he say for sure he's coming?"

"When I ran into him at the Witch's Brew yesterday, he told me he would be here."

It had been an awkward meeting, but I was determined to still be a friend to him. Maybe more now that I knew he was Dorothy's son. He was going to need all the friends he could get.

"I hope he does. I want us to be friends," she said, as though reading my mind.

"Just friends?" I asked, turning my stick just so. "Even now that you don't have to keep any secrets?"

The last I heard she was still thinking about her relationship with him. Wondering if she could, somehow, make it work.

She bit her lip. "Maybe even more now. When I found out, I was shocked of course . . . but it made me finally realize I'd been making excuses."

"How so?"

"For the past few months I've blamed my lack of romantic feelings for him on keeping this big secret from him. Because it's hard to get close to someone when you're keeping a secret that big, you know?"

I nodded and turned my marshmallow.

"But now that he's . . . and I don't have to keep the secret . . . the feelings still aren't there. They're just not there. I probably stayed too long in the relationship because of the secret, telling myself it was the only reason the relationship wasn't working. I should have gotten out sooner, but I don't like hurting anyone."

"I know you don't."

She wrinkled her nose. "I hurt him."

"Relationships that don't work out always hurt. But if it's not working, it's not working. Staying would have hurt worse in the long run. For both of you."

She jabbed another marshmallow onto her twig. "I know you're right. I just hope he'll forgive me one day."

I pulled my marshmallow from the fire and waited for it to cool a bit before I popped it into my mouth. Gooeyness oozed onto my fingers. "I hope you'll forgive *yourself* one day. You didn't do anything wrong."

Tears brimmed on her lashes. "Thanks, Darcy."

"Anytime."

We listened to Mimi belt out Abba's "Dancing Queen" and clapped as she finished the song with gusto.

"By the way," Starla said. "I've been thinking about it, and I believe I'm the reason Miles' body was found."

I froze. "What? Why do you think that?"

"As you know, it was Vince's birthday last week, and he made a wish on his cake candles. When I asked him what he wished for, at first he wouldn't say. Then he finally said he wished that he would finally learn the answers to some of the questions he'd been seeking. It was a vague wish, but he phrased it properly, so I cast the wish spell. I didn't think much more about it until his background came to light. If one of those questions was where Miles Babbage was . . ."

Then it made perfect sense that we had found Miles' body when we did, and it explained the timing I'd been questioning.

"I'm just sorry the wish brought with it such heartache for others, and that it almost got you killed."

"The wish didn't do that. Oliver did that."

"But still," she said softly.

I said, "Remember what I said about forgiving yourself?"

"Yeah, yeah." She smiled wanly.

I held up my sticky fingers. "I need to grab a napkin. Do you need one?"

She licked her fingers clean. "Nope."

I laughed and left her loading two marshmallows onto her stick. There was nothing like warm marshmallowy goodness to ease a troubled soul.

The French doors were wide-open, letting the music float through the house. I smiled as I spotted the framed clover on the mantel next to the acorn and little white bird. I washed my hands and grabbed a napkin. Nick was listening to Godfrey and Ve tout the merits of roasting walnuts versus leaving them raw when baking.

"Who knew?" Nick whispered to me. Cherise had fixed his ankle, as good as new. Sometimes it was wonderful to have magical friends.

Most of the time, in fact.

Smiling, I leaned up and pressed a kiss to his cheek. "I hope you're taking notes."

He pulled a notepad from his pocket. "Got some paper right here."

"No, really, what's the paper—" I was cut off by the pealing doorbell. "I'll get that."

"Good. I've got notes to take."

I smiled as I headed toward the front door. I happened to glance upward on my way, and through the spindles of the overlook, I barely made out Harper sitting all alone in the reading nook.

My heart hurt for her.

Marcus had moved back to his parents' house to focus his attention solely on Oliver's future trial. No charges had been filed against Penelope and wouldn't be since the statute of limitations on Miles' assault had long since expired, but Oliver was sitting in jail, his bail denied. They all had a long road ahead of them. One that Marcus apparently wanted to travel alone.

He would return to Harper. I was sure of it. I just hoped for her sake it was sooner rather than later.

As soon as I let in the new guests, I'd bring her a cupcake and sit with her awhile. See if she wanted to talk. And if not, I'd just hold her hand and trace hearts in her palm like I used to do when she was little.

I peeked through the sidelight on the door and smiled when I saw who'd arrived. "It's good to see you," I said when I pulled open the door. "I wasn't sure you'd come after . . . well, after everything that's happened this week."

"We wouldn't miss it," Glinda said. "Well, okay. We did think about skipping. But only for a minute. Life goes on. Might as well get all the questions over with, right?"

"I'm glad you're here," I said again, meaning it. "Come on in."

Tall and dark haired, Liam held out a cake plate. Under a domed glass sat a mouthwatering-looking coconut cake. "I made it myself."

"Is it poisoned?"

"Of course it is," he said with a twinkle in his blue eyes. He headed off to the kitchen.

Glinda lingered behind. I said, "He's cute, he's artsy, he bakes, and he clearly adores you. . . ."

A blush reddened her cheeks. "He's pretty amazing. I'm not sure I deserve him."

I frowned. "Why not?"

"I'm not the easiest to live with."

"I'm shocked! Shocked, I tell you."

She laughed. "I'm trying, though. That has to count for something."

"It counts for everything."

She held out a package carefully wrapped in muslin and tied with a twine bow. "For you. A housewarming gift."

"It's not another dead plant, is it?" I joked. She'd given me one when I first bought the place.

She cracked a smile. "Not this time."

I pulled the twine, and the muslin fell open, revealing a beautifully handmade besom, about three feet long. I gently touched the carved ash handle, the birch bristles. "You made this?"

She nodded. "It'll offer protection to keep evil from coming inside the house . . . and also it aids with fertility."

My eyebrows shot up at that last part.

"Just in case . . . you know," she stammered. "It's *tradition*."

I laughed. "It's gorgeous." I walked over to the blank wall next to the door. I held it above the basket that held all my house blessings. "Should I hang it here?"

"Perfect. Just make sure it's upright. And, Darcy?"

"Yeah?"

"Thanks for not making a joke about evil coming in when I came in. . . ."

"Cross my heart, I didn't even think it."

"We've come a long way."

"Yeah, we have." I closed the front door. "How are things on the home front? With, you know . . ."

"Weird," she said after a moment. "It's going to take some getting used to."

"I imagine so." I linked arms with her. "Well, come on in. Let's get that inquisition over with, so you can enjoy the party. Archie's in grand form if you're the karaoke type."

She laughed. "I can do a mean Aretha Franklin."

"Evan will be recruiting you for the stage in no time."

"He'll be wasting his breath. I'll leave the theater to my mother."

Dorothy was still complaining about being cast as

one of the nuns in the play instead of Maria. I thought it absolutely hysterical myself.

I left Glinda with Liam, who'd joined in the walnut conversation. I cut two pieces of the coconut cake—which to my delight had raspberry and cream filling—and set them on a plate. Once I found the right drawer, I grabbed two forks and headed for the stairs to see Harper.

On my way past the front door, I happened to glance outside and saw Vince standing at the front gate. I watched him for a moment step forward, then backward. He crossed the street, and I thought he was leaving until he stopped, turned around. He took another step forward, then back again.

I set the plate in my office so none of the pets would steal the cake, and grabbed my pea coat from the hat tree and went out to see what was going on.

Vince didn't look all that surprised to see me as I stepped up next to him. We stood near Mrs. P's bench and the beautiful birch tree that was raining yellow leaves onto its seat. I heard a coo come from the upper branches and knew I wasn't having this conversation with Vince alone.

My mother was here. I'd sensed her even before she'd given me the vocal heads-up.

As I was learning, the magic within was extremely powerful.

Vince looked . . . shell-shocked. Bloodshot eyes watched me from behind his glasses. One of his eyes was still bruised from the fight last weekend. Stubble covered his cheeks and chin, and his hair was disheveled.

"Vince, why don't you come on inside?"

He slid a look my way. "What do you think I've been trying to do, Darcy?"

I held out my hand. "Come with me. We'll go together."

He held out his hand to take mine but abruptly pulled it back, cradling it like it had been injured.

"I don't understand," he said, shaking his head.

That made two of us. "What's going on?"

"Every time I get near your house I get this little buzz, like I'm a dog wearing a shock collar. The closer I get, the more jarring the buzz. And I just felt it when I reached for your hand."

I glanced back at the house, then at my hand, then at him.

Realization hit me like a sucker punch, bringing with it a deep sadness. I reached into my coat pocket, pulled out the lone acorn I had left in there. I tossed it to him. "Catch!"

He snatched the nut out of the air and dropped it almost as quickly as he caught it. "What the hell?"

"You're practicing sorcery," I said. It wasn't a question.

His blue eyes darkened. "So?"

"You don't need it," I said, hearing the pleading tone in my voice. "You have the Craft, Vince."

He jammed the toe of his shoe into the grass, kicked up a divot. "Right. The *Craft*," he sneered. "I have the power to make brooms. Whoopty-freakin'-do."

I thought of the beautiful besom Glinda had just gifted me, and I wanted to hit him upside the head with it. He was being shortsighted.

"With sorcery I could have endless power," he said, throwing his arms wide. "I could make Starla love me again. I could make the whole village love me."

"Is that what you want? To be loved?"

He narrowed his gaze. "No. Love is for the weak," he spat. "I want power."

I shoved fisted hands into my coat pockets. "Dark magic isn't the way to go."

He kicked up another divot. "Maybe. Maybe not."

"I know you're hurting, Vince, but—"

"Don't tell me what *you* know, Darcy. I wasted more than a year on Starla."

I tipped my head. "Do you really think it's wasted time? You loved her. . . ."

He flicked me a wry look. "It wasn't her who told me about the Craft, now, was it?"

My jaw jutted. It sounded to me like maybe Starla had been right about his using her. I hated thinking it might be true. It made me feel sick that she was inside worried about *hurting his feelings* when he might not have cared about her after all. I wanted desperately to believe that he was just talking in anger. He'd been through a lot this past week.

But I wasn't sure.

Maybe he was more like his father than anyone thought and didn't know how to love . . .

I said, "I think you just need some time. To process."

"You think so?" he replied sarcastically.

I didn't know what to say. I wanted to cut him some slack, but I didn't like him very much right at the moment.

He motioned to the ground. "What's with the acorns?"

"Witches use them for protection from things like dark magic. Among other stuff. You're new to the Craft. You have a lot to learn. You have more abilities than just Broomcrafting, Vince. Spells, charms. You don't need the dark stuff."

He glanced toward my house and kicked up another divot but said nothing.

"You should talk to the Elder," I said.

"Yeah," he mumbled. "Maybe." Then he added, "Thanks for the invite, but I'm just going to go. See ya around."

He spun around and walked off.

"Vince!" I called out.

He looked over his shoulder.

My heart was in my throat when I asked, "Did you love her at all?"

Raw emotion flashed across his face for the briefest moment, and I saw the truth before he shuttered it behind a steely glare.

"It doesn't really matter now, does it?" he said and strode off.

I watched him walk away, then replaced the three divots. I sat on Mrs. P's bench and tried to digest the conversation I'd just had.

"He loved her."

"Yes, he did." My mother's voice came from the branches above my head. "Until the quest to learn dark magic took over. It became his new love and Starla was cast aside."

I didn't dare look upward for fear of giving away her position. This way to any onlookers who happened by I would simply look like I was talking to myself.

"This sorcery . . . ," I began.

"He's hurt and angry and confused," she said. "I'll talk to Dorothy. We'll work together to get this sorted. He'll come around."

I picked up the acorn from where it had fallen. I was glad my mother sounded so confident about Vince, because I wasn't. I dropped the acorn back in my pocket.

At all.

Chapter Twenty-seven

It had been a busy Sunday. The morning had been spent cleaning up after the housewarming. I'd told only Nick of my unsettling conversation with Vince, and he agreed that the situation with him was probably going to get worse before it got better.

The rest of the day I'd helped Nick and Mimi finish packing up their house, which was now officially on the market. We probably loaded and unloaded Nick's truck a dozen times, and would need to do it probably a dozen times more to fully empty the place. Our weekends were booked for the foreseeable future, which was a good thing because it excused me from helping with the yard sale Ve had planned for next weekend. She was determined to get that space cleaned out and smudged, to exorcise all its lingering bad memories.

I yawned and stretched, feeling knots in my back. Moving was exhausting work, but it had been worth every minute of it. Nick and Mimi had decided to head back to their old house to gather one last load of boxes for the night, and I'd stayed behind to feed Annie, Higgins, and Missy and to take the dogs for their nighttime walk around the square.

We'd just come back, and I'd fully expected to find Nick and Mimi here unloading their latest haul, but instead I found two notes beneath a dandelion paperweight on the kitchen island. The missives were being guarded by Annie.

Or perhaps she was lying in wait.

Annie loved making confetti.

The paperweight had been a good idea.

One note was from Mimi: *Went to Aunt Ve's for ice cream and to watch a movie. Be home later.* At the bottom, she'd signed an *M* inside a heart shape. Under that she added a PS: *We need to add ice cream to the grocery list ASAP. Chocolate chip. Double chocolate chunk. Anything chocolate.*

My first thought was that it was a bit late for a movie on a school night, but Mimi was thirteen and . . .

That's when my second thought hit, hard and powerful.

She'd written *home.*

She'd be *home* later.

I glanced around. This was now her home.

Our home.

Life was never going to be the same ever again.

And I couldn't have been happier about that.

Nick's note simply said *Meet me in front of Spellbound at 9:15.*

I looked at the furry faces watching me carefully. "Spellbound? What's this about?"

Not a single one answered me, though Higgins did slobber my hand. He slobbered everything, so I wasn't sure what it meant. Missy's stubby tail was wagging for

all it was worth, and she yapped happily. Annie's gaze
shifted to the piece of paper in my hand. She reached
a paw for it, and I quickly stuck the note in my pocket
and rubbed her head. "Nope. Not for you."

It was nine twelve, so I gave them all treats and told
them I'd be back soon. In the mudroom, I slipped on
my coat and my shoes and wondered why Nick had left
the note. Was Harper okay? Wouldn't she have called?
I knew she was having a rough time because of Marcus,
so my heart was in my throat as I hotfooted it across
the green.

As I jogged, I took a moment to breathe in that magical smell I loved so much. To appreciate it. The scent
seemed especially strong tonight as the faux gaslights
that lined the village sidewalks and the twinkle lights
twined through tree branches cast a soft glow upon the
village.

Moonbeams caught the colors of autumnal flowers
overflowing from tall planters that dotted the pathways.
It was a beautiful night, chilly but not too cold. Breezy
but not too windy.

Vibrantly colored leaves crunched under my feet as
I searched for answers as I neared Spellbound. The
storefront was dark, as were the windows of Harper's
apartment. My gaze settled on the manly silhouette
pacing in front of the shop.

"Is Harper okay?" I asked when I was close enough
for him to hear me. I noticed he'd showered. Damp hair
curled around his ears, and he smelled soapy fresh. He
wore jeans, a button-down, and a blazer. Definitely not
moving clothes.

Light thrown from a gaslight nearby lit his smile.
"She's fine. This isn't about Harper."

Utterly confused, I said, "Then what's it about? Apparently it's ice cream and movie night at Ve's, and I'm
sure we've only missed the opening cred—"

"It's about these," he said, cutting me off.

He reached into his blazer pocket and pulled out what looked like a small block of square notepaper. On closer inspection, it was just notes held together with a paper clip. A lot of notes.

"Recipes for toasted walnuts?" I teased.

He laughed. "No. That was just a ruse."

"What are they?" I reached for them, but he pulled them away.

I tipped my head in question, but he just kept on smiling.

I was starting to get a warm, mushy-gushy feeling in my stomach.

"Yesterday, at the housewarming party, I asked our guests to write down something they love about you." He held up the notes. "These are the results."

That mushy feeling bloomed into my chest. "When? How? Why?"

He ignored my questions. "This one is from Godfrey. He says, 'Everything. I love everything. Except her flip-flops. Those have to go.'"

He held it up and tears came unbidden to my eyes when I saw Godfrey's chicken-scratch scrawl. "Nick . . ."

He said, "This one is from Ve."

I blinked away tears. "I can't . . ."

He swallowed hard. "She says, 'Everything. Darcy is light and goodness and all that is right in this world. She owns a piece of my heart, always and forever, and now you will, too, Nick.'"

Tears spilled down my cheeks. He reached into his pants pocket and pulled out a handkerchief embroidered with tiny daisies and handed it to me.

I shot him a questioning glance.

Nick was not a handkerchief kind of guy. Daisies yes, handkerchiefs no.

"Pepe sent it for you. He thought you might need it."

Which only made the tears fall faster. "He's an intuitive kind of mouse."

"That he is." He held up a note. "This is from Archie via Terry: 'Darcy had me at hello.'"

I laughed. I loved that bird something fierce.

"From Harmony: 'Everything, of course, but especially her love of all creatures great and small and those slightly smelly from having been in a Dumpster . . .'"

"This one," Nick said, holding up the next note, "is from Glinda."

Smiling through tears, I said, "Oh no. I'm not sure I want to know. . . ."

"She says, 'Love? Let's not get crazy. But I do admire Darcy's ability to see the good in people who cannot see it in themselves.'"

Fresh tears filled my eyes.

"Starla says, 'Everything. Absolutely everything.'" He flipped to the next note. "This bundle is from Mimi."

It was three or four stapled pages, and my heart swelled.

"I'll let you read those on your own, or I might not get through this," he said, his voice strained. "Let's just say there are many, many things she loves about you."

The lump in my throat made it impossible to talk. I nodded.

"From Mrs. P and Pepe: '*Toutes les petites choses.* All the little things. Darcy *is* love.'"

I had to look away to just . . . catch my breath. My blurry eyes tried to focus on the flowers in the window box below Harper's display window, but the yellow geraniums and purple pansies blended together like something from an impressionist-style painting.

"From Terry: 'I consider Darcy to be the daughter Ve and I never had. I love her. If you hurt her, I will hurt you. Understood?'"

I couldn't help but sniffle and laugh at the same time as Nick read that one.

With a lifted eyebrow, he said, "Terry's kind of scary."

Which made me laugh harder.

"This one is from Evan. He says, 'Hello-o-o, everything! Simply, I love her.'"

I didn't know how much more of this I could take.

"From Harper . . ."

I set my hand on his. "I . . . Nick."

He took a step back and drew in a long, deep breath. "She says, 'Darcy already knows how much I love her. It's an indescribable love that can't truly be put into words. I think you know the feeling, Nick. I see it in your eyes when you look at her. For that, I love *you*, and I'm looking forward to the day when I become your sister, too. Welcome to our crazy family.'"

I had to sit down. There were no benches nearby, so I opted to sit on the curb. Nick sat next to me, his shoulder and leg touching mine as though we were connected.

I supposed we were. And had been for quite some time.

"You didn't have to do all this," I said, emotion cutting the words into shards.

"I didn't think so at first, either. Trust me—I tried asking you other ways, but I kept getting interrupted. By Vince, by Harper, by Terry . . . And I started thinking that maybe the universe was trying to tell me something. Because without them," he said, cupping the notes in his hands and lifting them up, "we wouldn't quite be us. They've shaped our relationship as much as we have, taught us lessons, helped us grow. . . . So I knew they had to be part of this."

This.

Nick was right. Absolutely right. The people in our

lives had helped shaped us. Loved us. Healed us. For Nick to think of including them tonight made me love him more than I ever dreamed possible.

He shifted sideways, to face me. "And if you didn't notice, the predominant trait that our friends love about you is *everything*. Just like I love everything about you. Your smile, your laugh, your kindness. I love the way you love Mimi. Oh God, the way you love her . . . I love that you don't mind Higgins' drool. I love the way when you're sleeping, you pull the covers up to your nose every . . . single . . . time. I even love that you try to talk to me when you're brushing your teeth. *Everything*. I love everything. Which is why I brought you back here, to where it all began on a stormy June night right about this time when we came upon each other right here at this doorway. . . ."

The memory was one I'd never forget. I'd been new in town, and I'd just come from a job acting as a tooth fairy that hadn't gone exactly as planned. I was running late for a town meeting . . . as was Nick.

It was the first time in such a long time that I'd felt *anything* for a man that it had taken me aback. It had scared me . . . and given me hope all at once.

He said, "I knew the moment I saw you standing there in your sparkles and tiara with that cautious look in your beautiful eyes that I could love you. It didn't take long for me to realize just how much. I can't imagine living the rest of my life without you by my side. Darcy Ann Merriweather, would you do me the honor of becoming my wife, of letting me love you for as long as I live? Longer, even . . ."

I'd tried to picture this moment a thousand times, maybe more. But I hadn't even come close to imagining the gift Nick had just given me. I wanted to tell him all the things I loved about *him*. The list was long. So long. But mostly I wanted to thank him for making me believe in love again. True love. The forever kind of love. But I couldn't find the words. They were trapped in a web of emotion in my throat. Later. I'd tell him later. I'd probably be talking his ear off all night long. I knew instinctively he wouldn't mind a bit.

I tried to pull myself together, but the knot in my throat just wouldn't let any words pass. I could barely swallow. Breathe. As he patiently waited for my answer, I couldn't even say "Yes, I'll marry you" like a normal person. I could only nod. And nod some more.

But Nick seemed to know what—and how—I was feeling. A smile stretched across his face as he set the notes he'd been holding on the ground behind us and reached into his inner coat pocket and pulled out a ring. He held my shaking hand tightly and slipped the ring on my finger.

As I gazed at the bright round diamond surrounded with smaller geometrically cut diamonds in a bezel setting, I almost started crying all over again when I realized what I was looking at. My chest ached but I managed to squeak out, "A starburst!"

"It reminded me of you when I saw it," Nick said, kissing my hand, "and I knew it had to be yours."

I threw my arms around him and held him tight. I felt like I could sit here with him all night. Holding him tight. Feeling his love. Feeling *our* love.

And breathing in that special magic in the air . . .

Across the village green, a little dog sat on the window bench in the master bedroom of her new home, watching the romantic scene in front of the bookshop unfold. Even without being able to hear the words, she could feel the emotion of the moment all the way down to her soul.

Next to her, the Elder sighed.

"It's everything we wanted, isn't it, Mel?" she asked.

"It's more than I ever dreamed when we collaborated to play matchmaker," Melina Sawyer replied. "Mimi is giddy, and nothing makes me happier than seeing her happy."

"How are you adjusting to living under the same roof as all three?" the Elder asked.

Melina shifted, suddenly uncomfortable. The Coven of Seven had denied her request to create a new Craft that would allow her to hop out of her canine form and into another at will. It had to be a unanimous vote, and there had been one holdout. Melina knew just the witch who'd denied her. It was no surprise, really.

"Mel?" the Elder asked, tenderness in her voice.

"The spell you gave me has been immensely helpful, but as you know, it leaves me drained."

"Adjustments are being made using your feedback. It's a new spell, so it will take time to work out all the kinks."

The spell allowed Mel's spirit form to lapse into a sleep state while her canine form remained awake. She'd been testing the spell these past few weeks and was slowly adjusting to its quirks. "I know, but . . ."

"But what?"

She looked at her friend, held her gaze. "I don't belong here. As much as I love Mimi and love being with her, this is Darcy and Nick and Mimi's house. Not mine." She drew in a deep breath. "I've made a decision."

The Elder tipped her head. "What is that?"

Mel told the Elder of the plan she'd devised. "It has to work. I believe it's the only way I can stay in the village and still be a big part of Mimi's life. What do you think?"

"I think it's the perfect resolution, but it could take some time to implement."

Mel laughed. "If there's one thing I have, it's time. I have all the time in the world."

The Elder smiled. "That you do."

Unless . . . No, she would not bring it up. No doubt it was already weighing on the Elder's mind. As if she didn't have enough to worry about with the Renewal looming, now she had to deal with Vince bringing sorcery into the village.

The fool had no idea that he could destroy the magical fabric that generations of witches had labored tirelessly to stitch.

Or perhaps he did.

It was a terrifying realization.

Mel did not envy the Elder one little bit.

The Elder's mind must have wandered to the same place as Mel's, because she said, "We're going to have quite the battle ahead of us, Mel. Especially if Harper doesn't . . ." She trailed off, shaking her head.

"She cast that spell, remember?"

The Elder nodded, then smiled weakly. "She did, but I fear her heart is not open to her birthright at this moment. It needs to be open to be fully receptive."

Melina sighed. She still couldn't believe that Marcus had walked away from Harper. If he were here now, she'd bite him. Hard. Harper had been making such progress. . . . "Can you not seek Darcy's help in this matter?"

"You know as well as I do that Harper has to do this on her own."

"There must be a loophole."

"No loopholes." She laughed, but it held no humor. "Trust me. I've looked."

Mel's gaze went to the dark windows above the bookshop. "Then we just need to trust the magic that's within Harper."

"Trust the magic," the Elder echoed, nodding. Then she solemnly added, "May it save us all."

Read on for an excerpt
from Heather Blake's

A POTION TO DIE FOR

Available now!

If there were a Wanted poster for witches, I was sure my freckled face would be on it.

Ducking behind a tree to catch my breath, I sucked in a deep lungful of humid air as I listened to the cries of the search party.

I didn't have much time before the frenzied mob would turn the corner and spot me, but I needed to take a rest or risk keeling over in the street.

It was times like these that I wished I were the kind of witch who had a broomstick. Then I could just fly off, safe and sound, and wouldn't be hiding behind a live oak, my hair sticking to its bark while my lungs were on fire.

But *noooo*. I had to be a healing witch from a long line of hoodoo practitioners (and one rogue voodoo-er, but no need to go into that this very moment). I was a love-potion expert, matchmaker, all-around relationship guru, and an unlikely medicine woman.

Fat lot of good all that did me right now.

In fact, my magic potions were why I was in this predicament in the first place.

I'd bet my life savings (which, admittedly, wasn't much) that my archnemesis, Delia Bell Barrows, had a broomstick. And though I had never before been envious of the black witch, I was feeling a stab of jealousy now.

Quickly glancing around, I suddenly hoped Delia lurked somewhere nearby—something she had been doing a lot of lately. I'd been trying my best to avoid a confrontation with her, but if she had a broomstick handy—and was willing to loan it to me—I would be more than willing to talk.

There were some things worth compromising principles for, obviously. Like a rabid mob.

But the brick-paved road, lined on both sides with tall shade trees, was deserted. If Delia was around, she had a good hiding spot. Smart, because there was a witch hunt going on in the streets of Hitching Post, Alabama.

And I was the hunted witch.

Again.

This really had to stop.

Ordinarily I would've ridden my bike, Bessie Blue, to work, but when I saw the crowd gathered on my curb that morning, I snuck out the back door. Unfortunately, someone had spotted me and the chase was on. I'd cut across to the next block over, then doubled back to my street. And now here I was, trying to catch my breath and hoping for a broomstick, of all things.

Pushing off from the tree, I spared a quick glance behind me as the crowd turned the corner.

"There she is!" someone shouted.

Heart pounding, I made a break for it. I jumped the rotting picket fence surrounding my aunt Marjoram's front yard, skipped over loose stepping-stones, brushed away overgrown shrubs, and then made a dash toward the back gate.

I nearly tripped as I tried to wade through a thigh-high weed patch, and heard the cackle of my aunt's voice.

"Carly Bell Hartwell, get your skinny ass out of my garden!"

Some garden. "Sorry, Aunt Marjie!" I yelled over my shoulder. "But they're after me."

"Again?" she shouted from the steps of her dilapidated deck.

The high-pitched cries of the crowd trying to find me carried easily in the quiet morning. "Mr. Dunwoody made his forecast."

"Land's end!" Marjie shouted. "I'll get my gun."

I didn't bother to try to talk my aunt out of it. The townsfolk would be safe enough—most knew better than to trespass in Marjie's yard. And if they blatantly ignored all the posted No Trespassing signs, they'd get what they deserved.

Just like those Birmingham lawyers who'd been sniffing around Marjie's place the past few weeks.

I didn't think those stuffed-shirt businessmen would be back anytime soon.

Shotgun blasts had that effect on city folk.

Taking a deep breath, I yanked open the wooden gate at the back of Marjie's property. Rusted hinges groaned in agony, and the brambles at my feet didn't want to give the gate an inch of swing, stubbornly digging their thorns into anything they could grab onto. Including my shins, which made me regret my choice of shorts over jeans that morning.

I yanked for all I was worth. The gate swung only a

foot, but it was all I needed. I wiggled through the narrow space. Safe on the sidewalk on the other side, I assessed the damage from the brambles (minimal), and wished I had a cell phone to call for backup.

Unfortunately, I didn't have a cell phone. No one in town did because there was no coverage, thanks to the surrounding mountains and the town's refusal to build an ugly cell-phone tower that would ruin the picturesque landscape. Except for a noisy few, we'd all embraced the quirk as a charming throwback to a simpler time. But right now, a cell would've been handy.

I headed for the town center, not having time to admire the sun-dappled view of the Appalachian foothills in the distance. I had lived in Hitching Post, Alabama— the wedding capital of the South—nearly my whole life, with only one brief, somewhat disastrous foray beyond its borders. I loved this town, but right now, I wished it were smaller. Much smaller. Like, a one-stoplight kind of place—because it seemed as if I'd been hotfooting it down side roads and back alleys for an hour now, even though it had been only ten minutes.

The heart of Hitching Post was made up of a large circle, nicknamed the Ring (very appropriate, considering it was a wedding town). In its charming middle was a grassy picnic park with twisting trails, big shade trees, flowers, and a gazebo smack-dab in its center. A wide cobblestone sidewalk (no roadways inside the Ring) connected the park to dozens of shops, offices, and restaurants.

Splintering outward from the Ring were parking areas, quaint neighborhoods, the scenic river walk, and the bread and butter of Hitching Post: the chapels, inns, and reception venues catering to the marriage crowd. People came from all over for quickie country weddings—more intimate and personal and less tacky than Vegas. Hitching Post looked postcard perfect, too, and was consistently named one of America's most beautiful small towns, which had a lot to do with the mountain backdrop, the river views, and all the effort the beautification committee expended to create the perfect idyllic Southern atmosphere.

Occasionally tossing looks over my shoulder as I stealthily entered the Ring, I zipped down the sidewalk toward Déjà Brew, the local coffee shop. Ordinarily I'd go in and visit with the shop owner, Jessamine Yadkin, pick up a muffin, linger over some coffee.

This morning, however, Jessa waited in the doorway of the shop with a to-go bag dangling from an outstretched arm. I grabbed it—kind of like a marathoner would snatch a cup of water—and kept on going. "Thanks, Jessa!"

"Run faster, Carly!" she yelled in her raspy, used-to-smoke-two-packs-a-day voice. "They're gaining on you!"

Run faster. Easy for her to say.

At this rate, I was going to need a defibrillator by the time I reached the safety of my store, the Little Shop of Potions. The crowd was gaining on me; I needed to pick up my pace.

Unfortunately, my shop was on the opposite side of the Ring from Déjà Brew. A good half mile at least if I followed the walkway; less if I cut diagonally across the picnic park and hurdled some shrubbery. The choice was a no-brainer. Thankfully, I had a head start. A small one, but it was enough.

Sweat dripped from my hairline as I dodged picnic tables and flower beds. Behind me, I heard pounding footsteps, along with hollers of "Carly! Carly!"

I ran at a dead sprint and finally my shop came fully into sight. The storefront was painted a dark purple with lavender trim, and the name of the shop was written in bold curlicue letters on the large picture window. Underneath was the shop's tagline: MIND, BODY, HEART, AND SOUL. Behind the glass, several vignettes featuring antique glass jars, mortars and pestles, apothecary scales, and weights I'd collected over the years filled the big display space.

At this point I should have felt nothing but utter relief. I was almost there. So . . . close.

But instead of relief, a new panic arose.

Because standing in front of my door was none other than Delia Bell Barrows.

I could hardly believe it. *Now* she showed up.

I grabbed the store key from my pocket and held it at the ready. "Out of the way, Delia!"

Delia stood firm, neck to toe in black—from her cape to her toenails, which stuck out from a pair of black patent flip-flops that were decorated with a skull and crossbones. A little black dog, tucked like Toto into the basket that hung from Delia's forearm, barked.

The dog and the basket were new. The cape, all the black, and the skull-and-crossbones fascination were not.

"I need to talk to you, Carly," Delia said. "Right now."

I hip-checked Delia out of the way, and the dog yapped again. Sticking the key into the lock, I said, "You're going to have to wait. Like everyone else." I threw a nod over my shoulder.

The crowd, at least forty strong, was bearing down.

Delia let out a gasp. "Did Mr. Dunwoody give a forecast this morning?"

"Yes." The lock tumbled, and I pushed open the door and scooted inside. Much to my dismay, Delia snuck in behind me.

I had two options: to kick out the black witch—which

would then let in the crowd . . . or keep Delia in and the crowd out.

Delia won.

I slammed the door and threw the lock.

Just in time. Fists pounded the wood frame, and dozens of eyes peered through the window.

I yelled through the leaded glass panel, "I'll be open in half an hour!" but the anxious crowd kept banging on the door.

Trying to catch my breath, I walked over the cash register counter, an old twelve-drawer chestnut filing cabinet. I set down my to-go bag, opened one of the drawers, and grabbed a small roll of numbered paper tickets. Walking back to the door, I shoved them through the wide mail slot. "Take numbers," I shouted at the eager faces. "You know the drill!"

Because, unfortunately, this wasn't the first time this had happened.

Turning my back to the crowd, I leaned against the door and then slid down its frame to the floor. For a second I rested against the wood, breathing in the comforting scents of my shop. The lavender, lemon balm, mint. The hint of peach leaf, sage, cinnamon. All brought back memories of my grandma Adelaide Hartwell, who'd opened the shop more than fifty years before.

"You should probably exercise more," Delia said. Her little dog barked.

My chest felt so tight, I thought any minute it might explode. "I think I just ran a 5K. Second time this month."

"What exactly did Mr. Dunwoody's forecast say?"

"Sunny with a chance of divorce."

Delia peeked out the window. "That explains why there are so many of them. I wonder whose marriage is on the chopping block."

The matrimonial predictions of Mr. Dunwoody, my septuagenarian neighbor, were never wrong. His occasional forecasts foretold of residential current affairs, so to speak. On a beautiful spring Friday in Hitching Post, one might think a wedding—or a few dozen—were on tap. But it had happened, a time or two, that a couple had a sudden change of heart over their recent nuptials (usually after the alcohol wore off the next morning) and set out to get the marriage immediately annulled or file for a quickie, uncontested divorce.

And even though Mr. Dunwoody was never wrong, I often wished he'd keep his forecasts to himself.

Being the owner of the Little Shop of Potions, a magic potion shop that specialized in love potions, was a bit like being a mystical bartender. People talked to me. A lot. About everything. Especially about falling in love and getting married, which was the height of irony, considering my mother's side of the family consisted of confirmed matrimonial cynics. Luckily, the hopeless romanticism on my father's side balanced things out for me. Mostly.

Somehow over the years I had become the town's unofficial relationship expert. It was at times rewarding . . . and a bit exasperating. The weight of responsibility was overwhelming, and I didn't always have the answers, magic potions or not.

Because Southerners embraced crazy like a warm blanket on a chilly night, not many here cared much that I called myself a witch, or that I practiced magic using a touch of hoodoo. But the town did believe I had all the answers—and expected me to find solutions.

My customers cared only about whether I could make their lives better. Be it an upset stomach or a relationship falling apart . . . they wanted healing.

And when there was a divorce forecast, they were relentless until I made them a love potion ensuring their marriage was secure. I had a lot of work to get done today. Work I'd rather not do with Delia around.

"Why are you here?" I asked her.

"You've been ignoring my calls."

If one was especially myopic and viewing us from afar, we might pass as sisters. The blond hair, the same height, the same nose and jawline. Which made sense. Seeing as how we were first cousins. Delia's mother, Neige, was my father's sister.

Delia (Hartwell) Bell Barrows was a snowy-white blonde with shoulder-length hair, ice-blue eyes, and creamy, pale skin. I was a cornfield blonde with golden wheat–colored hair, big milk chocolate–colored eyes, and dozens of freckles. Where I was the very image of a girl next door, Delia was ice-princess striking.

"You've been calling?" I asked, straight-faced.

My cousin was persistent, I'd give her that. I had been ignoring her phone calls for the past two days. I could only imagine what she wanted as she looked around the shop—it was the first time she'd been in here. Just as I'd yet to step foot in her shop, the Till Hex Do Us Part boutique, a mystically themed gift shop that featured her personalized liquid hexes.

"You know I have." She used minimal makeup, and that was the only thing that kept her from looking as though she'd completely lost her mind, with all the black she wore. "It's quite rude of you to make me track you down."

It wasn't the first time I'd been called rude. "Don't you have to get to work?"

Our businesses were yet another thing that set us apart. I used our hoodoo roots to heal people, and Delia used our voodoo roots to create hexes.

It was a divide that had defined our heritage, really, harking back to our great-great-grandparents, Leila Bell and Abraham Leroux. The legend of what happened to

them was infamous in Hitching Post as one of those
bittersweet stories of star-crossed lovers that was retold
over and over again as a warning to young girls as to
why they should never, *ever* marry a bad boy.

"Carly," she said, taking hold of an engraved round
silver locket, an orb that swung from an extra-long
chain around her neck. "This is serious."

The engraving on the locket was of two lilies en-
twined to form a heart, and inside it held a strand of
our great-great-grandmother Leila's golden hair.

I knew, because I had an identical locket around my
neck.

Beyond our looks, common middle name, and nail-
biting habit, Delia and I also shared one *big* similarity,
a trait passed down to all the women on my father's side
of the family.

We had all inherited Leila's ability to feel other people's emotions. Their pain, their joy.

The lockets, protective amulets given to us by our
grammy Adelaide when we were babies, weren't meant
as defense from others. They offered protection from
ourselves. From our own abilities. These lockets allowed
us to shut off our empathetic gift at will so we could live
as normally as possible.

Well, as normally as possible while practicing magic
in this crazy Southern town.

My ability was almost always turned off, way off,
except when I needed to tap into a client's energy in
order to create a perfect potion for him or her. However,
there were times, despite my charmed locket, when I
was overstressed or tired, that I couldn't control the
ability at all and was forced into hibernation until I
could handle society again.

My empathetic gift also came with an added bonus
that no one else—not even Delia—shared: a sixth sense

of sorts that I had no power over whatsoever. Warning signals that all wasn't quite right in my world. My best friend, Ainsley, called them my "witchy senses." It was as good a description as any.

"How serious?" I asked.

"Very."

I was feeling warning twinges now, and had to wonder if they were coming from the crowd outside . . . or Delia's dramatic pronouncement.

"Well, out with it already." I was very wary of Delia, and wondered if she was trying to trick me somehow. As a dabbler in the dark arts, one who used her magic with no concern for its consequences or side effects, Delia's magic was definitely dangerous but not nearly as potent as my magic.

She'd do just about anything to learn my spells and uncover the secret component that made my potions so successful—mostly because she was still in a snit that due to an unfortunate (for her) case of bad timing, I had possession of the secret magical ingredient and she didn't. And essentially, because of that one ingredient, my magic was more powerful than hers would ever be— and that bugged her to no end.

"Rude," she muttered.

"I'm kind of busy, if you can't tell."

Delia was six minutes younger than I—a source of contention that had created a chasm as deep as Alabama's Pisgah Gorge through the Hartwell family, splitting brother and sister apart.

All because I had been born two months prematurely, making *me* the oldest grandchild.

Making *me* the heir to the family grimoire and the keeper of the Leilara bottle and all its magical secrets.

Making *my* abilities superior to Delia's.

The grimoire was basically a recipe book for Leila's

hoodoo remedies, folk magic at its most natural. It had been handed down to the oldest child on my father's side of the family ever since Leila and Abraham died tragically. And the Leilara, well, that was pure magic born from their deaths. The way the Leilara drops mixed with specific herbs and minerals in a potion was what made that concoction effective. I couldn't rightly say I understood how it worked, but I firmly believed magic was one of those things to *feel* rather than study.

If my mother hadn't gone into labor two months early, the grimoire and the Leilara would have gone to Delia and the dark side. Aunt Neige had argued for years that gestational age should have taken precedence over actual birth dates, but her outcry had been overruled by Grammy Adelaide.

Currently, the grimoire and the Leilara were safely hidden, tucked inside a specially crafted hidey-hole in my shop's potion-making room. Hidden, because if Delia had her way and got her hands on the book of spells and the bottle of magic drops . . . Right now the Leilara drops were used for good, to heal. But with Delia, they'd be used for evil, to make her hexes that much more wicked.

"I had a dream," Delia said, fussing with her dog's basket.

"A Martin Luther King Jr. kind? Or an REM, drool-on-the-pillow kind?" I asked, looking up at her.

"REM. But I don't drool."

"Noted," I said, but didn't believe it for a minute. I shifted on the floor; my rear was going numb. "What was it about? The dream?"

Delia said, "You."

"Me? Why?"

Delia closed her eyes and shook her head. After a dramatic pause, she looked at me straight on. "Don't ask me. It's not like I have any control over what I dream. Trust me. Otherwise, I'd be dreaming of David Beckham, not you."

I could understand that. "Why are you telling me this?"

We weren't exactly on friendly terms.

Delia bit her thumbnail. All of her black-painted nails had been nibbled to the quick. "I don't like you. I've never liked you, and I daresay the feeling is mutual."

I didn't feel the need to agree aloud. I had *some* manners, after all. "But?" I knew there was one coming.

"I felt I had to warn you. Because even though I don't like you, I don't particularly want to see anything bad happen to you, us being family and all."

Now I was really worried. "Warn me about what?"

Caution filled Delia's ice-blue eyes. "You're in danger."

Danger of losing my sanity, maybe. This whole day had been more than a little surreal, and it wasn't even nine a.m. I laughed. "You know this from a dream?"

"It's not funny, Carly. At all. I . . . see things in dreams. Things that come true. You're in very real danger."

She said it so calmly, so easily, that I immediately believed her. I'd learned from a very early age not to dismiss things that weren't easily understood or explainable. Maybe Delia's dreams were akin to my witchy senses—which should always be taken seriously.

"What kind of danger?" I asked. I'd finally caught my breath and needed a glass of water. I hauled myself off the floor and headed for the small break room in the back of the shop. I wasn't the least bit surprised when Delia followed.

"I don't know," she admitted.

I flipped on a light. And froze. Delia bumped into my back.

We stood staring at the sight before us.

Delia said breathlessly, "It might have something to do with him."

Him being the dead man lying facedown on the floor, blood dried under his head, his stiff hands clutching a potion bottle.

Also available from

Heather Blake

The Wishcraft Mysteries

Darcy Merriweather hails from a long line of
Wishcrafters—witches with the power to grant wishes by
casting a spell. She's come to the Enchanted Village in
Salem, Massachusetts, to learn her trade, but she never
dreamed she'd have to learn about
magic *and* sleuthing...

It Takes a Witch
A Witch Before Dying
The Good, the Bad, and the Witchy
The Goodbye Witch
Some Like It Witchy
Gone with the Witch

**"Magic and murder...what could be better? It's
exactly the book you've been wishing for!"**
—Casey Daniels, author of *Supernatural Born Killers*

Available wherever books are sold or at
penguin.com

facebook.com/BerkleyPub

Connect with Berkley Publishing Online!

For sneak peeks into the newest releases, news on all your favorite authors, book giveaways, and a central place to connect with fellow fans—

"Like" and follow Berkley Publishing!

facebook.com/BerkleyPub
twitter.com/BerkleyPub
instagram.com/BerkleyPub

BERKLEY | Penguin Random House

1844